Bring It All

Mollie Goins

Aster Creek

SERIES BOOK 2

To my sister, you are stronger than you think and deserve more than you know.

I hope you never settle for anybody but an Owen West.

Disclaimer

Bring It All follows the story of Waverley Bennett and Owen West. It is important to note that Waverley is a sexual assault survivor (unrelated to MMC). In this book Waverley speaks openly about her past experience and details are given. While this topic is mentioned throughout the book, deeper details are given in the chapters listed below.

If you are needing to speak with someone regarding sexual assault, please reach out to 800-656-HOPE (4673). This is the National Sexual Assault Hotline (United States). Your voice deserves to be heard and know that you are not alone.

Chapters of note:
- **Chapter Twelve**

- **Chapter Twenty-four**

- **Chapter Thirty-six**

Additional topics that may be triggering:

Implications of child neglect and child endangerment - this is a topic that happens in present time and takes place throughout the book. Neither of the main characters are the source of said neglect.

Mentions of death in male main character's family - Mentions throughout the book but chapters of note listed down below.

- **Chapter Twenty-six**

- **Chapter Thirty-eight**

- **Chapter Forty**

Bring It All
playlist

In chapter order!

1. Diamonds Are Forever - Sabrina Carpenter

2. Golden - Harry Styles

3. Hurt Somebody - Noah Kahan (feat. Julia Michaels)

4. Sweet Creature - Harry Styles

5. Repercussions - Bea Miller

6. Woman - Harry Styles

7. Because You Live - Jesse McCartney

8. Choose Me - Brailey Lenderman

9. Not Like I'm In Love With You - Lauren Weintraub

10. Bad Liar - Selena Gomez

11. To The Grave - Bea Miller

12. I Can't Breathe - Bea Miller

13. Everything Has Changed - Taylor Swift (feat. Ed Sheeran)

14. On the Ride - Aly & Aj

15. Ruin My Life - Zara Larsson

16. Fetish - Selena Gomez (feat. Gucci Mane)

17. Don't You Know - Jaymes Young

18. Honeybee - The Head and The Heart

19. Body Talks - The Struts (feat. Kesha)

20. Collide - Rachel Platten

21. Home - Edward Sharpe & The Magnetic Zeros

22. Black and White - Niall Horan

23. From Now On - The Features

24. Learn To Let Go - Welshly Arms

25. You Are In Love - Taylor Swift

Contents

Chapter 1

Waverley

"Cheers! To a life full of love, happiness, and great sex," my younger sister, Wyla, says as she holds up her glass of champagne.

"Cheers!" We clink our glasses together. Throwing mine back, I feel the bubbles go all the way down.

My oldest sister, Winry, just got engaged to her amazing boyfriend, so we're celebrating. Graham organized the whole proposal at his old friends' bed and breakfast. Between the fairy tale theme of this place and all of the twinkling lights and candles, the back patio looks like a scene out of a book.

"Winry, let's see the ring again." Mary, one of the owners of the place and a friend of Winry's, reaches out for her hand. "Ugh, it's so beautiful."

"I know! I feel like I'm dreaming." Winry's smile is plastered to her face, and it hasn't faded once. Not that I blame her. After everything she went through with her ex, she deserves to be happy.

We fawn over the ring for a bit, and eventually, Graham pulls Winry away for a dance. I stare at my sister and her new fiancé as they sway together to the music.

A tinge of jealousy runs through me that I didn't expect. I haven't dated in so long, although I haven't really been looking to date. I was so focused on getting my degree, then I jumped straight into teaching the sixth grade.

More couples file in alongside Winry and Graham. "Oh, look how precious Owen is dancing with Annabelle." Wyla points in their direction.

"Who knew the devil had a soft spot," I say and swallow another sip of my champagne as I watch Owen twirl his eleven-year-old niece around.

"Oh, come on, Waverley. He's not that bad; you can't be mad at him forever." Wyla rolls her eyes.

"I'm not mad at him anymore. I simply don't like him." Owen West is an annoying, self-centered jerk. Yeah, he's mouthwateringly handsome, and he knows it too. He has no shortage of women at his disposal.

"Whatever, if you hate him so much, maybe you should stop staring." Wyla giggles.

"I wasn't staring. I was watching Mom and Dad," I deflect, but I was totally staring.

"Sure, Wav. Want to dance with me?" My sister holds out her hand and pulls me towards the dance floor.

"Alright, but I'm taking my glass with me."

We dance for a while but then the night starts to wind down. Winry and Graham excuse themselves—all too eager to celebrate their engagement in private. I hang out for a bit and help clean up. Unfortunately, I'm not the only one.

"Hey, Firecracker. Think you could pick up the pace? I want to get back to Aster Creek tonight before sunrise," Owen says as he ties off one of the full trash bags.

"One, stop calling me that. Two, just go, I can handle this myself." I push past him and blow out the last of the candles.

"But then who would make sure it's done right? You clearly require someone to follow behind you and make sure everything is complete." Owen reaches around me and grabs a candle that must have re-sparked. He brings the candle up to his mouth and blows it out. My eyes trail down from his dark green eyes to his mouth. *Damn it, why does he have to have perfect lips?*

The corners of his mouth turn up into a smile. "Quarter for your thoughts?"

His voice pulls me from my gaze. "The saying is a 'penny for your thoughts.'"

"I know, but I'd pay a whole lot more to know what you were thinking while staring at my mouth like that."

I scoff. "Don't flatter yourself. The only thought I had was how hard I would have to hit you to bust your lip."

"I highly doubt that." Owen takes a small step closer to me. The moment his cologne hits me, it fuels so many dirty thoughts. I stare up at him, unsure of what to do next. His short black hair has that messy but put-together look, and he has the perfect length of scruff on his face. It's just enough that I'm sure it would cause shivers to run down my spine if he kissed me.

"Uncle Owen, are you done yet? I'm tired." Annabelle's eyes look heavy, and she yawns.

"Sure thing, Belley. Waverley just said she was going to finish up for us." Owen winks, and I stick my tongue out at him.

"Thank you, Miss Waverley." Annabelle runs up and gives me a hug around my waist. She's too sweet.

"You're welcome, cutie. Hey, I'm doing a reading program this summer. Maybe you can sweet talk your uncle into bringing you." I smile wickedly, knowing good and well she will demand to go, and Owen will be the one stuck with bringing her every day. Goodness knows her mom won't do it.

Annabelle's eyes light up. "Are you really? Oh, can I do it, Uncle Owen? Please, please, please."

Owen shoots a quick look in my direction, and I smirk. "We'll talk about it, Belley. Let's head home."

They walk out, and I try not to admire his ass. He did look good tonight, in his all-black suit. And I hate it. Picture Prince Charming then throw that image in the trash because that's not Owen. He's the one you picture as the morally gray villain, with his dark hair, broad shoulders, and tattoos that go from his collarbone down to his fingers. Oh, and did I mention he's like 6'3? Tall, dark, and fucking handsome. *Blah.*

I collapse in my car ten minutes later. Most of the group decided to get a room to stay the night, but I have to drive back to help run Crossroads for the day tomorrow. Crossroads is a book and café store that Winry and her friend, Ivy, opened together over a year ago. Ivy had asked me a couple of weeks ago if I would be willing to help her cover since their part-time girl couldn't come in, and Winry will be thoroughly preoccupied with her new fiancé.

Again, a little bit of jealousy runs through me. I'm twenty-three, so settling down isn't exactly on my radar, but it would be a lie to say I'm not jealous of my sister. It's not really their relationship I'm jealous of, but it's the trust and comfort they have that gets me. A few months ago, Winry decided to open up about how she struggled with suicide, and Graham was there holding her hand the entire time.

I never expected that from her. She has always been the "bubbly" sister. But I guess it shows you never know the battles people fight, and I'm still not strong enough to share my own battle. Despite how close my sisters and I are, we each have our secrets. I came close to telling them mine when Winry gave us her confession but chickened out because it didn't seem like the right moment.

A wave of relief washes over me as I pull into my little two-bedroom house. It was actually my Mamaw's; we were always close and when she passed I begged my parents to let me take over the deed. Everyone knew how much I loved Mamaw and this house, so no one fought me over it. It's paid off, *thankfully*, or else I wouldn't be able to afford to live anywhere but my parent's house.

I have barely changed a thing—from the faded floral wallpaper to the oak cabinets, or the lace tablecloth on the kitchen table. The only furniture I changed was my bedroom set, but the rest was all hers. The house screams grandma-cottage core, and my favorite part of this house is the claw foot tub and shower. After a stressful day, you couldn't tear me out of that tub. Give me a glass of wine—scratch that, a bottle of wine—and I'm good to go.

I unlock my front door, and immediately kick off my heels. I crinkle my toes and stretch my feet trying to relieve the post-heel pain. *Ugh, heels are a bitch.*

Heading straight to the bathroom, I take out my contacts and wipe off all of my makeup. There are two things I refuse to do while sleeping, and they are wearing makeup or contacts in bed. Even on my twenty-first birthday when I was smashed, I still managed to take my contacts out and wash my face. Don't ask me how I did it; Wyla swears I didn't even open my eyes when I pulled out my contacts.

I walk to my bed and the wood creaks with each step. I peel off my dress, throw on an oversized t-shirt, and climb into bed. I relish in the comfort of my many blankets and pillows, and my mind drifts back to the close encounter with Owen earlier tonight. I hate how he gets under my skin. We can't even carry on a conversation without one of us losing our cool or making snarky comments to each other.

I roll back and forth in my bed; finding sleep seems to be out of reach. Why did he have to look and smell so good? Frustrated, I roll over and dig through my nightstand. I'm not proud to admit that I have fantasized about Owen West before, and I hate the fact that tonight probably won't be the last time.

I rummage through my drawer, finally finding my small pink vibrator that I picked out the one time my sisters and I went into an *adults only* store off some random exit while taking a road trip. We thought it would be a great idea for us to buy matching vibrators. Weird, I know, but I'm not complaining considering the only sexual relationship I intend on having is with *Mr. Efro*n here.

And yeah, I named my vibrator after Zac Efron. Old crushes die hard, man.

Laying on my back, I click it on and take myself back to the patio and play out my fantasy.

"Quarter for your thoughts?" Owen says with a smirk. That sexy smirk that makes me want to bite his lower lip.

I take a small step into him, our bodies just barely touch, but it's enough to send goosebumps down my arms. "I was thinking how nice it would be to have those lips on mine. How good it would feel to have them kissing all over my body."

"Don't tempt me, little Firecracker." *He backs me up against the cool rock wall. His hands find my hips first then slide down to my thighs.* "I'm willing to show you exactly how good it would feel."

"Well, come on, show me what I've been missing," *I say breathlessly.*

Owen lets out a low growl right before his tattooed hands move up to fist my hair, and his mouth crashes into mine.

The kiss is rough and dirty, each sweep of his tongue sends shockwaves down to my core. The kiss is full of built-up tension and dislike for each other. It's not sweet or romantic like most first kisses. It's pure need. I wrap my legs around his waist, and he grinds into me, leaving me with no questions about what he is packing.

He kisses up and down my neck and collarbone. I start to roll my hips, in need of more friction. The sensation fills me with so much desire, but I can only do two rolls before he cups my ass and carries me over to one of the nearby tables and lays me down.

He rips off his coat and stares at me hungrily. Tugging at the tie of my wrap dress, it easily comes undone, giving him a full view of my body.

Since this is a fantasy, I don't feel self-conscious of my body or afraid in any way. In this, there is no past, no distrust, just pure lust. I only dive deeper into the daydream.

Owen smiles wickedly then rips away my underwear and wastes no time going down for a taste. Fuck, my body feels like it's been ignited. He licks and sucks right where I need him to and I feel that need to explode building. I lean up on my elbows, needing to watch him devour me. And what a wonderful sight it is. When his green eyes peer up at me, there's nothing but need in those emeralds. He pushes one finger in, and my head falls back in pleasure. He doesn't let up, and when the second finger comes, I fall over the edge. Crying out his name, I writhe on the table, and ride out every second of my orgasm on Owen's face.

I slowly blink open my eyes. Feeling satisfied, I put my vibrator back in its drawer.

A little wave of uninvited sadness crosses over me for a moment, but I don't entertain it. I roll to my side and drift into a peaceful sleep.

Chapter 2

Owen

Driving down the road, Annabelle and I have the windows down in my truck and the wind is blowing her hair every which way. It feels amazing outside, not a cloud in the morning sky and not a single thing to do. So, I take Annabelle by Crossroads for some cinnamon rolls before she goes back to her mom's.

I hate taking Belley back to my sister's. Natalie is a bit of work in progress. She got pregnant with Belley when she was sixteen, and I partly blame myself for it. It was a year after our father passed away, and I was too busy drowning in my sorrows to pay attention to my sister. When Annabelle was born and her sperm donor gladly forfeited his rights to her, I cleaned up my act and decided I needed to be better for her. Natalie, however, has only gone further downhill.

My mom and I do what we can to shield Annabelle from it. No matter how much I beg, Natalie refuses to let me have full guardianship of her. I don't know why she fights me on it. She has no problem calling me or Mom when she wants to go out drinking or "needs a break."

Natalie's "breaks" usually come about every other day, if not multiple days in a row. Not to mention, I help pay for all of their living expenses. Natalie works at a diner in town. While most people can actually make pretty good pay in restaurants, Natalie doesn't really have the server personality.

"Uncle Owen, can we take a cinnamon roll to go for mom?" Annabelle asks as we walk in.

There's an ache in my chest. Annabelle is constantly wanting to get stuff for her mom, because that's the only time Natalie shows affection—when presents are involved—and what eleven-year-old *doesn't* want their mother's affection?

"Sure, Belley."

The door chimes as we walk in.

"Hi, welc—oh, it's just you." Waverley doesn't hide the disdain in her voice.

"Well, that's quite the greeting. I see you are your usual *sunshiny* self, Waverley," I reply, and Waverley rolls her sky-blue eyes.

If I'm not careful, I could get lost in those babies, just staring at them. Her hair is pulled back in a sleek ponytail, and she's wearing an oversized crewneck with some biker shorts that show off her long legs.

"I reserve it just for you," she sneers, but her face softens as she turns to Annabelle. "Hey there, Annabelle, what can I get you today?"

"Hi, Miss Waverley. Can we get three cinnamon rolls to go, please?"

"And a black coffee," I add.

"Bland like you, I suppose," Waverley mumbles.

"You know I like my coffee bitter. Maybe if you dip your finger in it that will do the trick."

Waverley gives me a snarky smile. "Oh, I'd love to put something in your coffee."

"Alright, you two. Weapons down." Ivy comes up. "I'll get his coffee if you wrap up the cinnamon rolls."

"Alright." Waverley gives me a side eye, and I return it with a wink and a charming smile.

Annabelle giggles next to me. "Waverley and Uncle Owen sitting in a tree, K-I-S-S-I-N-G," she sings.

"Excuse me, kid. I don't know what you just watched, but that song does not apply here," I tell her.

"Sure it does, you two are mean to each other. Mom said that when boys are mean to you, it usually means that they like you." Annabelle shrugs. "You're always mean to Miss Waverley, so you must really like her."

"Okay, first, don't listen to your mother about stuff like that because you should *never*, under any circumstances let a boy be mean to you. Second, I do not like Waverley," I say a little too defensively.

Sure, Waverley is gorgeous. Her long black hair is something any guy would dream of wrapping his fist around. With her olive skin and bright blue eyes, I can't help but be drawn to her beauty. And don't even get me started on her body. She's taller than her sisters, by probably four inches, and her curves should be nothing but appreciated—no, *worshiped*.

So what if she happens to pop into my head a time or two during certain... *physical activities*? That doesn't mean I *like* her; it's more fun to piss her off anyway.

Annabelle looks at me confused. "So, you're mean to Waverley because..."

I open my mouth then shut it. Did I just get called out by an eleven-year-old? I try to come up with something, anything to say, but Waverley comes back with the cinnamon rolls and my coffee saving me from giving "I'm an asshole" as my best excuse.

"Here you go." She gives me a tight smile then a genuine one to Annabelle. "I hope you have a wonderful day," she says to Belley.

"Thank you, Miss Waverley. I'll see you tomorrow at school," she says cheerfully.

"Bye, Firecracker," I muse and she scowls.

I've been calling her that since she nearly got hit with a firework a couple years ago on the Fourth of July, and knowing it irritates her to no end means I'll never stop.

I nudge Belley out the door and we get in my truck.

Pulling up to my sister's house, dread immediately comes over me. Trash is piled up on the front porch where Nat throws it out the door, and it looks like the screen door is broken again, even though I just fixed it. I don't want to think too much about what asshole probably broke it slamming the door on the way out.

"Nat, we're here," I holler as we walk in the door, but no answer. "Nat? Hello?"

I hear some fumbling around and then my sister stumbles out from her bedroom. Unfortunately, it's very obvious to me what she was just doing, considering she's wearing a man's t-shirt and boxers.

"Owen, what are you doing here? I thought you were bringing her back at ten?" Irritation is thick in her tone.

"It's ten-thirty, Nat," I huff.

"Hey, Momma. We stopped by Crossroads, and I got you a cinnamon roll." Annabelle bounces up to her, completely oblivious. "Also, did you know that Uncle Owen *loves* Miss Waverley?"

"Oh, thanks." Nat pats her on the head. Yup, that's Natalie's extent of affection.

"Okay, hey, why don't you eat your cinnamon roll in your room. I want to talk to your mom for a bit," I say to Belley, pulling her attention back to me.

"Okie, love you, Uncle Owen." Belley gives me a big hug then heads to her room.

Once her door closes, Natalie doesn't waste a second. "Waverley Bennett? Really, Owen?"

"I don't love her. Annabelle only thinks that because you told her that being mean to someone means they love you. Seriously, Nat? Oh, before I forget..." I march past her to her bedroom and open the door to see Corey Jenkins butt-naked on her bed. "You have two minutes to get the hell out, or I'll throw you out."

"She's wearing my clothes," Corey says with his hands in the air.

I turn back to my sister. "Give him his shit and put your own clothes on."

Nat rolls her eyes, but listens. I go back to the living room to wait with crossed arms and blood pressure steadily rising. She always does this shit, but for once could she not pick a total loser? This isn't my first run in with Corey by any means—most of our run ins usually result in him spending the night in a holding cell for eight hours while he sobers up. After a minute, she comes back out with Corey trailing behind her.

"Hey Owen, how—"

"Get out," I bark.

"Right, call me when you are free again, Nat." Corey winks at my sister on his way out.

"Was that really necessary, Owen? Annabelle is in her room, so what if he stays a little longer?" Natalie crosses her arms. "It's not like you're a saint; you have your fair share of women in your bed."

"Yeah, but not a single one of them has ever been at my house when I have Annabelle, or when I'm about to get her. Seriously, Natalie, she is your daughter. You have to set a good example."

She waves her hand in the air, all my words going in one ear and out the other. I let out an aggravated huff. "I'll be back in the morning to pick her up for school. Don't forget it's your turn to pick her up tomorrow; school lets out at three sharp. Also, there is a summer reading program at the school she wants to do. I'll pay for it, but you have to help out by getting her there and back more often."

"Why can't she just sit at home and do nothing like every other kid during the summer?"

I hold up my hand stopping her rant. "Nat, she is doing that program, and you will help, unless you want to reconsider giving me guardianship."

"No!" she exclaims quickly. "I have told you no already, so drop it." Natalie looks like she is going to start her fake tears, and I don't want to get into that right now.

"I'm not fighting with you, Natalie." I take a step towards her. "No more guys when she's here, and it won't kill you to help a little more. I'll see you in the morning." I squeeze her shoulder, and she nods.

Back in the car, I don't feel any better. I'm not supposed to feel uncomfortable with leaving Annabelle with her own mother, but I do. I know if I fought Natalie for legal guardianship, it would completely destroy our already fragile relationship, and there is no guarantee I would win.

Heading back to my place, I can't wait to crash in my bed. Working night shift is hard enough, but it's worse when you can't stick to that schedule. Sometimes I will be up for over twenty-four hours because I have to get Annabelle for the day after working all night.

Don't get me wrong, I'd make the sacrifice every time for her. So, for now and for the foreseeable future, I'll sleep whenever I can and if Annabelle needs me, then it will just have to wait.

I somehow manage five hours of sleep, and I'm feeling somewhat better. I decide to go to the gym for a quick workout and finish it with a run. After I shower at the gym, I'm starved so I head over to Bluebirds for a burger.

I grab a seat at the bar, and a new bartender comes up with a flirty look in her eye.

"Well, hello there. What can I get you, good looking?" she purrs.

She's cute. Her fiery red hair is pulled up in a bun, and she is wearing a Bluebirds tank top that shows more than enough cleavage and short jean cutoffs. Natalie wasn't wrong that I tend to sleep around a little bit, but I don't have Belley, so I'm free to take whoever I want home.

"How about the classic burger with a Bud Light"—I lean forward on my elbows—"and maybe you when you get off work."

The bartender blushes, and an annoyed snort comes from the person next to me.

I turn to see none other than Waverley Bennett. "I'm sorry, have something to share with the class, Miss Waverley?" I say.

Waverley puts down her burger. "Oh, nothing. It's absolutely nothing."

The bartender shoots daggers at Waverley then turns back to me. "I'll be back with your burger; I get off at ten tonight." She slides me a piece of paper with her number on it and winks.

I give her my best smile and when she walks away, I turn back to Waverley. "Come on, say it with your chest, Firecracker."

"That's all it takes for you, huh? You didn't even ask her for her name, and she is putty in your hands." She sips her drink.

"Jealous?"

She nearly chokes. "Not in the slightest."

The bartender returns with my beer and hands Waverley her check. "Here you go, thanks for stopping by," she says with a passive-aggressive smile. I don't know why, but it pisses me off. Waverly looks like she just got her food, and now is expected to leave.

"Right. Here." Waverley puts some cash on the bar, slides off her chair, and heads for the door.

She doesn't spare me a glance; I know because I watch her the whole way out. I turn back and jump at how far the bartender is leaning over the bar.

"I'm Summer, by the way." Her smile has lost its appeal.

"Summer, could I get my burger to go, and hers also."

"You want her food?" Summer asks, confused.

"If you don't mind." I give her another charming smile and after a minute, she brings me both meals boxed and bagged.

"So, I'll see you when I get off?" Her eyes practically undress me.

"Sorry, I don't think so. Have a good night."

I lay down cash to cover the food and then some, and walk out.

Chapter 3

Waverley

Screw Owen West.

I hope he gets an STI from that chick. I wanted that burger.

My stomach growls on my way back home. I know I have no food at home, and I can't go from a Bluebirds burger to a fast food burger—it's not the same. *Damn him.*

Flicking on the lights, I make my way to my kitchen to see if I have anything that I can scrounge together to eat but no luck.

I really need to go to the grocery store.

Defeated, I change into a matching pink lounge set, remove my makeup and contacts, then grab my glasses and plop on the couch. I should be getting some sleep since I work tomorrow, but I'm hungry and grumpy. So, I turn on an episode of *New Girl* and hope it will distract me.

Just as I get the show started, there's a knock at my door.

Only slightly freaked out, I get up and check the peephole. *What the hell?*

I swing my door open. "Owen, what are you doing here?"

"Food delivery." He holds up a bag and gives his signature smile.

"I'm not hungry," I lie. "Thanks, but no thanks."

"See, I don't believe you, but if you want me to throw away a perfectly good burger and onion rings, that's up to you." He shrugs and starts to turn.

My stomach grumbles at his words. "Okay, wait... I want the burger."

"That's what I thought." He walks in and sets the food down on the coffee table in my living room.

"Why'd you bring me my food?" I ask. There has to be an ulterior motive for Owen to be doing something *nice* for me. "You know I'm not going to sleep with you, right?"

"Jeez, Waverley. Quit being a brat and eat your food." He pulls out two boxes and hands me one.

My mouth waters as I pick up my burger and take a huge bite. I practically inhale it. Owen sits next to me on the couch, and I choose to ignore that he's sitting maybe five inches away, at most.

"You know, you should probably breathe in between bites." Owen chuckles.

"Mm, sorry. I guess I was hungrier than I thought." I take the last bite of the burger and search for a napkin.

"Here." He hands some over, and I wipe my hands and face.

"Um, you missed a spot." Owen reaches over and wipes the corner of my mouth gently.

We make unusual eye contact for a moment before I quickly pull away. "Thanks."

"Uh, yeah, sure." He shuffles in his seat, moving away from me slightly and goes back to his burger and fries.

This feels *weird*. Him being here, bringing me food... and being *nice*. I don't like it. It's not our normal *want to kill each other* vibe.

We finish eating in silence—painful silence.

I have to say something. It's killing me, and because I don't like this friendly Owen, I say something stupid. "Well, you better get going if you want to catch up with that bartender. Wouldn't want to miss an opportunity to add another notch to your bedpost."

"Wow, okay." Owen stands abruptly and shakes his head as if he can't believe what I said. "You know what, Waverley... never mind. Forget it. I think I will go catch up with whatever her name is." He pulls out his keys and walks out the door without another word.

What just happened?

With each passing day, I am losing my touch with my students. With only one month left to go, every one of them is feeling the pull of summer break, especially now that it is starting to stay warm outside.

The bell rings for dismissal, and all of my students rush out the door. The stack of ungraded work mocks me on my desk, and I spend the next two hours grading until I go cross-eyed. With a bit of a headache, I switch off my classroom lights and head out the door.

I'm supposed to meet Winry and Graham for dinner tonight, but I'm running late after staying to finish grading those papers. Instead of having time to relax for a little bit at home, I head straight over to Bluebirds.

Once I get there, Winry waves me over to the table. "Hey, guys. Sorry, I'm a little late," I apologize.

"It's no big deal. Don't worry about it." Winry stands to give me a hug.

"So, is Wyla in the bathroom?" I motion to the chair next to me.

"No, sorry. No Wyla tonight. She is studying for finals." Winry shifts in her seat. "Um, Owen is joining us though," she mumbles.

"What? Why?" I whine and rub my temples, my headache intensifying.

"Because they asked me to be here, Firecracker," Owen says smoothly, as he glides into the chair next to me.

"Again, *why*?" I ask Winry, ignoring Owen.

Win lightly kicks me under the table. "Come on, Waverley, be nice."

"Ow, don't kick me." I kick her back then glare at Owen. "He doesn't deserve nice."

He rolls his eyes. "Wow, thanks for inviting me out tonight, guys. If I had known you invited this ray of sunshine, I would have politely declined." He sends a sarcastic smile my way.

"Oh, believe me—" I start, but I don't get the chance to finish.

"Alright, that's enough," Graham cuts me off. "You're both ruining this. Sit and be quiet."

Ugh, it's like being scolded by my dad.

Winry gives him a smile and turns back to us. "Graham and I asked both of y'all to be here because we wanted to ask you something."

Owen and I look at each other with disdain in our eyes. I'm unsure what this question could possibly be, and why they would need the two of *us* to answer it. My stomach tightens with nerves.

Winry continues, "We wanted to officially ask you guys to be the best man and maid of honor at our wedding."

And with that, my mood changes. "Oh, Win. Of course, I want to!" I reach across the table and squeeze her hand. When we were in high school, we made a pact that Winry would be Wyla's maid of honor, Wyla would be mine, and

I would be Winry's. So, I knew this day was coming, but still.

"Good, not that you have much choice. I was going to make you do it either way." Winry squeezes back.

"Owen, what do you say?" Graham asks him.

"Hell yeah, man."

"Yay!" Winry claps her hands together and her smile is a mile wide. "So, we were thinking about getting married this fall. We will be a little rushed planning, but we want to do it October 20th. We do have your guys' first job though. We want to do a joint bachelor and bachelorette party, but we'll leave the rest of the details up to you two."

"We have to plan your bachelor/bachelorette party together?" I glance at Owen again and crinkle my nose at the thought of us working on this together.

Owen snorts out a laugh. "Seriously, Waverley. You sure are a real—"

"Don't y'all think you can play nice?" Graham interjects.

Owen huffs. "I can. Her, on the other hand, I don't think Firecracker here has a nice side."

I glare at him, hating that he uses that nickname just to bait me. I grit my teeth. "I can be nice."

Chapter 4

Owen

I pick Annabelle up from her last day of school, and her mood is bumming me out.

"Come on, Belley. Perk up. It's summer, and you get to spend more time with your amazing uncle. I mean, that's a pretty good deal, don't you think?"

Annabelle rolls her eyes. "I like school, Uncle Owen."

"I know you do, kiddo. But, hey—you've still got that summer program with Waverley. It starts in two weeks." I signed Annabelle up immediately after a knock-out-drag-out with Nat last week. Natalie being Natalie, doesn't want the responsibility of taking her. Really any responsibility is like pulling teeth with her.

"Really? I get to go?" Annabelle's voice goes up an octave.

"Are you kidding? Of course you get to go."

"But, what about Mom? I don't want her to be upset." Her shoulders slump.

"You don't need to worry about that, Annabelle. Do you hear me?" Annabelle's sad puppy eyes look at me.

"You're the best kid there is. You want to do this program, and I will be damned if you don't get to do it."

"Uncle Owen, no cussing." Annabelle giggles.

"You can't cuss," I say, pointing to her and then to myself. "I can." This makes her giggle even more. "Promise me you won't worry about making your mom upset."

She nods. "I promise."

"Good." We pull up to my mom's house. "Now remember, Grandma is still hurting, so be easy." Mom had hip replacement surgery last month, and her recovery has been hard on her.

I grab the groceries for dinner, and we head inside.

"Mom, we're here," I announce.

"Oh, my babies!" Mom starts to press the up button on the power lift chair I bought her.

I set the groceries down on the coffee table. "Mom, please sit. We'll come to you."

"Okay, if you insist." She lowers back down, and Annabelle and I both walk over to greet her with a gentle hug. I glance around the living room to make sure there isn't anything I need to do before starting dinner.

I try to come over every couple days to help mom clean up the house, but sometimes she tries to do it without me—which she clearly has done today.

All of Belley's books are back on the shelves, every throw blanket folded, and the carpet looks vacuumed. She can tell I'm about to get on to her, so she changes the subject before it starts. "What are you cooking tonight? Can I help you?"

"I'm making stuffed peppers and no, you can't help. Belley, why don't you keep Grandma company, and I'll start cooking."

"Okie." Annabelle plops down on the couch.

I have always loved cooking; my dad practically lived in the kitchen. He said it was a skill every husband should learn, so he started teaching me as soon as I was old enough to hold a mixing spoon.

I clean and prep the peppers and pop them in the oven before starting on the stuffing. Natalie comes in the kitchen as I finish seasoning the meat.

"Hey, bro, care to tell me why Annabelle said she is taking that summer whatever thing? I thought I said I didn't have time to take her." Nat has her arms crossed and her bitchiest face on.

"I signed her up, Nat. She wants to do it, so she's doing it and so help me, you better not make her feel bad about it. I mean it, Natalie."

She snorts. "Is this just a ploy for you to get into Waverley Bennett's pants? I didn't realize your standards were that low, Owen."

"This again?" I roll my eyes and shake my head. "I have no interest in sleeping with Waverley, and she has no interest in sleeping with me. Your daughter wants to take the reading program, and Waverley teaches it. What is your fascination with her anyway?"

"I'm not fascinated with *Waverley*." She says her name with so much venom. "I just don't like her, and I don't want Annabelle spending a lot of time with her."

That's her excuse? Really?

"You don't have to like her. Hell, I don't even like her, but I trust her with Annabelle. She's taking that program, so you better swallow your feelings and smile about it because it changes nothing." I turn back to my cooking leaving Natalie to pout.

As I finish up dinner, Annabelle sets the table while Natalie continues to sulk in one of the chairs. Her arms never come uncrossed, and the sourness doesn't leave her face.

Annabelle gives me pitiful looks because she knows her mother is unhappy. I hate it.

Mom shuffles into the kitchen slowly. "Annabelle, why don't you go in the bathroom and wash up?"

"Yes, ma'am." Annabelle bops out of the kitchen and down the hall.

"Natalie, dear, fix your face. You don't play the victim well," Mom scolds.

"You always side with Owen. For once, can't you side with me?" Natalie says, holding on to the woe-is-me attitude. "He isn't perfect, ya know. You constantly get on to me when he does shit too."

"The only side I'm on is Annabelle's, and you're making her feel bad. So suck it up. You're her mom. Act like it." Mom takes her seat at the table. "This isn't about who makes the worst choices. This is about your bad attitude and how it's directly affecting Annabelle. So I'll repeat myself—suck it up."

I hold back my smile. Nat was annoying the shit out of me with her pity party. I was going to say something if my mother hadn't.

Annabelle comes back in the kitchen before Natalie can give her "I'm the victim" speech. "It smells so good, Uncle Owen."

"Thanks, kid." I set the dish of peppers on the table. "Alright. Dig in, everyone."

Tonight's shift has been slow as shit.

Slow nights were much easier when I was training Graham. A few months ago, they decided he was good to have his own car, so I'm back to riding solo. Not a single call has come through so far, and I'm bored.

Another hour drags by at a snail's pace. It's a little past midnight when I notice a car on the side of the road with what looks like a flat tire. Finally, something productive to do.

It's dark as I get out of my car, but I can see it's a girl with long black waves thrown behind her shoulder, and she looks like she is struggling to get the lug nuts off.

"Damn it, damn it!" She drops the lug wrench, plops on the ground, and buries her face in her hands.

"ACPD, can I help you with that?" When she uncovers her face, I'm met with bright, sky-blue eyes. "Waverley, what are you doing?"

"Oh, you know, I thought I would start working the street corner." She pushes off the ground. "What the hell do you think I'm doing? I'm changing my flat tire."

This woman.

"I can see that you have a flat. What I meant was why are *you* changing it instead of calling your dad, Graham, or literally any one of your dad's officers on shift tonight? It's midnight, and you're fucking around on the side of the road."

What was she thinking doing all this by herself in the middle of the night? She's off on a damn back road. She has no lights other than her headlights and her phone. Anyone could have come up on her and there would have been no one else around to help her. The only benefit she has here is that there was a flat place for her to get over in the grass and off the road.

"I'm not fucking around. I know how to change a flat tire, asshat. I can do it myself if I could get this damn nut off." She kicks her tire.

"Hand me the wrench."

"No, I can do it," she protests.

"Hand me the wrench, Waverley," I demand again.

"I said I can do it. Just go, Owen. I don't need your help."

"Okay, fine. You want to do it, go right ahead." I step back and gesture at the tire.

"Thank you." She goes to start again. "You can leave now."

"No way. If you want to be stubborn, so be it. I'll stand here all night. When you're ready to ask for help, just let me know." I lay out the challenge, and I can see the determination in her eyes.

"Okay, fine." She squats back down and starts on getting the lug nut off again. I point my flashlight down at her tire, so she can see better while she works.

With all of her absolute might she tries to turn the lug counterclockwise, but it doesn't budge. She tries again... and again... and again. About five minutes goes by of watching her struggle, and I'm about to pull the wrench out of her hands when she finally gets the nut to twist halfway.

"Ah, I did it!" She looks up at me, and her smile is remarkable. A wave of pride rushes over me seeing her accomplish what she said she was going to do, even if she only did it to spite me. Then, Waverley being Waverley, she sticks her tongue out at me. "Told ya I could do it."

"Great, Wav. Now do the rest of them." I nod back at the tire. I can't let her see that I'm proud of her.

"Phew, okay." The rest of the lug nuts go pretty smoothly. She gets out her jack, and she does let me lift the car for her, but then she demands to take back over. She pulls the lug nuts the rest of the way out and removes her flat.

"Listen, don't tell my dad about this, okay?" she asks as she sets the new tire.

"I won't if you tell me why you insisted on not calling anyone to help you. I get that you can do it, but it's the middle of the night, Waverley. Anyone could have pulled up on you."

"Save me the lecture. I'm not a child, Owen. I'm perfectly capable of taking care of myself." She finishes putting the spare tire on and gestures for me to lower the jack.

"What are you even doing out this late?" I ask as I hand over the flashlight, then lower her car.

"I went to Bluebirds with Wyla and Winry for karaoke, which in case you haven't noticed—I. Am. An. Adult. I'm allowed to be out late, I'm allowed to make my own decisions, and I don't have to explain myself to you." She gathers up her tools and jack and loads them into her trunk.

"Okay, Miss Big Girl, why can't I tell your dad then, hmm? You're an adult, right? What's the big deal? Is it because he'll tell you how stupid it is for a girl to change a flat on the side of the road, in the middle of the night, all by herself?"

It seems I have struck a nerve because by the look on her face you would think I just hit her. "Fuck off, Owen. My tire is changed, and I don't have to stand here and listen to you."

"Waverley."

"Goodbye." She pushes past me while giving me the middle finger and climbs in her car. I stand there until she drives off then head back to my car.

Well, I feel shitty.

Chapter 5

Waverley

I comb through my planner for the summer reading program and prep the tables for our first day. This course was set up for kids entering 6th grade or for kids that are on the verge of being held back.

Once I have the material all set out, I relax in my chair for a bit and sip my coffee. The hot coffee burns on the way down, but it's a good burn. I lean back, closing my eyes for a moment, hoping to take in the last few minutes of quiet time before students start arriving.

"Miss Waverley?"

I jump and nearly knock over my mug. "Oh, good morning, Annabelle," I give her a soft smile. "Owen." He gets no smile.

"Morning, Firecracker. I know we're early, but I couldn't hold her back any longer." Owen ruffles Annabelle's hair.

"Stop, Uncle Owen. My hair is already bad enough." Annabelle combs her wild blonde hair with her fingers. I notice that it's a bit of a mess which tells me she was at her mom's last night. On the nights she stays with Owen, her hair is at least brushed.

It breaks my heart that her mom puts in the minimal effort. I get that Annabelle is old enough that she can get ready by herself, but at the same time, you can't expect an eleven-year-old to do *everything*. Annabelle has such long hair, it can't be easy for her to tame it on her own. Especially since she has no one to teach her.

"Hey, we've got twenty minutes before the other kids get here. Why don't you let me pull your hair up in a ponytail, like mine, or maybe we could do braids?"

"Really?" Annabelle goes wide-eyed. "You can braid?"

"I sure can. So, what do you say, braids or a ponytail?"

"Braids." She smiles brightly.

"Let's do it." I glance at Owen, and he has this weird look on his face. I don't like it. I ignore him and dig out my bag full of emergency girl stuff. I motion for Annabelle to come sit on the floor in front of me and start brushing out her tangles. I may not like Owen, but Annabelle doesn't deserve that grudge to be carried over to her.

"I, uh... I'm gonna go," Owen says with that same expression on his face. "Belley, your mom will pick you up today. Wav, um... thank you."

"Sure, no problem." I remain focused on brushing out Annabelle's knots.

"Bye, Uncle Owen."

"Bye, Belley." He waves and walks out the door.

I finish up brushing out Annabelle's long blonde hair, careful not to tug too hard at her tangles. "Do you want two braids or one big braid?"

"Two, please."

"Sure thing." I separate her hair, making sure it's even then start on her right side.

"Could you teach my mom to braid?" she asks.

"Um..." I hesitate, unsure of how to answer. Natalie isn't the easiest person to get along with, and I'm sure she wouldn't be down with me teaching her how to braid her daughter's hair. "Maybe, but I could teach you how to braid. That way you can do it yourself."

"That would be so cool."

"It sure would. Tell Owen to bring you early like today, and I can start teaching you braids and different ways to fix your hair before the other kids get here," I say as I finish up the first side and move onto the other.

"Are you for real? You'd do that?" Her voice is high and excited like I just promised her gold.

"Of course, it will be fun. Okay, we're done. Here, check it out." I take a picture with my phone and show it to her.

"Wow, it looks so good, Miss Waverley. Thank you." Annabelle turns and gives me a big hug.

"You're welcome, sweetie. Come on, the other kids will be here soon. Why don't you go pick out a seat?" I point to the desks, and she hops up from the floor.

"Okie."

The rest of the students file in shortly after, and we get the day started. Some students are more excited than others. The ones forced to be here are making it painfully obvious. I go over our plans for what we will be doing over the next few weeks, and the kids' eyes glaze over. Well, all except Annabelle's.

I try to start the first day off with some educational games and word puzzles that help set up the material we'll cover, and I manage to hold their interest for today. I want this program to be fun, however, I do have a curriculum that needs to be covered, but it can wait until tomorrow.

By 2:00 p.m., I have all of the kids pack up their stuff, and I walk them out to meet their parents. By 2:30, I'm still sitting with Annabelle on the bench outside.

"Annabelle, would you like for me to call your mom?"

"Um, no. I'm sure she will be here," Annabelle mumbles.

My heart breaks looking at her face. I know she's embarrassed, and I don't want to make it worse for her. Another fifteen minutes roll by with still no sign of Natalie.

I'm about to call Owen when Natalie comes screeching in looking like she just got off the hot mess express as she walks up to us. Her blonde hair has very clearly gone unbrushed, and the tangles are falling out of her bun in every direction. Makeup is smeared under her eyes, and she's still in her pajamas.

"Hey, Annabelle." Natalie yawns. "Come on, let's go."

"Hey, Mom." Annabelle beams, just happy that her mom is here. The idea that her mom didn't completely forget her makes up for her being late in her eyes. "Bye, Miss Waverley, see you tomorrow."

"See you tomorrow," I say as Annabelle bebops to her mom's car. "Um Natalie, can I talk to you for a second?" I stop her mid-turn to the car.

"Sure, what's up?" Natalie gives me her best condescending smile.

"I wanted to let you know I don't mind waiting a little while with Annabelle, but if we need to work out another pickup plan—"

"There's no need to do another plan; I can pick up my daughter," Natalie says, already on the defense.

Deep breaths, Wav. "I understand that but pick up is at two o'clock, if we—"

She rolls her eyes. "I said I can do it, gah, do you give this lecture to every parent that's a little late?"

I glance around her shoulder and find Annabelle watching us from the front seat. I need to be careful here, I don't want to cause a scene in front of her. "Natalie, I'm not trying to lecture you. I'm just asking if you are going to be late to—"

"Listen, Waverley, I didn't want Annabelle to do this 'little thing' you're doing here anyway. So yeah, I might be late picking her up from time to time. If it's a problem, I'll simply pull her out of this." Her threat is clear; she doesn't care what Annabelle wants or how it would crush her to be pulled from this program.

Biting my tongue and putting on my best fake smile, I grit out, "No, that won't be necessary."

"Perfect. Now, we really gotta get going. See you sometime tomorrow, *Miss Waverley*," Natalie throws back.

"See you tomorrow." *Bitch.* But that last part I say in my head.

Natalie is late the rest of the week. I bite my tongue and fake a smile at every pickup. Back in my classroom, I fall back into my chair. I can't wait to go home and take a nice bubble bath with a glass of wine.

My classroom door opens and in walks Anna. "Late again, huh?"

Anna and I both started teaching this year and have gotten rather close. We bonded over our dislike for Quinn, the 6th grade math teacher. She's only five years older than us, but she talks to us like we're stupid and couldn't possibly understand the struggles of her life.

"Oh yeah, no excuses either, just shows up late to spite me, I'm pretty sure. What are you still doing here?" Anna is the art teacher here and also decided to do a summer program.

"I wanted to get the prep ready for next week, so I don't have to worry about it over the weekend. What big plans do you have, Miss Waverley?" Anna asks as she leans on my desk.

"Oh, big plans, I'm thinking a bottle of wine, a bubble bath, then sleep."

"Aren't we exciting?"

"Hey, don't judge. What are your plans exactly?" I counter.

"Alright, no plans, but we could go do something," she says eagerly.

"Rain check, please?"

"Come on, Wav. Don't you want to go get some drinks, maybe meet some really cute guys? You need a little lovin' in your life. I've never seen you with a guy. I pray one-night stands happen, and I don't know about them."

"Ha! No, I'm not a one-night stand gal. I promise, one night I will let you drag me to whatever bar you want but tonight is not that night."

"Alright, deal, I'll see you Monday?"

"Yup, have a good weekend." Anna walks out, leaving me to go back to work.

I finish up my stuff and head for home a half hour later. About halfway there my phone starts to ring. I'm too tired to look at who's calling so I just answer. "Hello?"

"Hey, Firecracker. I'm surprised you answered," Owen says over the car speaker.

Damn it.

"Yeah, me too," I grumble. That's what I get for not looking.

"I see you are in your usual sunshiny mood. Listen, we need to start planning the group bachelor-bachelorette trip. Why don't you meet me at Bluebirds tonight to start planning?"

"Tonight?" I whine.

"Yeah, tonight. What, you got big plans or something?" There's a challenge in his tone.

"Maybe I do," I lie.

"Yeah, that was *very* convincing. Just come to Bluebirds."

"No," I snap.

"Come on, Wav, don't be difficult."

"I'm not being difficult, I'm tired. I've had a long day, and I want to go home." Where my bubbles, wine, and bed are waiting for me.

"Okay, I'll come to your house."

Nope, can't do that again.

"No, Owen. Why do we have to do this tonight anyway?"

"Because I'm off, and you're off. Plus, if I leave it up to you, you'll push it off as long as possible."

He's not wrong, and I promised Winry I would be nice. "Ugh, fine. But you're not coming to my house, I'll meet you at Bluebirds at six."

"See you then, Firecracker."

I let out an audible groan. I've already dealt with one West sibling today, and I'm about at my limit. I get home to change out of my school clothes, throw on some black leggings, a graphic tee, and put my hair up in a ponytail. I couldn't care less about how Owen thinks I look, so I take off my makeup too. When this is over, I want to be able to crawl in bed and go to sleep.

I walk into Bluebirds right at six. I spot Owen in a booth, typing on his phone. He looks so effortlessly sexy with a simple t-shirt and a black ball cap. I hate it.

I slide into the seat across from him. He notices me right away and puts down his phone, giving me his full attention. I hate that too.

"Let's get this over with," I grumble.

"I see your mood hasn't changed. Want to order something?" He hands me the menu like everyone in town doesn't have this menu memorized.

My stomach chooses that moment to growl.

"I'll take that as a yes," he chuckles.

"Shut up," I snap.

Our waiter comes over, and I'm a little relieved to not see the redheaded bombshell that Owen hit on last time. I order the house burger and a Michelob Ultra. Beer and burgers are a match made in heaven, and I'll need at least one drink to survive this dinner.

"Well, what were you thinking?" Owen asks. "They want to do a joint one because it's not a bunch of us."

"Who all is going again? Winry sent me a list, but my brain checked out after class today."

"It's me, you, Winry, Graham, Wyla, and Ivy. Mary and Jace aren't doing the trip because of the kids... oh, and Levi is coming. He's another officer on our shift that started a couple months ago."

"Okay, well, I was thinking not the beach. We have access to the beach easily. I think we should do something different."

"What, like Vegas?" Owen asks as the waiter drops off our drinks.

"No, too big, and flying will be expensive and too much to manage with a group. What about New Orleans?"

"I think we would still fly if we went there. What about Nashville? My uncle has a pretty big condo downtown we could use. We all drive up Friday, then leave Sunday night. Graham, Levi, and I will have to get back on our night shift schedule anyway, so we could drive through the night and have a full day on Sunday.

I contemplate shutting down his suggestion just because I hate that it's his idea, but Nashville does sound fun. "Okay, that's not a *horrible* plan."

"Wow, high praise. See, we can do this without fighting."

"I wouldn't get too excited. Our food isn't even here yet. The evening can change." I let out a rare smile. "Okay, I have three weeks off between when the summer program ends and before school starts. So, we could do it one of those weekends that would fall under your and Graham's off weekends. Levi's, too."

"Okay, so, Nashville? I'll message my uncle and see if it's available for the last weekend in July," Owen says as he types on his phone.

The waiter comes by and drops off our food. I dive into my burger. I love the food here, and Owen's not being completely insufferable. This night might not be a total bust.

"Hey, man. How's it going?" A blonde *Greek god* comes up to the table. *Holy hell, who is this?*

"Hey, Levi. It's going, what are you doing?" Owen gives Levi the bro handshake.

"I'm grabbing a beer with Graham, but it looks like he isn't here yet." Levi turns his blue eyes on me, and I fight the urge to melt. "And who is this?"

I guess I look too lovestruck to speak because Owen responds for me. "Uh, this is Waverley Bennett. One of Chief's daughters."

"Oh, really? Hi, it's nice to meet you, Waverley." Levi holds out his hand, and I'm all too happy to shake it.

"Nice to meet you too." I smile.

"Ah, Mich Ultra? My kind of girl. Lucky you, Owen."

"Oh, no, we aren't together," I say quickly—maybe too quickly based on the look Owen gives me. "We were actually meeting to plan the joint bachelor-bachelorette party."

"Yeah? Where are we going?" Levi smiles, and I melt... *again*.

"Uh, we are planning on doing Nashville," Owen says, still looking at me, but I'm too distracted to care.

"Sweet, I love Nashville," Levi says and turns to me. "I'm actually from a town about an hour away from there, I'll have to show you around."

I blush. "Yeah, that sounds great." We hold a gaze for a moment, but then Graham walks up to the table.

"Hey, guys. Sorry, I'm late, Levi."

"Nah, you're good. I was just getting to talk to Waverley." Levi smiles at me, and my blush deepens.

"I'm here too," Owen deadpans.

"I'm sorry. I must be imagining things. Waverley, are you eating dinner with Owen? *Willingly*?" Graham looks impressed and surprised.

"I know, it's shocking, right?" I laugh, but Owen is completely unamused. "We're planning y'alls trip. Where's Winry?"

"She's still at the bookstore helping Ivy bake some cupcakes. We'll let you guys get back to it. Win will be proud to know you two haven't killed each other yet." Graham claps Owen on the back and nods toward the bar at Levi.

"It was nice to meet you, Waverley. I hope to see you around sometime." Levi smiles.

"Yeah, I'd like that." *Oh my gosh. Oh, my gosh.*

"Bye, Levi," Owen says shortly.

"See ya later." Levi nods at him and heads to the bar. Do I watch him walk away? *Yes.* Does Owen notice? *Unfortunately, yes.*

"Wow, that was something," Owen grumbles.

"Excuse me? Is there a problem?" I snap.

"No. No problem." Owen takes a long swig of his beer.

"Yeah, right. Come on, spit it out."

"No, it's nothing. You just still have some drool still on your face." He hands me a napkin, and I swat it away.

"Shut up. I don't know what you're talking about," I deflect and deny.

"Oh yeah, sure." Owen rolls his eyes, and it infuriates me.

"Okay, so what? Am I not allowed to find other people attractive? It's not like I'm jumping into bed with him after just meeting him."

"What's that supposed to mean?"

"You know what it means. I mean, how dare you judge me when you have slept with all of Aster Creek," I bite back.

"Wow, okay. Not all of Aster. I haven't slept with you, and you bet your ass that will never happen. Doesn't seem like I've stooped that low yet."

That's it. That last part cuts me deep, but I'd never admit it. I grab my purse and throw down a twenty for my food.

"Waverley—" Owen starts, but I cut him off.

"Save it, Owen." I go to walk out but turn back to him. "Hey, do me a favor. In between your endless *sleepovers*, tell your sister to pick up her kid on time. I'm tired of staying an hour late every day waiting for another sorry-ass West sibling."

Owen opens his mouth but closes it—wisely so—and I stomp out the door.

Chapter 6

Owen

I'm an asshole. Yup, a big, dumb asshole.

Why did the way Waverley was looking at Levi bother me so much? Why did I say what I said? I didn't mean it... I just couldn't stand the way she was drooling over him.

I look down at my food, appetite gone with a queasy feeling taking its place. And because karma is a bitch, Graham and Levi slide into the seat where Waverley just sat.

"Well, I knew that was coming. Hell, I'm impressed y'all made it to your food arriving," Graham says with a chuckle.

"I don't know what you're talking about." Deflect, deflect.

"Really? Waverley stormed out of here like the place was on fire, and you don't know what I'm talking about?" Graham raises his eyebrows.

"Nope," I say, drinking the last of my beer.

Graham shakes his head. "Alright. Well, Levi here was going to call her tonight, but considering someone pissed her off, I told him to wait."

The queasy feeling in my stomach intensifies. Why do I absolutely loathe the fact that Levi is going to call her? Watching her drool over him gave me this strong feeling of needing to punch him. I like Levi. He's a good guy, and I don't have feelings for Waverley, so why do I care?

"You want to call Waverley?"

"Uh, yeah. She's gorgeous," Levi says and damn it—he's not wrong. "Unless this is a problem for you?"

"For me? No, no problem." Yes, it is a problem. A big problem.

"Okay, great, so I'll call her." Levi smiles, and I want to punch him again.

I pull up to Nat's house to get Annabelle on Monday morning. Annabelle sits eagerly on the front porch, barely letting me put my truck in park before she tries to jump in.

"Good morning," Annabelle says with a bright smile.

"Morning, Belley. Hey, is your mom up? I need to talk to her real quick."

"Um, yeah, I think she's up. I think I heard her moving around inside while I was waiting for you."

"Okay, be right back." I ruffle her wild hair and head into the house. "Nat? You up?" I ask, opening the front door.

"Natalie?" I holler again.

"Ugh, coming," Natalie groans from her room. I hear her fumble around for a minute then stumble out groggily. "What—what do you want this early? Annabelle was waiting for you on the porch."

"Yeah, she's in the truck. I need to talk to you about picking her up, Nat. Have you been picking her up an hour late?"

"She told on me. Wow, little childish," she mumbles. "Look, it's no big deal, so Waverley has to take some time out of her day to sit with Annabelle. She's the teacher, it's her job."

"It's not her job to wait around on you, so I'm telling you, Natalie—pick her up on time."

"Whatever, *Dad*. Bite me. I'm going back to bed." She turns around and slams her bedroom door like a child.

I drop Annabelle off early like she asks every morning, but this morning I don't go into the classroom with her. I drop her off at the front door like a coward because I still feel like shit about what I said to Waverly on Friday.

"Bye, Uncle Owen." Annabelle waves down the hallway to the classroom.

"Bye." I wave back and when I turn, I accidentally bump into someone. "Oh, I'm sorry."

I bend down to pick up the papers I knocked out of her hands. *Man, I'm on fire these days.* I stand up and hand over the papers to a woman who looks about my age. She's attractive, with blonde hair and blue eyes. Not blissfully blue like someone else I know, but pretty, nonetheless.

"Sorry about that."

"That's okay." She smiles at me. "I'm Quinn, one of the teachers here. I haven't seen you before. Does your child go here?"

"My niece, actually, Annabelle West. She's taking Waverley's reading program this summer."

"Oh, how nice. So, is Annabelle going into the sixth grade? I'm the sixth grade math teacher," Quinn says and takes a small step closer.

"Yeah, she's excited. Summertime is usually the worst for her. She loves school. Hence, the summer class."

"Yes, well, I look forward to having her in my class." She smiles. "Hopefully, I'll see you more too?"

I know what she's getting at, and she *is* pretty, but my mind has been occupied with Waverley lately... why? I don't know. I'm about to let Quinn down gently when I remember Waverley's face when she saw Levi, and that sick feeling comes back.

"Yeah, how about you give me your number, and we can get some coffee sometime?" I give my signature woman-winning smile.

"Yeah, I'd like that." She blushes as she pulls out a pen, writes her number on the corner of a page and rips it off.

"Great, I'll see you around." I finish off the conversation with a wink and head back to my truck.

Back at my house I grab a couple hours of sleep since I work tonight, but I set an alarm for 2:00 p.m. because I know I'm going to have to pick up Annabelle today. No matter what I said to Natalie, I know it went in one ear and out the other.

Sure enough, I pull up at the school at 2:20 and there sits Waverley and Annabelle. Annabelle's hair is in braids again, braids that I know weren't there this morning. Waverley is nodding along to whatever Annabelle is saying, listening to her intently. Wav's hair is also in braids and her light blue shirt matches her eyes perfectly.

"Hey, I thought Mom was picking me up?" Annabelle asks as I reach them.

"Yeah, I was just out in town, so I thought I would get you. Don't worry, I'll call your mom and let her know."

Waverley doesn't spare me a glance, not even a go to hell look.

"Okay, Annabelle. You were great as always. I'll see you tomorrow." Waverley smiles at her, still zilch for me.

"Thanks, Miss Waverley, see you tomorrow." Annabelle bounces her way to my truck.

When I turn back to Waverley, she has already started walking back to the school. I fight the urge to stop her and apologize; if this is how she wants to be, then so be it.

Back in the truck I shoot Natalie a text telling her I picked up Annabelle. I almost don't even bother sending it because I'm 99% sure that she knew I was going to show up to get her.

"Uncle Owen, what do you think of my hair? I did it all by myself." Annabelle whips the tails of her braids back and forth.

"You did that?" I ask, tugging on one.

"Yeah, Miss Waverley has been teaching me in the mornings before the rest of the kids get there. Tomorrow, she said she is going to start teaching me how to do a Dutch braid."

"Oh, well that's... nice of her. Has she been doing that every morning?"

I guess I shouldn't be too surprised; Waverley has a heart for kids.

"Yeah, she did it herself a few times, but she's been teaching me how to do it too. She even let me practice on her hair this morning. Uncle Owen, her hair is so soft and pretty. I wish my hair was like hers."

"There's nothing wrong with your hair, Belley. It's long and beautiful."

Waverley better not be making Annabelle feel bad about her hair.

"That's what Miss Waverley said." Damn it, of course she wouldn't.

Why did I even think that?

"Miss Waverley said her hair can be wild too, but she learned how to take care of it. She bought me a bunch of hair stuff. Look, it's in my backpack. She even wrote out instructions for each thing and how to use them."

Damn, this woman. Not that I want her to be mean to Annabelle, but it would make things a whole lot easier if she wasn't so fucking great with her.

"I want to get her something, like as a thank you. Do you know what she would want?" Annabelle asks.

"I don't know, Belley. I'm sure she would like whatever you got her."

"Can you take me to get it? I have some of my allowance saved, but can you take me, please?"

"You're not spending your allowance. I'll take you and pay for it. Something small though, and you have to pick it out." I tug at her braid again.

"You're the best uncle ever!" Annabelle squeals.

Best uncle? *I'd go with yes.* Still an asshole? *Big yes.*

We pull up to Natalie's, and Annabelle shoves the stuff Waverley bought her back in her backpack.

"Hey, um, is it wrong to hide this stuff from Mom?" Annabelle whispers.

I turn to her. "Why would you need to hide this stuff?"

"Mom won't like that Miss Waverley bought me it. I know she doesn't like her. She talks mean about her all the time, and I don't want to make her upset, but I really want to keep this stuff." Annabelle's eyes are big and pleading.

"Annabelle, listen to me. You've got to stop worrying about making your mom upset. The only person's feelings you can control are yours. You can't worry about everyone else's. You'll drive yourself crazy."

"But, what if she makes me throw it away?"

"She won't. I'll talk to her, but you have to pinky promise me you'll stop worrying so much about your mom." I hold out my pinky, waiting for hers.

"Okay, deal." Annabelle smiles a toothy grin as she wraps her pinky around mine, and we head in.

Once inside, I find Nat on the couch, all but sitting in Corey Jenkins' lap.

"Oh, hey guys." Natalie looks up at us but doesn't move. I guess I should just be thankful she's clothed, but her flannel—which is so clearly Corey's—is misbuttoned as if she rushed to get it on.

"Hey, Mom. How was your day?" Annabelle asks, trying to appear unfazed by the strange man in her living room, but I can tell by her body language and her fake happy tone that she's uncomfortable.

"It was great, Belley. Listen, I thought we would go out to eat tonight. How does Bluebirds sound?"

"Awesome." Annabelle jumps up and down.

"Okay, we'll leave in a couple of hours, why don't you watch some TV in your room until then?"

"Okie." Annabelle gives me a hug then walks back to her room.

Natalie finally stands up. "Thanks for picking her up today. I was about to head out the door when you texted."

"Yeah, I'm sure you were. Listen, I've got to talk to you about something." I pause and turn to Corey. "You. Get the hell out."

Corey goes to stand but Natalie pushes him back down on the couch.

"He doesn't have to go anywhere. Corey is my boyfriend, and he can stay as long as I say so." Natalie crosses her arms and gives me a "challenge me" look.

"You know what? I have other issues to talk to you about right now. For instance, you not picking up your daughter from school."

"This again? Owen, I was headed to pick her up, but you got her first."

"I told you to pick her up on time."

Natalie furrows her brows. "What, did it ruin your little girlfriend's day having to spend some time with Annabelle?"

"Nat, Waverley teaches her all day. The least you can do is pick her up on time. And while we are on the topic of Waverley, she bought Annabelle some stuff."

Fire blazes in Natalie's eyes. "What kind of stuff?"

"Just some stuff for her hair, it's not a big deal. You will let Annabelle keep the stuff, and you will not make her feel bad about it."

"You can't be serious. She's not keeping that shit."

"Yes, Nat, she is." I let out a deep breath. "If you let her keep the hair stuff and don't make her feel bad about it, I'll take over picking Annabelle up from school."

Natalie contemplates my offer for a moment, the fire in her eyes dimming. She may hate Waverley, but she hates responsibility more. "Alright, fine."

"So, we have a deal?" Natalie nods. "I mean it, Nat. If I find out—and I will find out—that you made her throw that stuff away, I will drag your ass to the school every morning and every afternoon with me."

"I said yes, now get out, you dick."

"Fine." I turn to Corey before I walk out. "If you so much as make Annabelle feel the least bit uncomfortable, I will kill you. And I won't care what happens to me."

Corey holds up his hands in surrender.

"Okay, Owen, he gets it," Natalie says, pushing me out the door.

Chapter 7

Owen

I'm dead tired at the start of my shift. I couldn't manage to get a quick nap after I dropped off Annabelle. I just had this sickly feeling that I couldn't get rid of. I'm not sure if it is guilt from leaving her there or how shitty I was to Waverley. Or both.

The first hour passes by and about halfway into the second, I get a call from Winry. *That's odd.*

"Hey Win, everything okay?"

"Um, not really. I hate to do this, but I think you should come down to Bluebirds. Natalie is here with some guy and Annabelle. I really hate this, but they are both hammered, and Annabelle is here and I—"

I stop listening after that and race to Bluebirds. My heart is in my stomach, and I know I'm not thinking clearly, so I radio Graham and Levi to meet me there.

I make it there in no time at all; Graham and Levi pull in right behind me. I don't wait on them, I just storm in. I have to make sure Annabelle is okay.

I scan Bluebirds, it's not a huge place, so I find Natalie pretty easily. Not only do I see her, but I *hear* her over the entire bar. She's practically yelling at Lacey, the head bartender—who just cut her off, I'm gathering.

"Natalie, hey, Nat. Calm down. Where's Annabelle?" I turn her toward me and steady her when she starts to stumble.

"Aw, man, what are you doing here?" Natalie slurs.

"Annabelle, Nat. Where's Annabelle?"

"She's fine, Owen. Relax I'm not a terrible mother, I know where she... oh hey, where'd she go?"

I follow Natalie's gaze to her table where Corey is staring off into space, panic immediately sets in.

"Owen, over here," Levi calls, pulling my attention over to the table where Annabelle is sitting at, between Waverley and Wyla while Winry hovers over them. Oh, thank fuck. Waverley has her arm over Annabelle and holds her close. When Annabelle sees me and races around the table to me, tears slip down her face.

"Uncle Owen, I—"

I wrap her up in the tightest hug possible, then lean back to look at her. "Are you okay, Belley?" I wipe her tears and she nods.

"Well, I guess I know who called you." Natalie stumbles over. "You're a real bitch, Waverley. How dare you try to mother my child."

"Natalie, enough!" I snap at her. "Annabelle, I'm going to need you to go wait outside with Graham for a bit, okay?"

Annabelle nods and walks quickly past her mom, Graham nods at me that he's got her, grabbing her hand, and Winry follows them out.

"Natalie, I'm trying really hard not to lose my cool right now, so I need you to walk out quietly. Levi will take you and Corey home, and I'll take Annabelle—"

"Fuck no, Owen, Annabelle stays with me. I'm her mother, she stays with me."

"Natalie, please." I take a deep breath. Raging at her like I want to will only make this situation worse. So, I put on my best calming voice. "Nat, Annabelle going with you isn't an option. You'll go home and sleep this off, and we will talk about this tomorrow."

Natalie looks at me then at Waverley. "This is all your fucking fault."

"Nat—" And before I can say anything more, Natalie grabs the nearest drink and throws it on Waverley. The shock on Wav's face is like a punch in the gut.

"Alright, that's it. Sorry, man... but we have to do our job. Natalie, hands behind your back," Levi says as he starts to cuff Natalie.

"What! Owen, tell him to stop!" Natalie demands.

"Not this time," I say to my sister. "Levi, do me a favor though. Radio to Graham to take Annabelle away from the cars, I don't want her to see this."

Levi nods and radios Graham, pulling Natalie out kicking and screaming. Some other people stand, gawking at the show, while others murmur to each quietly, but I don't pay them any mind. I look over at Waverly who is drying her face with some napkins with Wyla's help.

"Waverley, I'm so sorry. Are you okay?" I ask, kneeling beside her.

"I'm fine," she bites out.

"I'm going to get more napkins," Wyla says.

"Wav, come on, look at me." I take her hand and begrudgingly, she turns her sky-blue eyes to meet mine. "Are you okay?"

"I'm okay. Go take care of Annabelle, I'm fine, really." She tries to pull away, but I stop her, gently pulling her chin back to me.

"Wav... I'm so sorry. What she did was unacceptable. I didn't—"

Wav's eyes soften. "Owen, it's fine. Really. Worse things have happened to me than getting a drink thrown in my face. Now go make sure my girl's okay."

I study her, wanting to know more about what she just said, but she's right. I have to take care of Annabelle.

"Okay, we will need a statement from you before you leave, but I'm going to go check on Annabelle first."

She squeezes my hand. "Go, don't worry about me. I know the drill."

"Okay." I study her again but pull myself away. Annabelle—she's my priority right now.

Outside, I can hear Natalie screaming and crying in the back of Levi's car. I don't see Annabelle anywhere. Levi and Graham walk up with sorry-ass looks on their faces.

"Where's Annabelle?" I bark.

"Relax, Winry took her to Crossroads. It's just down the street, and she needed to get out of here." Graham places his hand on my shoulder. "She's safe with Win, you know that. Levi and I will finish this up. You know, we're going to have to charge her with child endangerment. Call Chief. He should be able to talk to CPS to get you emergency temporary custody."

I run my hands over my face. "She'll also be charged with public intoxication and assault if Wav wants to press charges," Levi adds, and I hate how he calls her Wav.

"Okay, I've got to go check on Annabelle first."

"Go, we've got this." Graham squeezes his grip on my shoulder, then they head back inside.

I head over to Crossroads and find Belley devouring one of Ivy's strawberry cupcakes but when I walk in, she drops it and runs into my arms.

"Hey, Belley. You alright?"

"Yeah, where's Mom? Is she okay? She was acting weird."

"She's okay, but you're going to have to stay with me and Grandma for a while. We'll talk more about it later. I have to make some calls. Can you stay with Winry for a little bit longer?"

Annabelle nods and heads back over to sit on the sofa by Winry. I step outside to call Chief.

"Hello?" Chief answers after the first ring.

"Hello, sir. I have a big favor to ask you." I fill him in on tonight's events. He keeps his cool during the drink throwing part, but knowing him, I know he's pissed. Just as I would be if it was Annabelle. And hell, *I'm* pissed that it happened to Wav. The look on her face gutted me. As much as I needed to make sure Annabelle was okay, I felt that same pull with Wav.

"Alright, well, I'll make some calls and see if I can get you temporary custody. Take the rest of the night off and take care of Annabelle. I'll call you when I get more information on the next steps."

"Thank you, sir. I appreciate it."

"Yeah, yeah. Now let me call and check on my daughter."

"Yes, sir." He hangs up, and I head back inside to take Annabelle home.

Chapter 8

Waverley

Well, tonight took a rather unfortunate turn.

I'm covered in sweet tea, and it's starting to get sticky. I just want to go home and shower, but now I have to give a statement... and decide if I'll press charges against Natalie.

"Hey, Wav, you alright?" Graham and Levi come up to the table where Wyla, Lacey, and I are wiping up sweet tea.

"Yeah, I'm good. Just wet and sticky. How's Annabelle?"

Graham sighs. "She's hanging in there. Win took her to the store. Owen is headed that way now."

"Good." She needs him right now. "And Natalie?"

"In the back of my car. We are taking her in for other charges, but we need to know if you want to press assault charges against her." Levi gives me a sweet smile that, in any other situation, would have me weak in the knees.

I contemplate charging her for a moment but ultimately decide against it. She's Annabelle's mom. I think I would feel guilty every time I saw Annabelle. "No, I'm not going to press charges. I'm fine, really. I just want to go home."

"Okay, Wav. Are you sure?" Graham asks.

"Yeah, I'm sure."

Wyla and I both give statements, and I head for my car.

"Waverley, wait up," Levi hollers behind me.

"Hey, sorry, I thought I was good to go." I turn toward him. *Man, he's so hot.*

"No, you are. I, uh...well, this may be the wrong time, but I was wondering if you would like to get dinner or something some time?"

"Are you asking me out? On a date?"

"Yeah, I am. Sorry, I probably should have waited to ask you another time, but I told myself the next time I saw you that I was going to ask you out. So, here I am."

Okay, that's hot. It makes me feel all giddy that he's thought about me. "Yeah, I'd like that a lot. Let me give you my number."

"Not for this to come off creepy, but I already asked Graham for it." He lets out a small laugh, and it's so cute.

"No, it's not creepy. It's sweet."

I'm rewarded with another small chuckle. "Good, I'll let you get home. I'll talk to you soon." Levi winks then walks back to his car.

Oh my gosh. Oh my gosh. Ahh.

Well, looks like the night has made another turn. This one for the better.

Annabelle doesn't come to class the next day, and my heart hurts thinking about it. I can't imagine what is going through her mind right now. I know Owen will always make sure she is taken care of, but that girl is a worrywart; I know she has to be sick about her mom.

Dad called me last night to check on me. I told him I was fine, but he wasn't happy to hear I'm not pressing charges. Dad's very much a *those who hurt his daughters will burn* type of dad. But he even knew, deep down, that it was the right call to make.

The day goes by like normal, nothing crazy happens, thank God. I'm about to leave when Anna knocks on my door.

"Hey, sugar. Look what was at the front office for you," Anna says holding a bouquet of flowers.

"For me?" I ask, puzzled. Who would have sent me flowers?

"Yeah, the card has your name on it. Check who they are from!" Anna squeaks.

"Okay, okay."

I open the card and it says:

> *Can't wait to take you out.*
> *Levi*

A big smile crosses my face.

"Oh, come on, let me read it," Anna says, pulling the card out of my hand. "Oh, who's Levi?" Anna's eyebrows do a little dance.

"None of your business, Miss Nosey." I take the card back out of her hands.

"Nuh uh, spill Waverley Bennett. Who is this mystery man?" Anna hops on my desk and crosses her legs.

I roll my eyes. "He's new-ish to town. He is one of dad's cops that started a couple months ago. His name is Levi, and he asked me out last night." I haven't told anyone about the mishap with Natalie yesterday. It seems like it's better left alone.

"Ah, this is so awesome for you! Is he hot? What does he look like?"

"Definitely hot."

"Okay, why does it feel like there is a but hanging there?"

"I don't know. He's hot, like jaw-dropping hot, but I don't know, it's probably just nerves from not being on a date in years."

The real reason—one that I have been mostly pushing away as soon as it enters my mind—is Owen. I even had a dream about him last night. I don't know, something ignited when he held my hand and when he looked at me when he asked if I was okay... I felt something.

"You haven't been on a date in years?" Anna's mouth gapes open.

"Nope, I mean I have dated before but not since my freshman year of college." I shrug.

"Hold up, when was the last time you had sex?"

I let out this weird snort laugh. We're not about to talk about this. "Alright, that's enough questions for today." I stand up to gather up my things. My blood pressure just shot through the roof, and I need to get out of here.

"What? No, we're talking about boys and sex." Anna hops off my desk and crosses her arms.

"And now, I'm going home. I'll see you tomorrow." I blow her a kiss.

"You suck," Anna huffs out.

"I know. Hey, turn off the lights when you leave. Love you, bye!"

I walk out, thankful I was able to escape *that* discussion.

I get home and put my flowers in a vase. That was really sweet of him to send those.

Owen and I would never work, so I have decided to let that moment I thought we had go and focus on Levi.

And as if his ears were burning.

Hey, it's Levi, are you free tomorrow night?

> For the man who bought me flowers? Yeah, I'm free. Thank you, by the way. They're beautiful.

I'm glad. I had a feeling you would need something to perk up your day. So, dinner tomorrow?

I'd love to.

Great, I'll pick you up at 7.

Ahh, I have a date. A real date, with an extremely attractive guy.

No cause for panic. Right?

I send Levi my address, and then just as I'm about to call both my sisters, there is a knock at my door. I'd love for it to be sister-telepathy and open the door to find Winry and Wyla on the other side, but that isn't the case.

Owen and Annabelle stand waiting on my little front porch. Annabelle is holding a big, pink gift bag in her hands and is practically shaking with anticipation.

"Hey you," I say to Annabelle. "What are you doing here?"

"I brought you a present! As a thank you for buying me that stuff for my hair." Annabelle beams.

"Oh, sweetie, you didn't have to buy me a present."

"Well, I didn't buy it. Uncle Owen bought it, technically." Annabelle looks up at Owen like he has hung the moon and damn, if that doesn't do something to me.

"Yeah, but you picked it out, so this is all you, Belley." Owen smiles so sweetly at her, and again, I get this tingly feeling.

"Well, come in, come in. I want to open it." I open the door wider for them, and they walk in and take a seat on the couch.

"Okay, let's see what we have here." I reach into the bag, "Oh Annabelle, how did you know I love peanut M&M'S?"

"Uncle Owen asked Winry this morning at breakfast what your favorite candy is. Keep going, there's more."

"Okay, ooh we got some scrunchies, love those. Some pink pens, wonderful, I needed some pretty pens. And oh, Annabelle, this is my favorite." I pull out a coffee mug that has "best teacher ever" on it.

"Do you really like it?"

"Yes, Annabelle, it's perfect, all of it. Thank you, my sweet girl." I wrap her up in a hug. "I missed you today. You know, no one laughed at my jokes today—not one person."

"Maybe because you're not funny?" Owen interjects.

Annabelle and I both shoot him the side eye. "I missed you too, Miss Waverley, and I think you're funny."

"That's all that matters to me." I give her another squeeze. "Why don't we dip into this bag of peanut M&M'S?" Annabelle nods eagerly. "Yeah, that's my girl.

Hold on, let me get a bowl so we can share. I'll be right back."

I head to the kitchen, and Owen follows me. "Hey, how are you doing today?" he asks sheepishly.

"I'm fine, Owen, really. No damage done. It was just a drink." I grab a small bowl out of a cabinet.

"You should have pressed charges, Wav. You know it legally qualifies as assault."

"I know that, and no, I shouldn't have. Come on, Owen, did you really expect me to press charges against your sister? I couldn't do that."

He takes a step into me, and his cologne hits me, making me weak in the knees. I can't put my finger on the smell exactly, it's just *Owen*. "You didn't press charges because of me?"

I did say that, didn't I? It's true though, deep down I couldn't do it to Owen as much as I couldn't do it to Annabelle. "Not just you... Annabelle too."

"Waverley, what did you mean when you said—" He stops mid-sentence and picks up the card from Levi that's sitting on the table. "He sent you flowers?" Owen asks, sounding oddly hurt.

"Um, yeah." Damn it, why do I feel guilty right now?

"So, you and Levi? Y'all a thing now?" He says it with disdain that makes my feeling guilty mode switch to defensive mode. His grip on the card tightens and clenches his jaw tight.

I yank the card out of his hand. "Not that it's any of your business, but he did ask me out."

"And you said yes?" he quips, almost like he can't believe it.

I stare into those deep green eyes; I would get lost in them if I weren't feeling waves of anger coming on. "Yeah, I said yes. What do you care?"

"I don't," Owen says, shortly.

"Okay, good." I brush past him and go back to the living room, ending the conversation. I have nothing to feel guilty about, but the look on Owen's face makes me question if we could ever be something.

No, that's crazy.

"Here we go." I plop down next to Annabelle and pour the jumbo bag of M&M'S in the bowl.

"Just a little bit, Annabelle. I've got to get you to Grandma's, so I can go to work," Owen says, standing as far away from me as possible.

"Okay." Annabelle dives into the bowl of candy.

We talk about school for a little bit as we munch. I fill her in on what she missed today, and she tells me about the book she started this morning. Owen stands firmly planted across the room. I can feel his eyes on me, and I can't help my gaze going to him every other bite. We lock eyes a few times, but I always turn away quickly.

With one more glance I turn away again. He walks up to us and finally speaks. "Alright, time to go."

"Aw man, why can't I stay here tonight? It would be easier for you anyway, Uncle Owen. She could take me to school in the morning so you don't have to." Annabelle puts on her best sad puppy eyes and bounces them between me and Owen.

"No, Belley, you're not Waverley's responsibility. Plus, it's rude to invite yourself to places, you know that."

"Sorry." Annabelle pouts.

Her sad face does me in. "Well, maybe not tonight but why don't we plan on you staying one day soon. That is, if you're okay with it?" I look to Owen.

"Oh please, Uncle Owen, please. Please!"

Owen gives me an unreadable look, then exhales. "We'll talk about it, but for now we have to go. Say goodbye."

"Bye, Miss Waverley." Annabelle's smile is a mile wide as she gives me a big hug.

"Bye, cutie, and thank you for my present. I love it." I squeeze her tight then walk them to the door.

Annabelle races to the truck, leaving Owen and I on my porch. The silence between us is deafening. "I don't mind keeping her one night."

"It wasn't your place to offer that in front of her, Waverley. Now I'm going to have to be the bad guy. She's not your responsibility, she's mine." His tone is harsh and irritated.

I'm taken back for a second. *Is he really upset?*

"I didn't mean to overstep. I thought I was helping. You know, it would be helpful if I kept her one night, and we would have fun."

"That's not the point," he snaps and shakes his head, looking anywhere but at me.

I throw my hands up. "Okay, then what is the point?"

Silence.

"I teach her every day, take care of her for hours. I would never let anything happen to her. Ever."

Silence again. He just scratches his jaw and continues to look off, and I'm getting more pissed by the second.

"Is this about Levi? Because you've been acting like I kicked your puppy."

Owen snorts out a sarcastic laugh and finally looks at me. "Please, this has nothing to do with you and Levi."

I throw my hands up again. "Okay, what then?"

"You're not her mom, Waverley," he barks.

"I'm not trying to be! Seriously, Owen. I offered to keep her because she's an awesome kid, but also because you've been running yourself ragged for years taking care of her. I wanted to help *you*, asshole. I was doing it for *you*." I poke him hard in the chest. "I *wanted* to do it for you!" I poke him hard again, and he grabs my wrist.

A thrill goes down my spine.

Owen doesn't speak, he just looks at me. The same look he gave me last night. I'm not sure if I'm imagining things, but there's this new tension between us, like *I want to find out what you taste like* tension.

Owen's eyes drop to my mouth and for a moment I think he may actually want to kiss me, but then Annabelle yells, "Come on, Uncle Owen."

Owen sighs and lets go of my wrist before walking away without another word.

When they drive off, I let out the breath I didn't realize I was holding.

Chapter 9

Owen

"You alright, man? I know this is a tough situation, but I don't know... you seem off," Graham says as we load some of Annabelle and Natalie's stuff into the moving truck.

Today sucks for many reasons.

One: I am completely moving Natalie and Annabelle out of their house when I just worked a 12-hour night shift.

Two: I have to take all of their stuff to three separate places. Natalie's necessities to my mom's house, Annabelle's to my house, and all their junk to a storage unit that I now pay for.

And three: Waverley is going on her date with Levi today.

I was doing it for you, replays in my head.

After hearing that, everything seemed to fade. I was just about to crash my lips to hers when Belley chose that very moment to interrupt.

Shit, was I really going to kiss Waverley?

I was doing it for you.

Fuck, I was. I was going to kiss Waverly Bennett.

Why, though? I mean I don't have... feelings for her.

I wanted to do it for you.

Fuck, fuck, I think I might.

And now she's going on a date with Levi?

Fuck that.

"I'm fine. Nothing I can't handle." I shrug. "Thanks for helping me. I know you're just as exhausted as I am."

"It's no problem. Win is working till six, and who needs sleep anyway? Personally, I love staying up for over twenty-four hours." The sarcasm is heavy in his tone.

"Fuck off," I joke.

"No, really. How is everything going?"

How is everything going? Let's see, I now have temporary custody of Annabelle. Natalie didn't put up too much of a fight during our hearing yesterday morning, as long as she could get supervised visitation. During our hearing, I found out Natalie lost her waitressing job at the diner in town, so now she's to moving back in with Mom. Thankfully, Chief knows her landlord and was able to get her out of her lease, just another reason I owe Chief Bennett my life. And to top it all off, I haven't been able to stop thinking about that moment with Waverley.

"It's going. I mean Natalie hasn't made matters worse—yet, that is. The living situation will be a little tricky. My mom is planning on coming to sleep at my house during the nights I work and then we're going to work out a few hours during the week that I will take Annabelle over to my mom's so she can visit with Nat."

"I'm sorry, man. Listen, if you ever need a break, you know Win and I can help take care of Annabelle."

"Yeah, I know you can but like I said, it's nothing I can't handle. Now, come on, let's get this shit over with."

After a long shitty day, we finally get everything out of Natalie's place. Stuff may still be shoved in the moving truck, but I have that for another day, so I'm not worrying about it right now.

I pick Annabelle up from Mom's house a little after eight. I'm dead tired, starving, and did I mention, dead tired? We load up in my truck and just when I think I'll get to go home, Annabelle asks, "Can we go get ice cream?"

"Ice cream? Come on, kid. I've been moving stuff all day."

"And you deserve ice cream. Please, Uncle Owen, we haven't gotten ice cream together in so long. Please, please, please." Annabelle turns her pleading puppy dog eyes on me. *Shit. I guess we're getting ice cream.*

"Alright, but we are getting it to go."

"Deal."

We pull into the ice cream shop, and Belley jumps out. I don't think I could jump right now if you paid me. I round the corner of my truck and *fuck me*.

"Uncle Owen, that's a bad word," Annabelle snaps.

I didn't even realize I said it out loud. I'm too busy staring at Waverley standing outside of the ice cream shop in a pink sundress that ties in a bow on the back. She looks fucking adorable. Her dark waves are pulled half up with one of the scrunchies Annabelle bought her.

For a moment, I feel all my stress fade away, but it all comes slamming back when Levi walks out the door and hands her some ice cream. "Fuckin' hell."

"Uncle Owen!" Annabelle smacks at me.

"Sorry, Belley. Come on, let's get it and go." And with any luck Annabelle won't see her and I can get the hell—

"Miss Waverley!" Annabelle squeals.

Why? Why me?

"Hi, cutie, what are you doing here?" Waverley turns and gives Belley a hug like she didn't just see her a couple hours ago at school.

"Uncle Owen brought me to get some ice cream, but I wouldn't talk to him if I were you, he's in a bad mood."

"Hey, I brought you here," I snap.

"See what I mean." Annabelle rolls her eyes.

Waverley's head falls back in laughter. *Man, that's a good sound.*

"Hey, Owen. How's it going?" Levi asks and drapes his arm over Waverley when he notices that I haven't been able to stop looking at her.

"Good. Long day," I say, shortly.

"Can we eat our ice cream with Miss Waverley? Pleaseeeeeee?" she begs.

"No, Annabelle, we made a deal. Ice cream to-go or no ice cream."

"But—"

"No buts."

"Ugh, you never let me do anything," Annabelle stomps past me with a huff.

"I know, I'm the worst. Right, Firecracker?"

A look of hesitation crosses her face briefly. "No arguments here."

"Well, that's a first." I laugh and before I can help it, I drag my eyes up and down her body, admiring how innocent, yet sexy, she looks.

Levi clears his throat, bringing me back to reality.

"Right." I cough into my fist. "Y'all have a good night," I say tightly.

"We will," Levi replies, tightening his arm around her waist, pulling her in closer. *Well, that hurts.* Waverley looks up at him and smiles.

And now, I'm dead. Great.

Chapter 10

Owen

"Quit being a dick and come," Graham says over the phone.

"Get off my ass, I'm not going," I grumble. I was kicked back on my couch peacefully scrolling through Netflix when Graham called with the third degree.

"Owen, it won't be the same without you there. If you come, I'll play cornhole left-handed during our game," Winry yells in the background.

Tonight is Chief Bennett's annual barbecue he hosts every summer. Normally, I'm all about it. We eat great food, play cornhole, drink some beers, and have a good time.

But it's been a shit week, and the last thing I want to do is watch Levi and Wav make googly eyes at each other all night. Levi didn't say much about their date to me but apparently, he told Graham it went really well. The thoughts of what "really well" could mean makes my stomach hurt.

"I'd still probably lose to you either way, Win. Graham can't even beat you."

One thing you need to know about Winry is that she doesn't lose games——any game——period.

"I can beat her at some things," Graham says adamantly.

"Yeah, who can come first doesn't count," I chuckle.

"Ha! Got 'em." Winry laughs.

"Fuck off, and Win—I'm going to spank your ass so hard tonight you won't be able to sit without thinking about me inside of you."

"Promise?" she replies.

"Oh gross. Come on, guys, I'm still on the phone. Save that shit for later." Graham and Winry truly deserve every bit of happiness and all that involves, but I don't need to hear about it.

"Sorry, Owen," Winry apologizes.

"I'm not sorry, because one: it's going to be awesome, and two: you're being a dick by not coming tonight," Graham says.

"I'm not being a dick. It's been a long week. I'll have to bring Annabelle with me, and she's been in a shit mood today too."

Annabelle is never in a bad mood. When I think about what could be causing the mood swings, my blood pressure goes sky-high.

"Have you asked her if she wants to go? I bet if you tell her that Wav will be there, she'll want to go," Winry suggests what I already know.

To add the nail on the coffin, Graham says, "Chief also helped your ass a lot last week, you need to come tonight."

I groan internally. Damn it, he's right.

"Fine, fine. I'll come, but I'm not playing cornhole."

"But it's tradition!" Winry whines.

"That's the deal. Beggars can't be choosers, Win."

"Fine," she groans.

"Okay, so it's settled. We'll see ya soon," Graham says happy with himself that he has won this argument.

"Yeah, yeah, see you soon."

After I hang up I holler for Annabelle to come out of her room.

"What's up?" Annabelle asks, poking her head out of her door.

"Get ready, we're going to a barbecue at the Bennett's in twenty minutes."

"Really?" she whines.

"Yes, really." Annabelle rolls her eyes, and I really don't think I can deal with a bad-mood Belley tonight, so I add, "Waverley will be there."

Her eyes change from irritated to bright and excited. "Okay, I'll go change."

Yeah, that's what I thought. I do the same, throwing on a pair of jeans and one of my ACPD t-shirts. I put some deodorant on and check my reflection in the bathroom mirror. *Damn, I look how I feel.* I fuss with my hair for a bit. When I can't seem to get it to do what I want, I give up and work on my beard. It's a little longer than I like, but I don't have time to fix it, so I put some beard oil on to help tame it.

Why am I even trying right now? I couldn't give two shits about how the guys I work with think I look but... I guess it's not *them* I'm thinking about.

"Come on, Belley. Let's go."

"I'm coming," Annabelle snaps. *Lord help me.*

We pull up to the Bennett's a little after six. Annabelle's mood has done a one-eighty turn, thankfully. I've been trying to give her some grace. Her life has been turned upside down this week.

I cooked at Mom's last night, and she got to spend some time with Natalie which went as well as it could with her. They mostly watched TV, but I know it made Annabelle happy to see her mom, so I didn't lecture Nat about not talking to her, even though I wanted to.

Everyone at the station is invited to this barbeque every year—it's not mandatory by any means, but everyone who can make it usually comes. It's something that the whole station looks forward to.

Chief is manning the grill on the upper deck, as always. There are tables all through the massive yard, and most importantly, cornhole boards are set up in the middle.

Mrs. Bennett spots us first. "Oh, hey guys. I'm so glad you came." She wraps us up in a hug. The Bennett women are huggers, you just have to accept it.

"Hi, Mrs. Bennett. Happy to be here."

"Owen, how many times do I have to tell you to call me Isabel." She gives me the sternest look she can manage, but it's about as menacing as a bunny. All of the Bennett women have dark hair and favor each other so much, but Wav and her mom share the same blue eyes.

"Just a few more times, ma'am."

"You're something else." She shakes her head. "Well, go enjoy. Graham and the girls are over there." She points them out, and Annabelle takes off with a squeal.

I follow behind at a snail's pace compared to how fast Annabelle is moving. Belley shouts Wav's name, then runs into her waiting arms and wraps her up tight. Waverley giggles at her embrace and returns the hug. My heart explodes right then and there.

"Hey there, Belley. I'm so happy you're here." Waverley gives her one more squeeze before letting go. "Oh look, we match." Wav pulls her long braid around her shoulder and does the same with Annabelle's.

"Oh my gosh, we do!" Annabelle looks like she has a coat hanger stuck in her mouth, her smile is so wide.

I'm completely enthralled watching them talk and laugh together, when Levi comes up and hugs Wav. My heart that just exploded from joy has now been stomped on.

"Hey, Owen. What's up, man?" Levi says with an arm still around Waverley.

I grit my teeth and force a smile. "Nothing much, just hanging out."

Wyla, Winry, and Graham join our party, and the girls all hug everyone. Like I said—huggers.

"Well, Levi, looks like you will have to be Graham's cornhole partner this year." Winry pats him on the back. "I know this is your first time, but Wyla and I win every year, so don't get too excited about your chances."

Waverley turns to me. "You're not playing?" It almost looks like concern crosses her face, but it fades quickly.

"Not this year, Firecracker."

"All the same, I guess—you're terrible." Wav snorts a laugh.

"Hey, you're just as bad. I can't even remember the last time you played."

"You don't play?" Levi asks her.

"No, I'll hang out with Annabelle and watch." Waverley smiles sweetly at Belley.

"Yay!" Annabelle cheers.

Chief whistles a standard loud dad whistle and yells, "Alright, who's hungry?"

We all get plates and devour Chief's burgers. The man knows how to grill, even Belley is eating hers, and she can be picky. I was hoping that I could get some space from Waverley while we ate, so I sat on the opposite side of the table. However, Annabelle decides to take the open seat right next to her and Levi. She keeps trying to talk to me from the opposite end, so I end up having to move.

I leave most of the talking to everyone else. I speak when Annabelle asks one of her million questions but otherwise, I just sit and do my best not to look at Wav. I'm doing pretty well until it's time for the cornhole tournament, and I'm left at the table with just Waverley and Annabelle.

"I'm going to grab another water. Annabelle, do you want something?" Waverley stands from the table.

"No, thank you. You're coming back here though, right?" Belley asks.

"I will, promise." Wav smiles at her then looks in my direction. I don't get the same smile but it's not a go-to-hell look either. "What about you, want a beer?"

"Water, please, I don't drink with..." I nod at Annabelle.

A strange look crosses her face. It almost looked like she was impressed by that. "Right... well, I'll be right back."

My eyes follow her as she walks away. Wav has on jean short overalls with a white tee underneath, her long hair is in a braid, and she has one of the scrunchies Annabelle bought her on her wrist. I think that's what gets me the most. She truly loves what Annabelle bought her and has worn it not once, but twice that I know of.

"What are you staring at, Uncle Owen?"

"Hmm, what?"

"You were staring." Annabelle laughs.

"Hush, you." I steal some chips off her plate and shove them in my mouth.

Waverley comes back, and we sit in comfortable silence watching everyone play, except when Annabelle asks what the score is after every turn. After a few games, Annabelle excuses herself to go to the bathroom, leaving me alone with my firecracker.

"So, how's she really doing?" Wav asks.

"She's hanging in there, been a little moody, but I figured that's normal given everything that has happened."

"It could also be—"

"Don't say it, don't even think it."

Waverley laughs. "I'm going to say something, but don't make a thing out of it, okay? You're doing what's right for her, Owen. I imagine what happened has been extremely difficult for her, but you can't even tell she's been through something traumatic because of you. She's lucky to have you."

"Thank you, Waverley. That means a lot to me." We stare at each other, searching, studying for answers that we aren't even sure are there. Annabelle comes back and slides into her seat next to Wav, pulling her gaze away from mine.

"What's the score now?" Annabelle asks for the thousandth time.

"Um, I'm not sure, actually, but I'm pretty sure Win and Wyla are about to finish it." Graham has his hands folded on the top of his head as Levi throws his last sack. It misses, and I'd be lying if it didn't bring a bit of a smile to my face.

Winry and Wyla jump and cheer, rubbing their victory in everyone's faces. Waverley jumps up to join them, and all is right in the world until Levi has Waverley back in his arms. Needing to get a little space, I tell Annabelle to stay put while I go to the bathroom.

I splash some water on my face and head back out. When I look out over the yard, I wish I had never even come tonight. Everyone is now sitting around the fire. Wav's head is back in laughter, a full, genuine laugh at whatever Levi just said. *Fuck.*

"Do all of my officers have feelings for my daughters?" Chief Bennett steps up next to me and I panic.

"I don't have feelings for Waverley," I blurt out.

"I didn't say which daughter. But sorry, son. It's been pretty obvious to everyone tonight who you've got your mind on."

"Aw, hell, everyone?"

"Everyone but Waverley, that is. I thought Levi was going to hit you a few times, but then he probably remembered what I told him when I hired him."

"What was that?"

"I told him I pride myself on my officers. How they conduct themselves in and out of uniform is important. I told him if he ever needed an example to look at you."

My head whips to face Chief. "Me?"

"Yes, it's shocking, I know, but also true. You're an outstanding officer, Owen, and what you do for that girl of yours. Well, if you gave Waverley a tenth of what you give Annabelle, there'd be no complaints from me."

I'm too shocked to speak. Did Chief give me his blessing, all the while telling me how great I was while doing it? "Thank you, sir. It means more to me than you know."

"Alright enough of the soft stuff, just don't let obstacles deter you from going after what you want." He claps me on the back and heads to join the party.

I take another look at Waverley. Her beautiful blue eyes seem to find mine from across the yard, but she looks away quickly. Levi seems to notice because he pulls her back into his hold. I hate it. Levi is a good guy— I'd even go as far as to call him a friend, but I'm going to have to ruin our friendship because I'm fighting for my girl.

Huh, my girl? You'd think that should feel weird to me, but it doesn't because that's what she is now. *Mine.*

Chapter 11

Waverley

I pull into Crossroads a little before nine to meet my sisters like we do every Sunday morning ever since Win opened. Winry and Wyla occupy our usual table already gossiping about something.

"Hey, sorry I'm a little late. What are we talking about?" I pull out my chair to slide in. A coffee mug with my regular order of a hot hazelnut latte and a big cinnamon roll sit on the table in front of me. "Mm, thanks for this."

"Of course. We were actually just talking about you," Winry says with her eyebrows raised, sipping her coffee.

"Oh no, what'd I do?" I laugh.

"More like *who'd* you do," Wyla snickers.

"Who'd I do? What are y'all talking about?"

"Oh, how you had two guys eye fucking you all night last night. Taking bets on which one you'll actually do." Wyla wiggles her eyebrows at me.

"Two guys? Y'all are going to have to spell it out for me because I have no idea what you're talking about."

"Oh, come on. Wav. Did you seriously not notice?" Winry asks.

I take a sip of my coffee. "Well, Levi seemed a little clingier last night than usual, but I don't know which other guy you're talking about."

"Yeah." Win chuckles. "Clingier because Owen kept looking at you like he wanted to steal you away."

"What? No, you guys are crazy. He was not." I nearly laugh at their accusation, but I'd be lying if I said this weird, excited, tingly feeling didn't come over me. Sitting with him and Annabelle during the cornhole tournament yesterday was actually... nice. We didn't poke at each other or fight. Talking to him felt *right*.

"You were looking at Owen too," Winry says, taking a bite of her muffin, and Wyla nods.

My face heats. I did catch myself gravitating to Owen yesterday. It was like my gaze would just drift to him.

"Okay, I definitely was not looking at Owen. You two have lost your minds."

"Right, are you forgetting who you are talking to right now? Cut the crap and talk to us. What's going on?" Winry gives me a little shove.

"That's part of my problem, I don't know what is going on," I blurt out. It's true though, I really don't know what has changed between me and Owen, but something has shifted. I find myself thinking about him ever since the drink throwing incident. Not to mention Annabelle—I love that girl and seeing how Owen is with her is enough to make any girl melt. And then to add fuel to fire, that moment on the porch messed my brain right up.

"Alright, start from the top." Wyla sets down her mug and they both give me their full attention.

I take a deep breath then let it all out. That's one of the benefits of having sisters, they're always there to listen to your drama.

Winry rests her chin on her hand. "What about Levi? How is that going?"

"It's fine, but that's it—it's just fine. We've only been on one date, and we didn't even have like a real kiss."

"A real kiss? What does that mean?" Wyla asks.

"It was just kind of like a kiss but with no *humph*. It felt like I was kissing a friend, which sucks because he's so hot and really nice, but it's not—"

"Making your lady bits dance." Winry laughs. "You think Owen can?"

"I don't know, but part of me wants to find out. And sometimes, it feels like something may happen but then one of us gets pissed off at the other."

"You two sure do like to argue," Winry agrees. "I bet the sex would be so good."

"It's not even about sex though." As far as my sisters know, I'm a sex-positive participant, but truthfully, I couldn't be more terrified. "Owen and I—we would be a mess together."

"You don't know that. You haven't even given him a chance yet." Winry takes another bite of her muffin.

"I don't know. I still think Levi is the better choice. He seems to really like you." Wyla shrugs.

"Sorry, but I'm team Owen. I think you should give him a shot." Winry gives me a soft smile. "But ultimately, it's your choice and frankly, you don't have to choose either of them."

"Yeah, okay, different topic now, please." I take a sip of my coffee. "Let's talk about wedding dress shopping," I suggest, knowing that will most definitely do the trick.

"Ah, yes!" Winry starts vibrating with joy.

We talk wedding for a while and about Wyla's classes that she's taking this summer to finish her vet tech license. All while I have an internal argument with myself the rest of the time, but I manage to hide it well from my sisters.

Could I actually give Owen a chance?

I roam down the aisles of Walmart. I need some vitamins, mousse, and I should probably grab some tampons while I'm here. I shouldn't start my period for another week, but I'm here, so I make a mental note to grab some.

I grab the mousse, the vitamins, and head toward the feminine aisle. I round the corner and there stands the man I just spent half of the morning thinking about, looking confused as hell holding two different boxes of tampons.

"Owen?"

He jumps and nearly drops both boxes. "Fuck, Waverley, you scared me."

I laugh. "I could tell. Um, what are you doing here?"

Owen gives me a look of pure terror and desperation. "I'll give you one guess as to why I'm standing in this aisle."

It takes me a minute but then it dawns on me... *Annabelle*. I was about eleven when I first got my period.

"How is she? How are you?"

"Both mortified. She's in the truck now. She has been crying all day, and I don't know what to do. Part of me wants to call Natalie, but I'm also terrified of what she will tell her this means and if she'll even tell her the right stuff. Like am I supposed to have the "talk" with her now? I don't think I'm ready for this." Panic riddles his voice.

"Slow down, honey." The endearment slips out before I realize it, but it seems to help calm him down. "Let me help. Go take Annabelle back to your place and order a giant pizza. I'll get everything she needs and meet you there. Just text me your address."

Owen deflates and puts the boxes in his hands back. "You don't have to, Wav. I can figure this out."

"Do you even truly know what a period is?"

Owen's eyes grow wide. "You're right. Here. Take my card. Buy both of y'alls stuff with it. I mean it—*both*—and I'll see you at my house."

He shoves the card in my hand and swiftly exits the store. I get to work picking out some pads in various sizes, some tampons in the brand I use, some panty liners, and some Midol.

My phone dings with a message from Owen with his address and asks if I'm good with pepperoni on my pizza. I text him back and get back to my shopping. I swing by the underwear section and grab a pack of cotton panties, then hit the chocolate aisle. I stock up on sweets and absolute junk and head for Owen's.

I pull in just as the pizza guy is leaving. I grab all the bags and ring the doorbell, to which a very stressed Owen answers.

"How's it going?" I ask.

"Let's see, she has locked herself in her room because I told you. She said, 'you've ruined my life.' Here, let me take those." Owen takes the bags out of my hands and takes them to the counter.

"Oof, that's rough. Don't worry, I've got the stuff to help."

I walk into his house, and I'm a little stunned. I didn't expect it to look so cozy and clean. It's simple but homey. He has pictures up on the walls of him and Annabelle. There are pillows and blankets that actually match on the sectional. Not a single dish is in the sink, and the best part is the whole place smells just like him.

After a second of breathing in the amazing scent that is Owen West, I remember why I'm actually here, and start to sift through the bags to grab everything I need.

"Which room is she in?"

"First door on your right. Should I go in there with you?" Owen runs his hands through his hair nervously.

"You can if you want to. It might be good, but it might also make it worse." Owen contemplates both options, and I know this is killing him, not knowing what's best for her. He always does his best for her, but this is a little out of his wheelhouse.

I take his hand in mine. "Why don't we ask her?"

Panic still holds him tightly, but he nods and squeezes my hand gently before letting go. I lightly knock on her door, "Annabelle, it's Waverley. Can I come in, please?"

For a moment there's no answer, but then she opens her door. "Hi, Miss Waverley," she mumbles.

"You know it's okay to call me Wav outside of school, Belley." I chuckle. "Listen, I know you are upset at your uncle for telling me, but it wasn't his fault. We just ran into each other in the aisle. I know this is all confusing and scary, but let us in, and we can talk about it."

"Okay." Annabelle opens the door the rest of the way to let us in and I take a seat at the foot of her bed.

"I got you some stuff. I'll go over how all of it works and the rules to follow with them. I also got you some new underwear, some pain medicine, and an obscene amount of junk food for when we're done. I'm not going to lie to you, Annabelle. I want you to ask me whatever comes to your mind. Okay?"

Annabelle nods, and I start with the basics, what's happening, and some changes she may notice in her body. She asks some standard questions, and I answer. When she's comfortable, I go over the differences in the feminine products, when it's best to wear what and for how long. Owen sits quietly, but I can tell he's listening just as intently as Annabelle is. I steer clear of any sexual talk; we didn't really discuss doing the "talk", so I keep it to a minimum.

"Okay, now believe me when I tell you that sometimes periods suck. I promised I wouldn't lie, and I won't. Most of the time it's a pain, but it's part of being a woman. I want you to know you can always talk to me and your uncle about anything, got it?"

Annabelle nods in agreement.

"Okay, do you have any more questions?"

"Not right now, I don't think."

"Okay, well if you think of any, ask away." I smile, and she smiles back. "Let's go eat."

We head back into the kitchen and Owen gets some plates for the pizza. We eat the whole thing and half of the chocolate and treats I bought while we watch a little TV and hang out. It's so comfortable. It feels *safe*.

"Alright, Annabelle, time to turn in. You've got to go to some silly school program tomorrow." Owen winks at me. "Say good night to Wav."

"Night, Miss... Wav. Thank you for your help."

Annabelle gives me a big hug, then Owen, and heads to her room leaving Owen and I alone.

"Oh, before I forget." I head to my bag and pull out my phone. I pull up the notes I made and send them to Owen. "Here, I typed out a list of the brands I bought today and the general rules to follow with them. I know you were listening in there, but I thought just in case."

"Wav, this is amazing... you're amazing. Thank you for helping me." He's standing so close now, just a small step and there wouldn't be anything but our clothes between us. My heart pounds in my chest, I'm afraid even he can hear it. Owen brushes a strand of hair from my face, and I suck in a breath.

"I'm going to kiss you now," he whispers as if he may scare this moment away.

"Okay," I whisper back, feeling the same.

His lips brush against mine. It starts a slow, soft kiss, but when I part my lips giving him a little more room to work with, he deepens the kisses. With the first sweep of his tongue, I let out an involuntary moan, and he loses all restraint.

The kiss becomes manic, demanding, passionate. It's everything you would want in a kiss. I tangle my hands in his hair, and he starts to roam my body. Everything is amazing and all I have ever wanted... until it's not. This kiss feels like it's leading somewhere, images flash in my head, that night, the room, the—

"Stop," I croak. "Stop, please."

Owen lets go immediately and steps back, giving me space. "Okay, Wav, it's okay." I'm breathing erratically, and this place is starting to feel very small. "Waverley, are you okay? Talk to me."

I close my eyes, willing the panic attack away, locking those memories back tightly in a box in my brain. Strong hands gently touch my shoulders but even that's too much, I jump back. Kissing Levi was nothing—I felt nothing. But kissing Owen? I'm feeling everything. That kiss made me want more and that... that thought terrifies me.

"Wav, hey, it's okay, baby."

I finally open my eyes and see those emerald-green ones studying me, almost like he is trying to memorize my face.

"I need to go," I blurt out and walk past him grabbing my stuff.

"Waverley, talk to me, did I do something wrong? I'm so sorry if I did. Please talk to me."

I can't—I can't tell him but... I want to. I want so badly to lay it all out there, to get this off my chest, but I've never said it out loud before. I don't think I can. Tears start to well in my eyes. I've got to get out of here.

The way he's looking at me, pleading with me to tell him what he did wrong, apologizing for something completely out of his control, it's breaking me down piece by piece.

"Waverley, will you at least look at me?"

But I can't, and he doesn't stop me on my way out.

Chapter 12

Owen

This kiss, this woman. Her lips are so soft, and she tastes like sweet chocolate. When she lets out a low moan, I nearly come right then. Her hands go up to my hair, and mine start to travel up and down her curves. This is heaven.

"Stop," she pants out. "Stop, please." Her voice trembles, and I let her go immediately.

"Okay, Wav, it's okay." Absolute terror mars her beautiful face, and she is starting to hyperventilate. I lightly place my hand on her shoulders, trying to ground her, but she jumps back, almost like she's scared of me. "Wav, hey, it's okay, baby."

Her eyes shoot open. "I need to go." She pushes past me to get her things.

I'm dying to hold her here and find out what's going on, but something is telling me not to touch her.

"Waverley, talk to me, did I do something wrong? I'm so sorry if I did. Please talk to me."

She stops in her tracks, back turned to me with her hand on the doorknob. I can see her battling something, her breath still uneven. I don't want her to leave like this.

"Waverley, will you at least look at me?"

But she doesn't, she turns the knob and walks out without another word.

I fold my hands behind my head. *What just happened?* Everything felt right tonight. Her being the one to talk to Annabelle, being here with us, laughing with us.

Was she more serious with Levi than I thought? I wasn't thinking about him. I was thinking about her and how badly I wanted to kiss her.

Yet again, I'm an asshole. I shouldn't have put her in this situation.

I'm about to kick my sorry-ass all the way to my bed when there's a soft knock at my door. *Please let it be her, please let it be her.*

I open the door, "Wav, I—"

"I was raped when I was sixteen."

Her words feel like a bullet to the chest. They startle me to my very core. I physically have to take a step back. "What did you say?"

"I can't say it again, Owen. Please don't make me." A tear escapes down her face, and she wipes it away.

I stare at her, processing the words that just left her mouth. So many emotions run through my brain, so many questions, so much hurt and pain for my girl.

"Words. I need you to say some words," she says softly.

"I... uh... I... Do you want to come back in?"

"Okay." She presses her lips together and wipes another tear. She takes a seat on my couch, and I try to sit close but not too close.

We sit in silence, but my mind is anything but quiet. My mind is screaming a very specific question that I need an answer to, *who did this to you*? But I won't push her to talk about this.

"I'll sit here all night in silence with you, Wav. Don't feel like you have to talk about it, if you're not ready."

We sit quietly for a minute longer, tears silently falling down her face, then she takes a deep breath and starts. "I was sixteen. I was staying the night at my friend's house with a group of girls." She takes another breath. "Her parents were gone for the weekend. I knew this but didn't tell Mom or Dad, or even Wyla or Winry. After a few hours, some of the girls wanted to go meet up with some guys we went to school with. I knew if I went out with them, I would get busted. Dad has always had eyes and ears everywhere, and I didn't want to be grounded, so I stayed at her house while they all went out.

"I kicked back on her couch thinking I made the right decision." She lets out a pained laugh and wraps her arms around herself. "About an hour later, her older brother came home. I didn't really know him, other than he was in Winry's grade and had just seen him around town, but

I wasn't too worried. He came in stumbling, obviously drunk from being at a party, and sat on the couch next to me."

Her arms only unwrap from herself to wipe her tears then they go back around her body.

"He was cute and older, so I didn't get up. I talked to him, even a little smitten by him. It was so stupid." Her tears fall harder, and every fiber of my being is begging me to go to her, to hold her, take her pain away.

She takes another shaky breath. "He started to kiss me, and at first everything was fine. Then things started to progress, and I just...wasn't ready, so I told him to stop. He...um, he didn't." Waverley chokes out the words as she falls apart.

Every second of watching her cry is like another bullet to the chest. I want to hold her. No, I *need* to hold her and remind her that she's safe here.

Before I can scoot closer she turns to me and falls into my chest.

"Let it out, baby, you're safe here." I comb my fingers through her hair as my shirt soaks up her tears. Her body trembles, and I pull her in closer. "You're safe, Wav. I promise."

"Why? Why did he do this to me? He hurt me," she cries. "God, he hurt me and all I did was let him kiss me. I didn't"—she chokes on her tears—"I didn't want—"

"Waverley, listen to me. This is not your fault," I cut her off and hold her tightly as she continues to cry. I want to rage and track down whoever did this to her, but I know that's not what she needs from me. She needs this. To let it out and to have a shoulder to cry on, and damn it, I want to be that shoulder for the rest of her life.

After a few minutes, her tears slow and she pulls back to wipe her cheeks and under her eyes. "He passed out after. I had to get out of there, so I drove to my Mamaw's house. I told her I got in a fight with my friends and needed a place to stay because I didn't want to get in trouble. She never asked another question. I always felt like she knew it was something more. I still have never told anyone what happened that night. Ever."

"Waverley..." All this time she's dealt with this alone.

"I've debated telling my sisters so many times and there are so many times I've convinced myself to tell my parents, but I never did. Two years after, I decided to tell Dad. He came home late. There was a single car fatality that night that kept him over. A drunk driver had gone off the road and hit a tree. He wasn't wearing a seatbelt and was ejected out of the car. Mom asked who the guy was and when he said his name, it was almost like I could breathe again." A few more tears fall and I reach to wipe them away.

"He was gone, and I know it's terrible, but I started getting my confidence back. I still had the weight of this, but knowing I would never see him again... I started working on myself and figuring out who I am. I decided I wasn't going to let this control me anymore and I would take back my love life and my body. I made a promise that the next time a man saw me—any part of me—it would be my choice." Waverley swallows and looks down at her lap. "I stuck to that for another three years. Never letting anyone take that from me, until...the Fourth of July."

No, no, no, no. I flash back to that day. A group of friends and I decided to go to the beach to set off some fireworks. I'm slightly older than Winry, but our families have always been friends, so I invited her to come. Naturally, she brought her sisters. When it came time to set them off, one fell sideways and was headed straight toward Waverley. I reached her in time, tackling her to the ground so it didn't hit her, but in the process, I accidentally knocked her top off. Everyone saw her boobs.

"Fuck. I took that from you." I stand up and start to pace, no longer able to be still. Not only did I take that from her, I've been constantly reminding her of that day by calling her Firecracker.

"Yeah, and I wanted to hate you for it." She lets out another pained laugh and it breaks my heart. "You know, I actually had a crush on you. I had thought you would be the one I would let in, but then the fireworks incident happened. I know it was an accident, but it was another thing taken away from me."

I kneel in front of her and take her hands in mine. "Waverley, I am so, so sorry. I–I can't describe how sorry I am that I took that from you. I—"

"Hey, it's okay. It was an accident."

"No, don't do that. Don't make it sound like it wasn't a big deal. Waverley, hate me, please hate me for it. I deserve it."

"I don't think I've ever truly hated you. Yeah, I've been a bitch to you every opportunity, but I've never hated you." Waverley takes a breath. "I've been thinking a lot about you lately, and that kiss tonight—it was everything I've always dreamed a first kiss would be, but then I got scared. I let him take over my mind again, and I don't want to do that anymore, Owen. I want to kiss the guy I like and enjoy sex. I'm so fucking tired of letting it control me."

I gently wipe some tears from her face, and she leans into the touch. "You have taken over my thoughts and dreams these past two weeks. I don't want to pretend that you don't affect me anymore, but I will never, ever, force or guilt you into anything. If you tell me to fuck off, I'll leave you alone, I promise."

"Will you kiss me again?"

Still kneeling in front of her I cup her face and lean in for a slow and tender kiss. My hands move and tangle in her hair, but I keep the kiss at the same pace.

She pulls back. "Owen, I trust you. Kiss me like you mean it."

I smile at her confidence. "Okay, baby."

I move back to the couch and pull her on top of me. My hands grip her waist, and the kiss turns into pure passion and need. Her hands wrap around my neck, and she starts to rock her hips. When I let out a low growl of satisfaction, she does it again.

"You better quit that before I embarrass myself," I growl, and Wav snickers.

I brush the hair out of her face and stare into those sky-blue eyes. "Stay here tonight. It's late, and I don't want you driving. You can stay in my bed. I'll stay out here." I pull her in lightly and kiss her forehead.

Waverley frowns. "Do you not want to?"

I cup her face again and she tries to look away. "Hey, look at me, Waverley." There's some hesitation, but then she rolls her eyes my way. "I want to. I want to, more than I want to breathe, but we have all the time in the world. I don't want this to be some quick fuck that we have to be quiet for so we don't wake up Annabelle. I want to take my time and worship every inch of this body." I pepper her face with kisses and her smile returns.

"You're right." She giggles.

"Ah, fuck, say that again." I bring her in for another demanding kiss.

We finally break apart for air. "Are you sure it's okay for me to stay? I don't want to kick you out of your bed," Wav says.

"It's no big deal, I'll be up all night anyway. You know—night shift hours."

"What about Annabelle? What time does she get up? I'll try to sneak out before she's awake."

"You most definitely will not sneak out. If you are out before she gets up, then fine—one less thing for us to explain to her right now, but you will not sneak out. If she sees you, then we'll deal with it. I'm serious about us, Wav, you're not going to be a secret."

The corners of her mouth turn up into a cheesy grin. "Okay, I like that."

"Good, now come on. I'll lend you one of my shirts to sleep in."

I get her set up in my bed, and it takes all of my willpower not to crawl in there with her, especially when she comes out of the bathroom in my t-shirt.

"Mm, smells like you." Waverley snuggles into the bed.

"That's a good thing, I hope."

"It is. That's one thing that would kill me. You always smell good. I hate it." She laughs.

"Well, your big blue eyes kill me, so I guess we're even." I plant a kiss to her head. "Good night, Wav."

"Goodnight, honey."

Honey? Yeah, I could get used to this.

Chapter 13

Waverley

My alarm goes off at 5:00 a.m. With only a few hours of sleep, I actually feel pretty good this morning. Last night was raw and emotional, but it felt good telling Owen. It felt right.

I put on my leggings and have an internal debate about if I should put my shirt back on or stay in his. I know which one I want to do, but would he think that's too much too soon, keeping his shirt?

It's just a shirt, Waverley. Be confident.

Okay, his shirt it is. I shove my shirt in my bag and head to the living room quietly. I know Owen said not to sneak, but I also don't want to wake Annabelle. I'd rather not have the period talk and the sex talk back-to-back.

When I get to the living room, the smell of bacon wafts over me. I head toward the kitchen and discover one of the best sights I think I have ever seen. Owen cooking... *shirtless*. He has on some basketball shorts that are hanging low on his hips displaying his muscular tattooed back with two sexy dimples right above his ass. He hasn't noticed me come in, so I take some time to enjoy the view, but I'm also dying to see the front.

"Well, this certainly makes my morning," I say, while obviously checking him out.

He turns, and his smile is just as sexy as his chiseled torso that is also scattered with tattoos.

Hello, abs. We'll talk later.

Owen abandons the bacon and walks over to me.

"Good morning." He smiles and before I can respond, his lips are on mine. His arms wrap around my waist and lift me up causing me to do that cheesy little leg lift you see in romance movies.

I giggle, and he sets me back down but doesn't let me go. "How'd you sleep, darlin'?"

"Good, I don't think my bed will ever compare again."

"Perfect." He smiles. "You hungry?"

"Starved," I say, staring at his lips. With a chuckle he leans back in and kisses me like I want.

Kissing him is great. His lips are so soft, and when he slides his tongue against mine, my knees start to wobble a little. His grip tightens to steady me, then he lifts me up on the counter. I wrap my legs around his waist and pull him closer.

I've never been kissed like this. Owen's kiss makes me feel alive and confident, like he wants me just as badly.

This moment is everything, except for that burnt smell.

"Owen," I say breathlessly, and place my hands on his chest. He hums in approval and starts to kiss my neck. "Owen, the bacon." I laugh.

"Oh fuck." He breaks away and races over to take the pan off the hot eye. Owen laughs. "You know I haven't burnt any food, let alone bacon, since I was ten. Then you walk in here wearing my shirt and ruin my record."

He gives me that damn smile and we're fused back together, our lips locked, fighting each other for what we don't know, but it's fucking awesome.

I don't know how I manage it, but I leave before Annabelle gets up. I smile the whole drive home. I'm running on about four-ish hours of sleep, but it doesn't feel like it.

I flit through my house getting ready, and reluctantly take Owen's shirt off. I throw on some white jeans, a pink V-neck tee and some fun pencil earrings. I toss my hair up in a bun and opt to wear my glasses instead of my contacts. Satisfied that I look somewhat put together, I grab my bag and head to work.

Once at school, I get out of my car with a little pep in my step. Is it normal to feel this giddy? It's a weird feeling, but good. Almost like a too good to be true feeling.

Shit. Levi.

I come to an abrupt halt because sitting on the bench in front of the school is Levi with two coffees in his hand.

I'm a terrible, terrible person.

"Hey, Wav." Levi smiles at me when he sees me and walks over. "I wanted to bring you some coffee."

"Oh, that's so sweet, thank you." I take the coffee and take a nice burning sip. I deserve this pain.

Of course, it's my go-to coffee order too.

Damn him.

I open my mouth to word vomit my confessions and apologies, but because the universe thinks it's funny, Annabelle comes racing up to me with Owen in tow. Owen and I hold a gaze for a moment, then he sees Levi. Well, this will be fun.

"Good morning, Wav. Oops, Miss Waverley." She tilts her head, thinking. "Do I call you Wav out here or Miss Waverley, since we are in the school parking lot?"

I let out a little laugh, "How about in the building, I'm Miss Waverley. Outside, you call me Wav. Sound good?"

"Sounds good." She cheeses. "Oh! We got you something." Annabelle turns to Owen gleefully, completely oblivious to the painfully thick tension.

Owen clenches his jaw when he notices the coffee in my hand, "We brought you some coffee but—"

I waste no time taking it with my free hand. "Thank you, this is perfect. Seems like a two cups of coffee morning." I nervously laugh and take a sip of Owen's coffee. Yep… it's my usual order too. Damn them both for being attractive and observant.

"Mm. Hey, Annabelle, why don't you head on in my classroom and get all the lights turned on and clean the board." I manage a smile and she bops along inside.

Owen and Levi both stare at me, waiting for me to say something, and I'm just about to when again the universe says, *"Hey, I know what would make this better."*

"Owen? Hi, how are you?" Quinn says, joining our little party. She walks in front of me, nudging me away from him. She places her hand on his shoulder then starts to rake it up and down his bicep. "I'm so glad I ran into you. I was hoping we could get together again."

Together? *Again?* Yup, that hurts. Last night all I was thinking about was him and the moment. I wasn't thinking about Levi. I wasn't thinking about Owen's… experiences. I wasn't thinking I would have both shoved in my face at seven in the morning either.

I must wear my emotions on my face because Owen's eyes go from tense to panicked and pleading.

"Listen, I—"

"Oops, hold that thought." Quinn moves her hand from his arm and places it on his chest. Owen tries to take a step back, but then she leans into him more. "Waverley, I saw Owen's niece Annabelle go in the school. She's part of your program, maybe you should go inside."

Of course Owen would sleep with her, out of all people—*her*. This is what I get, this is karma.

I grit my teeth and put on a fake-ass smile. "You're right. Thanks for the coffee, guys."

"Waverley—" Owen starts but is cut off by Quinn, and I start walking.

"Hey, Wav, wait up." Levi follows behind me. "Can I ask you a question?"

Oof, okay here we go. "Sure."

"Am I fighting a losing battle? I mean you smiled when you saw me this morning, but your eyes lit up when you saw him."

"I'm sorry, I really am. You're so great, and I'm a terrible person. I didn't mean, I, uh... we—" I get lost in my ramble.

"Waverley, it's okay. Don't beat yourself up about it. We aren't exclusive; we went on one date. It sucks, but I knew I was fighting an uphill battle when I first met you. I thought Owen was going to kill me when I told him I was interested in you."

"I'm really sorry."

"Don't be. Drink both those coffees and don't worry about it anymore. Friends?" Levi holds out his coffee.

I tap one of my cups to his. "Friends. Thank you."

"No problem, have a good day, Wav." With a quick wink, he heads back to his truck.

I glance back at Quinn still talking away to Owen. His hands are in his pockets, and he is rocking on his feet.

He must feel my gaze because he looks up at me and mouths, "Sorry."

I give him a half smile and head inside.

I shouldn't be upset about Owen's past, there's no point. I can't change it, but it sucks when it's right there in front of me. I mean, he said he was serious about me, but what is his definition of serious? We didn't really talk about anything this morning.

Why didn't we talk about it?

Probably because you're scared... oh, and you had your tongue down his throat.

By the time I enter my room I decide there's nothing to worry about. Everything between Owen and I is great.

By ten o'clock, I'm pulled back into the spiral. He's so experienced and I'm in the negatives when it comes to that area. What if I'm not good enough? How can I even compete with his past?

By lunch, I have typed and deleted at least twenty messages to Owen, some asking what we are doing, some about Quinn, some about forgetting this whole thing, and some asking about when we can see each other again. To my better judgment, I don't send a single one.

By two o'clock, my subconscious has decided that last night and this morning was a total dream. No matter how many times I stare at the coffee cup as proof of this morning, it's easier to pretend it didn't happen.

I walk all of my kids out to the front to meet their parents. My body is vibrating with anticipation and nerves at the thought of seeing Owen. I don't get worked up over guys. Granted, I never told a guy my secret, never told anyone really, but I told Owen. I suppose that's what has me in a tizzy.

I hate being vulnerable. I hate that he has this effect on me so quickly. I mean, yeah, I've been harboring mixed feelings for him for years, but everything changed last night. My complicated feelings for him are trying to untangle but as one gets free, it tangles with another.

Students start to leave one by one, and soon I see his truck pull up to the school. *Phew, okay, I can do this.*

Be cool.

Why must he always look hot, and in a baseball cap, nonetheless. I just want to turn that thing around backwards and kiss him senselessly.

"Hey, Belley." Owen smiles at her as he walks up to us. *Okay, and what about me?* He glances at me for a moment, his face unreadable. *Great, maybe I did dream this all up.* That or he just doesn't want there to be an us anymore. *Bottle it up, now is not the time to get emotional.* I turn my attention back to getting kids back with their parents.

I notice out of the corner of my eye that Owen walks Annabelle back to his truck without a word. *Well, this is going to hurt like a bitch.* I get the last kid with his mom and start back to my room. *No tears, Wav. Not until you're home.*

"Waverley, hold on," Owen hollers, jogging to catch me.

I want to keep walking, but my stupid heart makes me stop. I stop, but I'm feeling sassy. "Can I help you?" I ask, shortly, avoiding all eye contact with those deep green beauties.

"Oh come on, Wav, don't be like that." He smiles and lifts my chin, drawing my attention to his face. "I wanted to talk to the boss about us before I made anything official."

"What?" I cross my arms still on the defense.

"I told you I was serious about this, Waverley, but I'm also serious about Annabelle, so yeah, I had to ask her if she was comfortable if I started dating her teacher. Considering it's you, it's safe to say she's good with it."

I bite back a smile.

"I'm sorry about this morning, I want you to know that there is nothing going on with Quinn. I want you. I want to date you. And I'm hoping that feeling is mutual." Owen taps my nose.

"Owen, are you asking me out on a date?"

"Not just a date, darlin'. I'm asking for it all. A relationship, and everything that entails." He winks and gives me that damn smile. "What do you say, Wav?"

"I'm sorry—Owen West wants a relationship with Waverley Bennett? Man, hell must have frozen over," I tease.

Owen tugs on my hips pulling me into him. "And I'm pretty positive if you say yes, pigs will start flying. So what's it going to be, Wav?"

"Yeah, I'd like that."

"Good. I work tonight and tomorrow, but what do you say I pick you up Wednesday for dinner?"

"Shoot, I can't—we're going wedding dress shopping right after school. What about Thursday?"

"It's a date. I'll pick you up at your place at seven."

"Okay." I smile a stupid wide grin.

"I just want to kiss those pretty lips of yours, but I don't think I'll stop if I start, and I know Annabelle is watching." Owen lets out a low sigh.

"Hmm..." I peek around his broad shoulders over to his truck where Annabelle is practically about to bust out the windshield. I give her a little wave. "Yes, she's very much watching." I laugh when she waves back.

Owen lets out another sigh and shakes his head. "The little shit... she's going to tell me 'I told you so' as soon as I get in that truck."

"I told you so?"

"Oh yeah, she's been banking on this happening for a while now. She squealed when I asked her if it was okay."

"Well, you better go tell her I said yes before she busts out your windshield." I lay a hand on his chest, unable to resist not touching him.

Owen tucks my hair behind my ears and his hands trail down my neck.

"I better go before I become a very bad example." His eyes are trained on my lips.

"Go before I let you," I whisper.

He smiles. "I'll talk to you later."

"Okay, be safe tonight."

"I will."

With another wink he walks back to his truck, and I can't help but smile idiotically.

I'm in a relationship... with Owen.

Yup, hell really is frozen.

Chapter 14

Waverley

When I pull up the bridal shop, my sisters and mom are already inside. I walk in the shop and scan the store. Laughter erupts—I recognize my mother's laugh a mile away, so I follow the sound as it echoes through the room.

Peering down each aisle, I finally find them in the back, each with a champagne glass in hand, sitting on some ritzy couches and talking to a sales lady. The lady seems to be asking Winry all sorts of questions about her and Graham and their wedding.

Winry pauses mid-sentence when she sees me sliding into the seat next to mom.

"Oh, this is my other sister and maid of honor, Waverley." Winry gives me a big smile and holds out her hand for a squeeze.

"How lovely, I'm Elise, your bridal consultant for the day." Elise gives me a warm smile and turns back to Win. "So tell me—what you are looking for today?"

"Well, we are having the wedding in my parents' backyard, so I would like something light and flowy. I know you will have some options, but I would really like for my sisters to pick some out too." Winry beams.

"Not a problem. Why don't you and your mom hang out here, and we will start to pull some dresses."

Elise motions for me and Wyla to follow her. She takes us back up to the front where there are aisles and aisles of dresses.

"Okay, why don't you two look around and grab some dresses, grab any you like. There is a rack right over there, just place them on that and I'll take them to her dressing room."

"Wonderful, thank you," Wyla says to her, and Elise nods and walks to grab some dresses of her own.

"Okay, where to start?" I ask, interlocking my arm around Wyla's as we stare at the six rows in front of us.

"Divide and conquer? You take the front. I'll start at the back and we'll meet in the middle."

"Sounds like a plan."

Filing through the dresses, I find one or two that fit Winry's style and take them to the rack. As I'm filing through again, I pause, I come across a dress that is in no way is Winry's style but is totally me. It's simple and classy with a V-neckline and silky soft material. It's a mermaid style fit with a low back and ruching on the back that leads to a long silk train. I sigh as I try to envision myself in it. While my sisters are both 5'2 and tiny, I'm 5'7 with a big ass and tits to match. I've learned to appreciate my body and feel confident in my own skin, but it's been years in the making.

Still, trying on things isn't always fun. Some things are just not meant for my body type. It can be so frustrating, just as I'm sure trying on this dress would be. My boobs would probably topple out, and the tight silhouette would most likely not do me any favors. With another sigh, I move on to the next.

Wyla and I find two dresses each, and Elise pulled three to start. Winry starts with Elise's picks; each are gorgeous but just doesn't seem like her. Next is Wyla's. They're closer but something's still missing.

I chose two lace dresses, each with an A-line shape, with a deep V down the front and back. But one has a flowy lace overlay and the other has a layered tulle skirt.

Winry comes out in the tulle one first. "Okay, so far I have liked this one the best," she says as she steps out of the dressing room.

"Oh, Win, this one is beautiful," Mom says with tears rolling down her face. She has cried the whole appointment—with each dress she cries more.

"It still doesn't feel like *the one* though." Win scrunches her face in indifference.

"Try on the other one. I liked it the best." I give her an encouraging smile.

"Okay, one more." She takes a deep breath and heads back to the dressing room.

Wyla nudges me with her shoulder, "So, anymore thought to the whole Owen versus Levi debate?"

I try not to blush. "There may have been a new development in that department." I cross my legs and adjust my skirt, avoiding all eye contact with my sister.

Wyla is the sister that can read me like a book. She can read anyone like a book really, she has the best bullshit detector out of all of us.

"Do tell, Miss Waverley." She smiles and nudges me again.

"Well... oh, here comes Win."

Saved by the bride, thank goodness.

Winry comes out and her smile lights up the whole room, and tears fill her eyes. "This one, this is the one."

She's right, this is the one. It's perfect. Wyla grabs my hand, and tears pool in our eyes as well.

"Win, you look beautiful," Wyla cries.

"Let's doll you up for the full effect." Elise walks over to the veils and pulls out an extra-long veil with matching lace. She adjusts it in her hair, and it makes all of our tears spill over.

"It's perfect." I wipe some tears and stand to hug my sister.

"Wait for me." Wyla stands, going in for a hug also.

"Group hug," Mom yells and joins in our embrace.

"I love you guys," Winry says, squeezing tighter.

"But you love me most because I found your dress."

"Shh, we all know I'm her favorite," Wyla mocks, and we all laugh.

After the appointment, we go to this little café two blocks down from the store. We all order and talk more about the wedding for a little bit, then Wyla perks up.

"Oh, Waverley was just about to tell me about a new change in her love life. Story time, Miss Waverley."

I take an avoiding sip of my water. *Should I tell them the full story?* No, now is not the time.

"Come on, tell us, did you pick Owen or Levi?" Winry asks, resting her chin on her hand, leaning on the table.

"Ohh, let it be Owen. He is so precious with Annabelle, I could just eat them up." Mom beams.

"But Levi is so hot," Wyla says.

"Owen's hot too," I respond instinctively.

"Well, there's our answer." Winry laughs.

"You picked Owen?" Wyla turns in her chair to face me.

"Yeah I did, or he picked me. I don't know."

"You don't know? What does that mean?" Mom questions.

I tell them about running into him at the store and the talk with Annabelle, and how good it felt being there with them. I tell them about the kiss, then I tell them that I freaked out but I don't tell them the real reason for that. I skip over the spending the night and tell them about the next day run-in with both Levi and Owen. Then finish off with our relationship talk.

"Wow, that's a lot for twenty-four hours." Wyla laughs. "But it sounds like Owen's your boyfriend to me."

Mom and Winry both nod in agreement. "Have you talked to him anymore since Monday?"

"Yeah, we've been texting, and I've seen him when he drops off and picks up Annabelle from school. We have a date tomorrow night too." I bite back a smile.

"Oh, how exciting." Mom clasps her hands together. "What are you going to wear?"

Damn, what am I going to wear?

"Um, I don't know, I didn't think about that until just now. What should I wear?"

"I guess we better go shopping!" Wyla beams.

Chapter 15

Owen

Today's the same as it was yesterday. It's been a real struggle to not kiss Waverley every time I get Annabelle from school. She's always so adorable and sexy, especially when she is wearing her glasses. I just want to take her and run my hands all over her curves and through her long hair.

I'm taking her out tonight, and Annabelle is going to a sleepover at one of her friend's houses. Much to Annabelle's protest, I most definitely will not be bringing her on our date. She begged me all night last night for her to come to dinner with us. She stomped off to her room when I told her not a chance in hell.

I get out of the truck when I see Waverley bringing the kids out. Walking over, Wav notices me and gives me her beautiful smile.

"Hi," she greets me.

"Hi, Wav." The urge to touch her is strong, but I hold back.

"Hi," Annabelle says with a bit of attitude.

"Still mad at me?"

"Yup," Annabelle says, popping the P.

Wav laughs. "Come on, Annabelle. Next time, okay?"

"Okay," she grumbles but seems pacified for now.

"Go hop in the truck, grumpy." I ruffle her hair and send her on the way to the truck. I turn back to Wav and with a wink, I tell her, "I'll see you soon, darlin'."

"Can't wait." She blushes.

Begrudgingly, I walk back to my truck and head to get Annabelle ready for her sleepover.

"Are you sure I can't go with you tonight?" Annabelle asks.

"I'm sure, Belley. Look, we will do something together soon. You'll have tons of fun tonight at—what's her name again?"

"Madeline." Belley rolls her eyes.

"Right. You'll have fun at the sleepover."

"I guess so," she grumbles.

I take her to Madeline's at six and run back home to get myself ready. I plan on taking Wav to an Italian restaurant called Valentino's in the Northshore area, just outside of Aster Creek.

I shape up my beard and take a quick shower. I put on some black dress pants and a black button up. I opt out of a tie and go for a black sport coat.

I head to Wav's house and honestly, I'm a little nervous. I don't think I've ever been nervous for a date, but it's different with Waverley. It has to be different with her; I don't want to fuck around with her, and not just because she's my boss' daughter, but because I want it to be different. I want her to be mine.

I knock on her door. *I can do this.*

Waverley opens the door, and I don't think I can breathe anymore.

"Wow, you look..." I trail off.

Wav is wearing a fitted black dress with a slit up one side. The dress shows off her curves beautifully, and she's finished off the look with hot pink heels.

"Just wow."

Waverley blushes and tucks her curled hair behind her ears. "Thank you."

I don't want to go another second without touching her, so my hands wrap around her waist. "Can I kiss you now?"

"Finally."

My lips go to hers and it starts innocently enough, romantic even, but when her lips part I can't help but turn it up a notch. My hands go up to her long silky hair, and hers wrap around my waist.

Man, why have I waited this long to kiss her. Kissing her is like finding solace and a vice at the same time.

"Wow," she whispers as we break for air.

"Word of the night, I guess." I laugh, still resting my forehead on hers. I want to go back in, but that's not what tonight's about. "Come on, darlin', we've got reservations at Valentino's."

"Ooh, very nice." Wav grabs her small bag and I lead her out to the truck and open up her door. She smiles at me, and I can't wait to see that smile for the rest of the night. She hops in and I round the truck, ready to get this date started.

"So, how upset was Annabelle that she couldn't come tonight?"

"Very, she barely spoke to me today, pouted the whole morning and right up until I took her to her friend's house."

"Bless her, she's so sweet. While I don't mind for next time, I'm glad it's just us for tonight."

I rest one hand on her thigh. "Me too. I'm also happy to hear there will be a next time."

"Well, you said relationship. Are you thinking about backing out already?" Waverley laughs, but I know there is a hint of nervousness in that laugh.

"Absolutely not, you don't even realize the boyfriend jackpot you hit," I joke trying to ease her anxieties.

"Oh, really? Boyfriend jackpot, huh? Someone's awfully cocky for a first-time boyfriend. But I'm a first-time girlfriend, so who am I to talk?" Waverley rests her hand on top of mine.

"Really? You've never been in a relationship before?"

"Nope, but you haven't either."

"That's different. I'm an asshole who wants to do better to earn you." I squeeze her thigh and wink at her.

"I just never found someone I wanted to date, I guess. After... it... the thought of being with anyone made me want to be sick. After high school, I dated a bit. I've been on maybe a handful of dates but none of them felt like they would go anywhere." She shrugs.

"Even Levi?" I hate asking, but it slips out.

"Jealous?" She laughs lightly. "Yeah, even Levi. It was nice, but something was still missing."

"Obviously. The thing you've been missing is me."

"And I can't wait to see what I've been missing out on." She gives me a wicked smile.

"Oh fuck, Wav, you're killing me."

"I've been trying to kill you for a few years now, I'm just trying a new tactic."

I glance over at her; she really is something else and this dress... *mercy*. "I surrender, take me captive, torture me... kill me for all I care, but you have to do it in this dress."

"Deal."

Talking to her is easy. Our conversations flow and for the rest of the drive, my hand lays promptly on her thigh.

I give myself a mental high-five for this restaurant, it's low lit with all the fancy stuff, tablecloths, and candles at every table. I pull out her chair, and she smiles at me as she slides in.

So far, so good. *Let's not fuck this up, Owen.*

I take off my coat and before I sit across from her, I notice she has her arms wrapped around her. "Want my jacket?"

"Yeah, that would be great, thank you."

I drape it over her shoulders, and she relaxes, just a little bit though. "Quarter for your thoughts?"

She lets out a small giggle. "I thought we covered this already. It's a *penny for your thoughts.*"

"Yeah, but your thoughts are worth a lot more."

Wav gives me a soft smile. "I guess I'm just nervous. I didn't really think I'd ever be on a date like this," she says sheepishly.

"It's okay, do you want to go somewhere else?"

"No, I like it. It's a good nervous." She smiles, and I think the room got brighter.

The waiter comes and takes our drink order. Trying to impress her, I order a bottle of her favorite wine. I might have called Winry before we left to find out her drink of choice. It only took a "don't hurt her" speech from Graham to find out that Wav likes Michelob Ultra with her burgers, lime margaritas with tacos. Otherwise, it's a white zinfandel.

Waverley's long hair is flipped around to one side. She bites her bottom lip while she contemplates her menu. Then she flips her hair back behind her shoulder. It's a simple move, but I find it so sexy. *She really is trying to kill me, isn't she?*

Waverley sets her menu down. "So, how are things going with Annabelle?"

"It's good, I mean she thinks I'm less cool now that she's living with me. It can be a little difficult though. I don't want to have to drag her back and forth on the days I work. So my mom comes over on the nights I work, and I take her twice a week to see her mom for a couple hours. I'm a little nervous for the Nashville weekend. She's going to stay at my mom's house with Natalie. My mom will be there too, but now that Belley is my responsibility, it feels wrong to leave her."

"I get that. Do you think you won't go?"

"No, I'm going. No way am I giving up a weekend away with you."

Waverley's cheeks turn a light pink color. "Other people will be there too, Owen. Plus, you may tire of me by then."

I know she didn't mean it as a jab, but it feels a little bit like one. "Wav, you don't really think that do you?" I hold my breath waiting for her answer.

"I don't know." Waverley looks down at her lap, avoiding my eyes. "I mean this is our first date; we haven't even had sex. I don't know if I'm ready for it, you could get bored waiting for me."

I shake my head. "Jesus, Waverley, do you really think that low of me, that I would be upset at *you* for not being ready for sex?"

"No, of course not, I didn't... I just meant it's not fair—"

"What's not fair is assuming I wouldn't want to be with you because you aren't ready. Listen to me, I have all the patience in the world. We are doing this at *your* pace. So I don't care if it takes weeks, months, even years. I'll wait. I want to be with you, but there is no pressure. No is a full sentence in my mind, Waverley. All you have to say is no."

Wav bites her lip, and her shoulders slump. "You're right, I shouldn't have said that. I'm sorry."

"Don't be sorry, Wav. I know I have a bit of a history, so I don't blame you, but I want you to know that this is different."

Waverley's smile returns, and the waiter comes back with some water and glasses for the wine. We order and after our little talk, Wav seems a little more comfortable. We talk about our days, and again, the conversation flows easily.

"Come on, tell me, what's the stupidest thing you've ever done?" Waverley pesters.

"Why would I tell you? It's embarrassing, and I'm trying to impress you."

"I think you've impressed me too much with the fancy restaurant and my favorite wine. I think you need to be taken down a notch."

I wipe my hand with my napkin and toss it on the table. "Alright, alright. I was about seventeen, I think. Do you remember Greg Pritchett?"

"Nuh-uh." Wav shakes her head. "I'm younger than you, remember?"

"Right, well, he was a fucking prick. I couldn't stand him. Anyway, he was having a bonfire at his house. Nothing too crazy, but we were drinking. The whole night he was acting like he was the shit, and I just wanted to take him down a peg. So, I started poking at him, calling him anything to get him going. Well, I called him a pussy, so naturally he put out the cigarette he was smoking on his arm, thinking I would find that intimidating. So I grabbed someone else's cigarette and did the same. Then it was a challenge to see who would tap out first. Greg went with another cigarette, but I decided I wasn't going to fuck around. I grabbed one of the metal grill forks and put it in the fire, waited until it turned red then put it out on my arm."

"No, you didn't!" She gasps.

"I did, with a straight face too, thanks to all the alcohol I drank. Granted, the next day I thought my arm was going to fall off, but I won. And no one ever fucked with me during school. I have a scar on my forearm, it's covered by tattoos now, but you can still see it."

"I bet your mom just about died. What did you tell her?"

"Not the truth, obviously. I told her that I burnt myself cooking." I take the last sip of my wine. Not gonna lie, it's pretty good.

"Oh my word, you're insane." Waverley smiles and snorts a laugh.

"Hindsight, I know my mom didn't buy that shit, but I'll never admit the truth. I'm swearing you to secrecy, darlin'."

"Hmm, I think you'll have to buy my loyalty." She smirks wickedly.

When our waiter walks past our table, I stop him eagerly.

"Check, please."

Waverley's head falls back in laughter.

Chapter 16

Waverley

We pull back into my driveway, and I hate that this night will end. But maybe it can end later.

I could invite him to come inside, right? He said we're going to do things at my pace, so maybe I'm not ready for sex, but we can do some other things.

The wine is hitting me, probably because he only had one glass, and I drank the remainder of the bottle. We don't waste good wine. Plus, I needed a little liquid courage. I so badly want to be that girl that throws caution to the wind and does what feels good. While things with Owen feel right, I still can't get myself to relax completely. But I don't want this night to be over yet either.

"Do you want to come in?" I ask with no confidence in my tone. *Fuck.*

"If you want me to, then yes. I want to." Owen tucks some of my hair behind my ear.

"And if I didn't want you to?"

"I'd walk you to your door and kiss you goodnight if you wanted. Then tomorrow, I'd call and ask you to go out with me again." Owen lifts my chin toward him. "Your pace, Wav. I'm just along for the ride."

"I want you to come in, but maybe not for that, but maybe something..." Oh my word, stop talking. "I mean..."

"Wav," Owen chuckles, his hand still on my chin. "Your pace."

"Right, thank you." We get out of his truck and walk in my house. I immediately kick off my heels. Again, heels are a bitch or at least definitely made by one.

"Want to watch some TV?" I ask, plopping on the couch.

"Sure, what do you want to watch?" Owen crashes beside me, pulls my feet in his lap, and starts to rub them.

"What are you doing?" I smile, damn that feels good.

"What? Your feet are sore. You kicked those heels off like they offended you when you walked in."

I can't help the grin that has been permanently glued to my face all evening. He just keeps surprising me.

I start scrolling through Netflix, but it's hard to focus with him sitting right next to me. Looking fine as hell in all black, with his tattooed hands on my body.

I can do this.

I set down the remote.

"What are you doing?" Owen asks, but I respond by climbing in his lap straddling him. "I like it, though."

"I promise, I'll tell you when to stop," I whisper, hoping he understands.

"And I'll stop—no questions, no pushing, no guilt. I promise."

"Okay, will you kiss me now?" I close my eyes in anticipation.

His hands go from my hips up to my back, pulling me toward him. His mouth latches on to mine. Our kiss earlier started with restraint, but this one—our restraint is long gone. Only pure *need* is present in this kiss.

My dress is hiked all the way up to my hips, which just leaves his pants and my underwear between us. I know I'm making an absolute mess of my underwear right now with how turned on I am, and since I can feel his erection pressed against my center, I'm sure I'm making a mess of his pants too. With my newfound confidence, I roll my hips which earns me a low growl.

"Fuckin' hell, Wav."

I roll them again and again. I think I may come like this, with his hands in my hair, his lips on mine, and grinding against him. I want more. No, I need more of him. Blame it on the wine, blame it on the way he's affecting me, but now, I'm feeling confident and bold.

"Touch me," I beg.

"Tell me when to stop and I'll stop, understand?"

Owen kisses down my neck and collarbone.

"Yes. Please, Owen."

"Such a good girl, asking so nicely. Take off your dress."

I practically rip it over my head and toss it to the side. I'm not wearing any overtly sexy underwear—like my sisters suggested—just a simple black strapless bra and a seamless black thong, but Owen is looking at me like he has won a fucking prize.

"Fuck. This body should be illegal."

My hands move for the buttons of his shirt, working them one by one. "Your turn," I say, sliding his shirt off.

Hi, abs, I told you we'd meet again. My hands start to trace over the lines of his muscles and twirl around his tattoos.

"And now, it's my turn." Owen's hands start to roam my body as well, and with each pass of my breasts, my need grows. I separate only for a moment to unhook my bra. Owen wastes no time taking one of my nipples in his mouth and massages the other one with his hand. Rolling the buds with his tongue and his fingers, it's almost too much. The burn between my legs is begging for some relief.

"Owen, I need—"

"I know what you need," he cuts me off. He switches breasts but one hand starts to travel down my stomach. "Are you good, baby?"

I feel a small beat of hesitation, but I let it go. I remind myself that I'm in his arms and the fear melts away.

"Yes, please." With the one swift tug, and the sound of ripped fabric, shreds of my underwear go flying. I yelp in excitement.

"I'll buy you new ones." Owen slides a finger down my center, and *holy fuck*. "You're drenched. Tell me, did you ever think I would get you this wet?"

"Little confession, this technically isn't the first time you've made me wet." Where is this confidence coming from? He is pulling a different side out of me.

"Oh, really? Tell me, baby. Tell me all about it while I play with your pussy."

"Let's see, the most recent time was at the engagement party." Owen starts sliding his hand up and down, in and out, and right around where I need him most. My words now completely lost to me.

"Keep going, or I'll stop."

"You looked so hot in that suit, and you smelled so good. You always smell so damn good. When you leaned in close to me and blew out that candle, you got me so worked up I had to come home and take care of myself with only you on my mind."

"That's my good girl. Keep going, tell me your fantasy."

Owen circles my clit three times, bringing me on the brink but then stops.

"Fuck, Owen."

"Tell me, Waverley." He kisses down my neck and collarbone.

"When you leaned in, we weren't interrupted. I challenged you to kiss me, to show me what I was missing. So you backed me up against the cool brick wall, and kissed me just as passionately as you did a few moments ago. Madly, senselessly. Then I wrapped my legs around your waist, and you carried me over to the nearest table and fucked me with your tongue until I came."

"Is that what you want? You want my tongue, baby?"

He makes passes around my clit again, and my eyes fall shut, the sensation is incredible. All I can manage is a head nod.

"No, Wav. I want to hear it."

"I want you to fuck me with your tongue," I say breathlessly.

Owen quickly grabs my hips and lays me on my back, propped up by a pillow. He takes my legs and spreads them open.

"So beautiful." He peppers my thighs with kisses before diving in.

With the first pass of his tongue, I nearly come off the couch.

"Fuck, fuck, I'm not going to last long."

"I think you've earned it. Come for me, baby." Owen licks and sucks me up and down. When he takes the bud of nerves in his mouth, it's like everything else fades away. There's only us, only this moment. I call out his name just like the fantasy, only this time it's a million times better.

Owen doesn't let up until my hips slow, and my breath becomes less jagged. "I think I just found my new favorite dessert."

My cheeks blush, and I giggle.

Owen eases back up on the couch next to me and pulls my legs in his lap. He brushes my hair out of my face and tucks it behind my ear.

"That was perfect."

"Now for you," I say with less confidence. I've never even attempted a blowjob before, but now seems like a good time to learn.

"Don't worry, tonight isn't about me, darlin'."

"No way, what about blue balls or something?" I seriously have no idea what I'm talking about.

Owen chuckles. "I'll live, I swear."

"But... I want to... I want to try at least," I whisper, my newfound confidence dwindling. "I might not be good at it, but I thought..." My words trail off. I'm feeling self-conscious again. *Confidence, come back.*

"Hey, come here." Owen pulls me back to straddling his lap. "You feel that?" Owen presses his erection against me. "You did that to me. Don't for one second think that I don't want you. Because I do. *Badly.* But I want you to feel good about this. I don't want to push you."

"You're not pushing," I mumble. *Deep breath, Waverley.* "I want to. You'll just have to tell me what to do."

Owen studies my face, I almost give up but then he picks me up to where we are both standing.

"Okay, baby. Why don't you start by undoing my pants?"

Chapter 17

Owen

Waverley smiles as she undoes my belt, then the button, and then the zipper. She pauses for a moment, waiting for more instructions.

"Take 'em off, Wav. Then get on your knees."

Waverley hooks her thumbs in my pants then pulls them down, all while maintaining eye contact. I kick my pants to the side. My cock is absolutely raging right now. The thought of her on her knees makes me want to come undone.

Waverley bends down and when she looks at my dick, she mutters, "Fuck."

I laugh. "Backing out, baby?"

"No. What now?" She keeps her voice steady, but I can tell she's nervous.

"You can lick it to start if you want or hold it in your hand. Take your time, Wav. When you're ready, take me in as much as you want."

The anticipation is killing me.

Let's take this slow, asshole, and in no way are we going to come in her mouth her first time.

Waverley nods, takes her hand and wraps it around my shaft, then licks the tip. *Holy hell.* Those sky-blue eyes peer up at me. *Shit, I'm so fucked.*

Waverley licks the tip one more time then takes me in her mouth. She bobs her head slowly, I thread my fingers through her hair, pulling it back away from her face. After a few more strokes, she picks up her pace.

"You're doing so good, baby. Do you like having my cock in your mouth?"

Waverley moans then takes me a little deeper.

"Fuck, Waverley Such a good girl." I can't help it; I start to thrust my hips ever so slightly. Waverley moans again, and I'm about to lose all control. I keep my thrusts small, letting her keep the pace. Wav starts to go a little deeper. "That's it, baby. Take it all. You're doing so good."

She takes me to the back of her throat, then peers those blue eyes back up at me. *Fuck.* I pull her head back and cover her hand with mine, stroking out what has to be the hardest I have come, ever. I come all over our hands as Waverley beams up at me.

I grab my shirt and wipe off her hand, then mine.

"I figured pulling out was the best way to start, but when you are ready, you can swallow it." I lift her off her knees and pull her down on the couch with me. Our naked bodies tangle together.

"I liked it, it felt good having you at my mercy."

"Darlin', you have me wrapped around your damn finger."

Waverley nestles her head on my chest. "Owen, thank you for tonight. For the date and you know... I might not be ready for the other stuff yet, but tonight helped."

"We'll take all the time you need; I'll be here when you're ready. No matter how long, I'll be here." I kiss the top of her head and wrap her up tighter.

"Can you stay tonight?" Wav asks barely above a whisper.

"Yeah, I can. Madeline's mom is taking Annabelle to the school in the morning. What time will you need to be there?"

I hate that we both work tomorrow. I want to spend as much alone time with her as I can.

"Oh man, I forgot about work tomorrow. Well, I like to get there around 7:15, but 7:30 at the latest. I usually get up around 5:30. I like to take my time in the mornings."

"Good, because I want to take my time with you in the morning." I yank her body up and she lets out a little yelp, but I swallow it up with a kiss. "Come on, darlin', let's get you to bed."

With another quick kiss, we untangle from each other on the couch to tangle back together in her bed.

Chapter 18

Waverley

Finally, it's the last day of my summer program. Now, I'm free for three glorious weeks of no work, no kids, and no lesson plans.

After the rest of the kids are picked up, Annabelle and I head back to my classroom to get it locked up for break. Then we're heading to Crossroads to meet Owen for a celebratory treat.

"So, Belley, how was it? Everything you ever hoped and dreamed?" I ask her, walking back.

"Yes, I doubled my reading goal for this summer already, and it's only July. I still have a whole other month to go. I think I'll be able to triple it." She smiles.

"I don't doubt that for a second. I bet if you play your cards right, Owen will buy you some books today at Crossroads. Get those puppy dog eyes ready, kid."

"I could do them in my sleep." Annabelle laughs.

"I believe it." We walk back into my classroom, and as we are about to open my door Quinn walks out of hers.

"Oh, hi Annabelle, forget something today?"

Annabelle shakes her head. "Nope, Miss Waverley is taking me to Crossroads with Uncle Owen." Annabelle looks back up to me, beaming. "We better hurry so we can get a strawberry cupcake before they run out."

I smile back at her. "I'm sure there'll still be some but go ahead and grab your bag."

Annabelle bounces in my room as Quinn stares at me like she's confused.

"Does Owen know Annabelle will be riding with you?" Quinn asks sharply.

"Yes, he does. Don't worry, he added me to her pickup list this morning. Is there anything else I can help you with?"

Quinn furrows her brow. "Uh... no, I suppose not." She goes to walk away but stops and peaks her head in my room. "Annabelle— do tell your uncle that I said hi."

Annabelle nods but doesn't say anything.

Quinn flashes me a snarky smile. "Enjoy the rest of your break, Waverley."

I choose to not entertain her anymore and give her a quick "you too" as I shut my classroom door.

I give Annabelle a warm smile as I head to grab my stuff.

"I'm not telling Uncle Owen she says hi," she says quietly, almost like she's not sure if she should have said it.

I snort a laugh. "It's good you already know girl code. Come on, let's go."

We grab our bags, and I lock up my room.

When we walk into Crossroads, Owen is sitting at one of the tables with our coffees and three strawberry cupcakes. I smile as Annabelle races over.

"I get a frappe *and* a cupcake?" she squeals.

"Hell yeah, we're celebrating. Celebrations call for special treats." Owen stands and cups my face. "Speaking of special treats." He places a quick kiss on my lips, then gives me that stupid hot smile of his.

"Hey, honey." I smile back, and we all take a seat at the table and grab our cupcakes.

"So, how are my favorite girls?"

"Good," Annabelle and I mumble as we take our first bites.

Owen chuckles. "Girls, please, that's too many details."

"You're right, sorry, honey. We had a good last day. Annabelle doubled her reading goal for this summer, and I'm excited to not be getting up at 5:30 every morning for the next three weeks."

"Ya know, Uncle Owen, if I got some more books I could probably triple my reading goal." Annabelle smiles at him and bats her eyes.

"You know, Annabelle, I think you might be right." Owen reaches under the table, grabs a gift bag, and hands it to her.

"For me?" Annabelle squeals.

"Yeah, for you. Go on, open it."

Annabelle rips out the tissue paper. "Ahh, you got me a Kindle?"

Owen's smile is so big at the sight of her joy, and I think I might just melt here.

"Yeah, I know you like physical copies, but I signed you up for this unlimited thing, so you can download a bunch of books for free."

"No way! This is the best gift ever! Thank you so much." Annabelle stands up and hugs Owen tightly.

Owen's chair nearly tilts back, he leans forward and hugs her. "I'm glad you like it, kiddo."

"I love it," she corrects him. "Oh, there's Winry, can I go show her?"

"Sure, go ahead, but don't linger, she's working." Annabelle shoots out of her chair. "She wasn't listening, was she?" Owen asks me.

"Nope." I laugh. "That was really sweet of you to get her that. Be prepared though, she'll still want physical copies of the ones she really loves."

"Yeah, I figured. Oh well, better her be obsessed with books than boys." Owen shutters. "I don't even like to think about it."

"Oh, honey." I rub his back. "That day is closer than you think."

"Absolutely not." Owen pulls my chair closer and places a kiss to my temple.

"Hey, can I ask you something?" I ask hesitantly.

"Yeah, what's on your mind?"

"Um, what happened between you and Quinn?" I twist my coffee cup anxiously, I hate to bring up pasts, but his past with Quinn has been bothering me.

"Nothing much to tell. We had coffee one time. She was nice enough." He shrugs.

"So, you two never...?"

"No, we didn't. Truthfully, I only asked her out because I was upset with you for making googly eyes at Levi during that awful dinner."

"Oh yeah, that dinner where you said you'd never, *ever*, sleep with me."

Owen tenses. "Wav, I'm sorry. I never should have said that. I was jealous and mad, and at that time I didn't know why. I'm sorry."

"It's okay. At that time, I didn't want to sleep with your dumb ass anyway," I tease.

"What about that time after the engagement party?" Owen smirks.

"Fantasies and *actually* wanting to are two different things."

"Mhm... well, just so we're clear, whenever you are ready, I totally want to sleep with you but not a moment before."

Chapter 19

Owen

Graham, Levi, and I sit at the kitchen table playing a bit of no-bet poker, waiting on the girls to get ready. Tonight's the first night in Nashville, and we drove all day to get here.

But, that's not stopping us from going out.

"Ha, straight." Levi flips his cards over.

"Damn it." Graham throws his cards down. "Owen, what you got?"

"I almost hate to do it. Nah, I don't." I flip mine. "Flush."

Levi throws his hands in the air. "Come on, man, you counting cards or something? You've won the past three rounds."

"I'm dealing this time." Graham gathers up the cards and starts shuffling them.

"Whatever, I'll still kick y'all's asses."

"Come on, Owen. I let you have the girl. Let me have something," Levi jokes. We cleared the air one night after mine and Waverley's first date at Bluebirds when Graham—being the peacemaker he is—invited us both for drinks.

"Ha! Well, I'd rather give you the game than the girl."

"Damn." Levi laughs. "Should we check on them? They're taking forever."

"Yeah, that's the girls. Knowing them they're probably ready but are up there goofing around, drinking, and talking shit about us." Graham deals out another round.

"There was minimal shit-talking," Winry says, walking in the kitchen. "Deal me in, babe."

"Fuck no, you win at everything." Graham pulls her in his lap. "I need you as a good luck charm. Owen keeps winning."

"Yeah, he does." Waverley slides her arms around the back of my shoulders and leans around giving me a kiss on my cheek.

"Hey, Wav, come here." I pull her in my lap.

"Ah damn it. Wyla, Ivy, get your asses over here. I need double the luck." Levi pulls Wyla on one side and Ivy on the other. "Ha, fuck you guys."

"Okay, last round. The person with the worst hand buys the first round tonight. We all flip at the same time," Winry says.

"You're on."

"Okay, one... two... three."

We all flip our cards; Graham has a high pair, I have two pairs, and Levi has shit.

"Fuck, seriously?" Levi throws his head back in defeat. "Ladies, come on. You were supposed to be lucky."

"Ha, I'll take a shot of Jack Daniels, please." Wyla laughs.

"Oh, is it a whiskey night? You alright?" Waverley asks her.

"Yeah, just feel like letting go this weekend." Wyla stands up. "Let's roll, party people."

We call some Ubers and head for this bar that Levi said was awesome and is supposed to have a band playing tonight.

Once there, we grab a table on the far side of the bar. The stage is directly to the back of the building with a small dance floor in front of it. It's your typical country bar. The lighting is dark, and they have some neon beer signs scattered about.

Levi orders our first round. "To Graham and Winry!" we shout and throw back our shots.

"Ah, that's a good burn." Waverley smiles.

I tug her chair closer. "You look breathtaking tonight, darlin'."

She is wearing a pair of denim shorts with a black silk top and black cowgirl boots. Her hair is down in loose curls, and her lips are pink and glossy.

She smiles. "Thank you, honey. You're looking rather sexy too."

"You're just trying—"

"No way. Waverley Bennett." This random dude cuts me off.

"Ahhh, no way!" Waverley squeals and jumps up to give the guy a hug.

Who the fuck is this?

"What are you doing here?" the rando asks.

"Bach trip. One of my sisters is getting married. What are you doing here?" Wav hits his shoulder.

"Our band is playing tonight."

Waverley's eyes grow wide with excitement. "Nuh uh, everyone's here?"

"Hell yeah. Guys!" The guy whistles to another group.

"Ahh!" Waverley claps and hugs the group. I look around the table. Graham gives me a look that says 'cool it', but I'm about to lose it.

Waverley turns back to the table. "Guys, this is Tyler, Drake, James, and Emmett. I met them in college while working with Tyler's girlfriend, Jackie."

"Uh, wife now. We had a drunken Vegas wedding," he says, flashing his wedding band. Alright, he passes, but the rest—I'm not loving. Especially James who keeps looking Wav up and down.

"Oh, congratulations!" Waverley beams. "Is she here?"

"She's talking business with the manager, you know her. I'll make sure she comes by before we leave."

"Yes, please do." Waverley finally turns to me and takes my hand pulling me up. "This is Owen, my boyfriend."

Fucking finally.

"Hey, man. Nice to meet you." Tyler holds out his hand. "You've got a good one."

I shake his hand. "I couldn't agree more." I wink at Wav and wrap my arm around her possessively.

"Wav, you singing with us tonight?" James asks.

Waverley leans into me. "Oh, no. Guys, come on."

"Your ass is singing," a woman says behind us.

"Jackie!" Waverley races over and wraps her up in a hug.

"Hey, Wav. Look at you. Damn girl, lookin' fine as hell." Jackie playfully smacks her ass.

"Oh, fuck yeah," James mumbles under his breath.

My head whips toward him with a murderous look on my face. I open my mouth to rip him a new one, but Waverley pulls me to her. "Jack, this is my boyfriend, Owen. Owen, this is Jackie, my best friend from college."

"Oh, boyfriend? Okay, girl... nice work." Jackie nudges Wav.

"Hey, Jack... remember me? Your husband?" Tyler wraps his arms around her and kisses her temple.

"Baby, I could never forget you." She smiles. "Listen, we will catch up with you at their break, but it's time, guys. Love you lots, babe." Jackie hugs Wav again, then pulls the guys backstage.

Waverley wraps her arms around me and gives me a quick kiss.

"Let's order, I'm starving."

Feeling a little relieved they're gone; I hold her tight. "Okay, darlin'."

We go back to our conversations at the table. I order the next round of shots, and we throw them back as the band takes the stage.

I push the image of Waverley hugging them all out of mind. Waverley's mine, and I don't share, but she knows that. I need to let it go.

We order another round and finish eating our food. We're back on track, all having a good time.

The band starts their next song.

"Oh no," Waverley says.

"What?"

"Well..."

"Come on, Bennett, you're singing." Jackie stands with a microphone in hand.

"Jack, come on," Waverley protests.

"No way, get your ass up." Jackie waves her to come on.

"Go, Wav! Please? For me," Winry begs.

Waverley turns to me; I think she is looking for permission, not that she needs it. "Go, baby." I give her a quick kiss for encouragement.

"Okay." She gives a shy smile. "Jack, if I mess up, I'm killing you."

"Come on, hurry, you're going to miss your part." Jackie pulls her away from me and pushes her up on stage.

Tyler smiles at her and pulls her up to the center with him. Waverley shakes her head at him, then starts to sing with him and fuck, can she sing. Graham and Levi whistle and the girls cheer her on.

When the chorus comes, Waverley doesn't hold back. Her energy bleeds into the crowd. More people start to move to the dance floor in front of the stage. Waverley sings the bridge, then lifts one of her hands in the air and hits a high note.

Fuck, she's incredible.

"I swear, if you don't marry her, I'm taking her back." Levi hits my shoulder then whistles again.

"Fuck off." I give him a shove, then whistle and cheer Wav on with the rest of the group.

The song ends, and we all stand, clapping for my girl.

"Waverley Bennett, everybody." Tyler holds out his hands, gesturing to her. Waverley takes a bow and laughs as the crowd cheers louder.

"Come on, everyone, one more time," James says in his microphone, then walks over to Waverley and wraps his arms around her and kisses her right on the lips. Waverley's eyes go wide, and she takes a step back. The smile that was on her face is now gone.

Fuck, no. I start to move instantly.

"Owen, don't." Levi grabs my arm.

Graham walks up. "I'll go get her, you calm down."

But I can't, I'm seeing red. They don't get it, not only did someone touch my girl, but someone touched her without her permission, *again.*

"Let me go," I growl at Levi.

"What are you going to do? Storm on stage and punch him? You'll get your ass arrested."

"I don't fucking care," I bite out.

The band announces they are taking a break, so I shake off Levi's hold and push around Graham.

I make it to the stage when Waverley catches me. "Owen, honey, it's okay. Please let it go."

I walk past her. Wav, Graham, and Levi follow me behind the stage where I spot the

band.

"Hey, asshole. You think you can touch my girl without her permission?"

"Hey, man." Tyler steps in front. "He didn't—"

"And you would be okay with someone touching your girl like that?"

Tyler shuts his mouth and steps to the side. "Sorry, J. You're on your own on this one."

I storm past him and push James against the wall.

"Dude, chill out. It was just a little kiss."

"I don't fucking care if you high-fived her." I pull back and slam him against the wall again. "No one touches Waverley without her permission. I refuse to let her feel like someone can just touch her whenever they please without her consent, *ever again*."

The room goes silent for a moment. I know they are processing the "again" part. *Fuck, I probably shouldn't have said that*, but it's true. *Never again.*

The thought of him kissing her flashes back through my mind, and I slam him against the wall again.

"You're right, okay. Waverley, I'm sorry. I shouldn't have done that."

"Thank you," Waverley mutters. "You can let him go now, Owen."

With one more feral look, I drop him. I walk back over to Waverley, Graham, and Levi.

"You okay?" I wrap my arms around Wav, and she nods. "Okay, let's get out of here."

We walk silently back to our table. "I'm going to go pay my tab." I kiss the top of her head.

"Me too." Levi nods.

"I'll call us some Ubers," Graham says.

Levi and I make our way to the bar. "Hey, what did you mean without her consent *again*? Did something happen?"

I don't know how to answer because it's not my story to tell, but my hesitation is a good enough answer for Levi.

"Fuck, who?" Levi asks with the same anger in his eyes that I had.

"Doesn't matter. He's dead. Car accident, unfortunately. I sure would have loved to be the one to kill him. But listen, don't say anything. I'm the only one she's told, and she probably hates that I even hinted at it with people around."

"Got it, not a word."

Chapter 20

Waverley

"Well, the drinks were good," Wyla says, trying to lighten the mood in the Uber.

Owen is still fuming silently. He has a firm grip on my thigh but hasn't looked at me since we left the bar.

"Yeah, I'm sure. You drank the most, Wyla," Levi says from the front seat.

"Hey, I told y'all I'm letting go this weekend. Don't kill my vibe."

"I wouldn't dream of it." Levi jokes.

The rest of the ride is just Wyla and Levi making small talk with the driver. I don't know what to do or say. It's not like I asked to sing or asked for James to kiss me, so why won't Owen look at me?

Back at the condo, Graham pulls out the deck of cards again. "We were thinking of actually betting this time. Owen, Wav, you two in?"

"Nah, I'm good." Owen shakes his head and heads to our room. I follow and shut our door behind him.

"You didn't have to come up here, Wav. You can play if you want."

"No, I want to know why you are pissed at me for no reason." I cross my arms and huff.

Owen turns on his heels. "Pissed at you? You think I'm pissed at you?"

"Well, you haven't spoken or even looked at me since we left the bar." I throw my hands up. "You know, I didn't even really want to sing, and I *definitely* didn't want him to kiss me."

"Exactly, Waverley. That's why I'm pissed. I'm pissed because that fucker added one more layer of brick to that wall of fear you have. I'm pissed that he touched what's mine without any care or regard. I'm fucking pissed that another man has taken it upon himself to touch you without your permission, and there wasn't a damn thing I could do to stop it, Wav. That's why I'm pissed."

"Owen, you might not have been able to prevent it, but you stood up for me." I place my hands on the sides of his face and force him to meet my eyes. "You were there for me. You made sure he knew what he did was wrong and ensured it didn't go any further. You scared the shit out of him." I laugh lightly.

"Waverley, I don't ever want you to not feel safe and protected around me."

"I know, honey, but you can't protect me from everything."

"I'm going to fucking try." Owen leans down and gives me a light kiss. I wrap my arms around his waist, he rests his chin on my head. "I'm calmed down now. Do you want to go back downstairs?"

"No, I think I want to show you my appreciation for sticking up for me." I fiddle with the button of his jeans then undo the zipper and sink to my knees.

We still haven't had sex yet, and while Owen thinks that James added more bricks to my wall, Owen doesn't realize that he's been tearing them down two at a time for the past few weeks. With each coffee he brings me in the morning, with each text asking about my day, with each smile, with each kiss, and with each touch, he tears them all down.

"Morning, beautiful." Owen kisses my shoulder then brushes my hair away from my neck and kisses me again. For a moment, his lips make me feel something other than the absolute pounding headache. "Come on, Wav, time to open those bright blue eyes."

I grumble inaudible noises and roll into him, pinning him back down on the bed to rest my head on his bare chest. "Wav—"

"Shhh." I cover his mouth because talking is a big no right now.

"Alright, five more minutes." Owen kisses my head and lightly rubs my back.

We're leaving today and last night was definitely our crazy night. We decided to go bar hopping, and to say we all drank double our weight would put it lightly. It was care-free and straight up fun. All the stuff from the night before was completely forgotten.

A knock sounds on our door.

"Ugh, make it stop." I bury my head deeper in Owen's chest, and he laughs.

"Y'all decent?" Graham asks from behind the door.

"Yeah, we're good," Owen answers.

Graham peeks his head in. "Hey, we're all going to get some breakfast at this small diner, y'all coming?"

Greasy breakfast food? Now that gets me to open my eyes.

"Oh look, she lives." Owen laughs. "Yeah give us ten minutes and we'll be down."

"Okay, no rush. We are still waiting for Wyla to get back here."

"Wyla's not here?" I ask, confused.

"Goodness, baby, how much did you drink?" Owen plants a kiss to the back of my throbbing head.

"She snuck off halfway through the night with some guy. You sure she's okay? She's been a little off this weekend," Graham says.

"I think so, probably just some school stress. She starts her last year this fall." I shrug.

"Yeah, that's what Win said. Well, she should be back soon, and we'll head out."

"Alright man, we'll be down in a bit." Owen wraps me up in his arms, and I rest my head back down on his chest.

"Sounds good. Wav, Winry has Advil. Just in case you need some." Graham chuckles and shuts the door.

"How are you feeling, darlin'?" Owen asks me.

"Like my head is going to explode, and the room is sideways," I grumble.

Owen laughs. "Do you remember anything about last night?"

"I remember there was a bar—correction, bars. There was definitely tequila, and I believe a very strong, sexy tattooed man carried me to bed."

"Hmm, what a lucky guy."

"And he's about to be even luckier." I roll out of the bed. "Want to hop in the shower with me?"

"Most definitely, but I have to call and check on Annabelle first. Go ahead and start. I'll be there in a second."

"Okay, honey." I crawl back on the bed for a quick kiss. "Tell her I say hi."

"You got it." He smiles.

I start the shower and let the hot water fall over my body. I start shampooing my hair, and I decide to leave the body washing portion of this shower to Owen. I wash the conditioner out of my hair and when Owen still hasn't joined after a couple more minutes, I decide to finish washing and turn off the water.

I grab a towel off the rack and dry off. As I wrap the towel around my body, Owen opens the door to the bathroom.

"Sorry, you missed the party." I tuck the towel tightly at the top.

"I'm sorry, Wav. I got talking to Annabelle then ended up arguing with Natalie." Owen runs his hands over his face and leans against the door frame.

"Oh no, what happened?"

"Natalie wants to have Annabelle stay with her even though I'm the one legally responsible for her until Nat's next court date in September. I told her we could add a sleepover or two a week to our deal, but full time isn't up for discussion." Owen exhales.

"I take it that didn't go over well?" I give him a half smile.

"Not in the slightest," Owen huffs. "I'm not trying to keep her daughter away from her, but Belley is my responsibility now. I have to do what's best for her. For both of them."

"Hey, you don't have to explain yourself to me, honey. Everyone—except maybe Natalie—knows that you always do what's best for Annabelle. Even Annabelle knows it."

"I hope so." He pushes off the door frame and in just two steps we're chest to chest with his hands resting on my shoulders. "I know I missed the party, but can I still see the show?" He smirks as his hands move to brush the top of my towel.

"Hmm, okay, but you can only look, no touching." Owen groans. "We've run out of touching time, honey, we've got to get ready," I say, not entirely confident. I can easily be persuaded, and Owen smiles knowing it.

Our ten-minute get-ready request turned into half an hour, but finally we make our way downstairs.

Winry, Graham, Levi, and Ivy are sitting around the kitchen table. "Morning, sorry we took so long." I take the chair next to Win, really not feeling sorry at all.

"That's okay, Wyla just got here ten minutes ago. She's showering and changing real quick." Winry passes the bottle of Advil to me. "We all already took our share." She laughs.

"Oh, hallelujah." I shake out two pills for me and two for Owen.

"I'll take some too," Wyla says behind my shoulder.

"Oh hey, sure." I shake out two more and pass them over.

"Alright, are we ready?" Wyla asks quickly.

"Yeah, let's go." Winry stands, and everyone follows. We drive quietly to the nearest diner, all of us too hungover for big conversions right now.

We grab a table and order right away, desperate to get some substance in our stomachs. Finally, after we all get some food in our system, we slowly all start coming back to life.

"I definitely wasn't that bad." Winry chuckles.

"Win, come on now. I love you, and I know you like to win at everything, but this time you definitely came in last riding the bull." Graham rubs her shoulder.

"Uh, I did not. Wyla didn't even ride, so she's last." Winry crosses her arms. "Speaking about Wyla, why don't you tell us about your little departure from the group last night?"

"Mmm, yes, Wyla, do tell." I wink at her and she shrinks in her chair.

"Come on, guys, it was a one-night thing. No big deal." Wyla fiddles with her food and blushes.

"Oh, that good, huh?" Winry asks.

"Oh, please no sister sex talk at the table," Graham grumbles.

"Hush, you." Winry shoves him playfully. "I believe the question I was asked with Graham was 'how big was it,' so spill."

"Hey, Waverley asked you that question." Wyla points her finger my way, and Owen's head whips around.

"You asked that question?" he asks, eyes wide.

"What? It's a standard girl question, but this isn't about me. Let's go back to Wyla."

"How about I tell y'all over the next girls night?" Wyla counters.

"Yes," all of the guys say together.

"Fine, fine." Winry puts her hands in the air. "Ivy, you're joining that night too. I want to know all about that girl's number you got last night."

"Girl's and guy's actually, options are better." Ivy winks.

Chapter 21

Owen

I walk in the door to my mom's house Monday afternoon to pick up Annabelle. "Hello, anybody home?"

"In here, dear," Mom calls from the kitchen.

I round the corner, Mom and Annabelle are mixing some brownie batter on the table and Natalie sits on her phone. "Oh, brownies. Perfect timing."

"Yeah, and I've made them pretty much all by myself too." Annabelle smiles.

"Well then, I'm sure they'll be amazing, Belley. I can't wait to try one." I pull out a chair at the table and sit down.

"Okay, I think they're ready to go in the oven." Mom pours the mix in a pan then puts them in the oven. "How was Nashville, dear?" she asks me.

"It was great. We had a good time, ate good food."

"Waverley didn't choke to death on her food, did she?" Natalie sneers but still not looking up from her phone.

Annabelle's eyes droop. She loves her mom, but she also loves Waverley, and I know Natalie likes to make her feel guilty about it.

"Natalie, don't. You don't have to like Waverley, but I'm not going to let you talk bad about her."

"What? I was just asking about her wellbeing." Natalie shrugs.

I want to snap at her and tell her that she's being a real bitch, but since I'm an adult—unlike her—I ignore her and focus on Annabelle. "So, kid, read any books while I was gone?"

"Duh, Uncle Owen, who do you think you are talking to?" She laughs.

We talk for the half hour it takes for the brownies to bake about the two books Annabelle read over the weekend. She gives me a complete recap for each one, then starts telling me about the one she started last night.

I sit, listening intently while Natalie is still glued to her phone. Two minutes into Annabelle talking, Natalie puts her headphones in. I wish she would give this kid just a second of genuine attention.

"Alright, brownies are ready. Who wants one?" Mom asks.

I check my watch. "Annabelle and I will have to take ours to go. I need to get home to get ready for work."

"Okay, dear, and you're sure about tonight?"

"Yes, Mom, take a break. Don't worry, you'll be back on night shift tomorrow." I give her a hug.

"Is Grandma not coming over tonight?" Annabelle tilts her head and furrows her eyebrows.

"We'll talk about it later, okay? Come on, say goodbye to your mom and Grandma, then you carry the brownies, and I'll carry your bag." I grab Annabelle's bag while she says goodbye and throw it in my truck.

"Hey, I want to talk to you," Natalie says from the porch.

Great.

"Go ahead," I say, walking up to her.

"Annabelle needs to stay with me full-time," she says with her arms crossed and a scowl on her face.

"Nat, that's not going to happen. We already talked about this. We can add a sleepover or two during the week as long as Mom is here, but she's not staying here full-time."

"And why the hell not? I'm her mother, Owen. You're just her uncle."

"No, Nat, I'm not just her uncle. I'm her legal guardian, which means I get to decide where she stays, who she stays with, and for how long. You agreed to a few hours of visitation during the week. Me allowing more time is not something I have to do, and frankly, if you are just going to be on your fucking phone the whole damn time, maybe she won't stay more."

"This isn't fair. She's my daughter."

"Then maybe start acting like her mother. Let's go, Annabelle," I holler, ending this senseless bickering.

Annabelle walks out the front door with a tub of brownies. "Grandma gave me a bunch, said I'd need them later."

"I'm sure you will. Come on, tell your mom bye then hop in the truck." I grab the brownies so she can give Natalie a hug. They say bye, and we head back to my house.

"So, are you not working tonight?" Annabelle asks.

"No, I am."

"Then why is Grandma not coming over to stay with me? I don't know if I'm ready to stay alone all night."

I smile. "Don't worry, Belley, you won't be alone."

"But, who—" We pull into my driveway. "Is that Wav's car? Is she staying with me?"

"I don't know." I put my truck in park. "Why don't you go in and see."

Annabelle squeals then jumps out of the truck and races to the door. I barely make it out of the truck when I hear girlish screams coming from inside. I laugh and head inside to find Annabelle and Waverley wrapped up in a big hug. I can't help the smile that spreads across my face or the tug in my chest.

"I've missed you, cutie." Wav squeezes her tightly.

"I've missed you." Annabelle finally lets Wav go. "Are you staying with me tonight?"

"I sure am. We are having a full-on girl's sleepover. We've got pizza, chocolate, face masks, nail polish, a girlie princess movie, and... matching pajamas!" Waverley holds out some pink striped pajamas and Annabelle squeals again.

"And we brought brownies," I say, putting the tub on the counter then walk over to Wav.

"Hey darlin'. Avert your eyes, kid." I turn Annabelle's head the other direction and give Wav a quick kiss.

Annabelle giggles. "Stop it, I'm not a baby. I know you two kiss."

"I don't know what you are talking about. We would never do such a thing, and you better not be either."

Annabelle rolls her eyes. "Sure, Uncle Owen, whatever you say."

"Don't worry, we can talk boys when he leaves." Waverley winks at her.

"The only boy you can talk about is me and good things only."

"Yeah, yeah, we have plenty to say about you, don't we?" Waverley jokes, and Annabelle nods enthusiastically.

"Oh, really? Well, just for that, I'm stealing some of y'alls pizza." I walk over to the table and steal a slice of pepperoni pizza. "Alright, I have to get ready for work. You girls get started, and I'll be out of here shortly."

"Annabelle, why don't we put on our pajamas, then we can destroy the living room and make what me and my sisters call 'the sister pile'." Waverley hands Annabelle her pajamas.

"Awesome." Annabelle beams then skips off to her room to change.

The moment her door closes, I throw down my slice of pizza and toss Waverley over my shoulder.

She yelps and laughs. "What are you doing?"

"Taking advantage of a moment alone." I start toward my room.

"Wait, grab my pajamas."

"Ugh, wasting precious time, woman." I turn around, grab the pajamas, and stalk back to my room. Once inside, I toss her on the bed.

Waverley giggles as I climb on top of her. "We've been together for the past seventy-two hours and counting. You're bound to be tired of me."

"Wav, I don't think I'll ever tire of you." I kiss down one side of her neck and then up the other.

"Mmm, have I told you how much I love the feel of your beard on my skin." Waverley brings her hands up to my face and scratches my beard.

"Any spot in particular you love the most?"

"I know what you're getting at, and we don't have time for that." Wav smiles and places her hands on my chest pushing me up. "I've gotta change and get back out there."

"Well, we may not have time for everything, but I'll be damned if I don't get to be the one to undress you." I grab the hem of her shirt and tug her closer. Waverley bites her lower lip. "Arms up, darlin'."

Chapter 22
Waverley

"Owen, I have to get back out there," I say breathlessly as our lips break apart for just a moment, but then we go back in.

"And I need to get ready for work," Owen says but still we don't break apart. His tongue glides in, sweeping against mine. He has a firm grip on the back of my neck and the other wrapped around my waist, holding me close. "Fuck it, I'll be late." He kisses up and down my neck.

"I don't think being late because you were making out with the boss' daughter will go over well." I snort a laugh.

"Maybe not, but it's so worth it," he says before returning to my lips.

"Mmm, okay, honey." I place my hands on his bare chest. "You need to get ready, and I need to go back out there."

Owen groans. "I know." He gives me one more quick peck. "You've got five seconds to get out of here before I start kissing you again."

I contemplate calling his bluff, but I do need to go back to the living room. I don't need the "what were y'all doing in there" question.

"Go, Wav. I'm not kidding." Owen smacks my butt, hurrying me along.

"Okay, okay, I'm going." I throw on my pink pajamas as Owen goes into the bathroom.

I walk back to the living room. Annabelle is sitting on the couch with a slice of pizza in hand.

"Hey, cutie. I like your pajamas," I say plopping down next to her.

She laughs, "I like your pajamas, Wav."

"You ready to make a sister pile?"

"Yes! What do we need?"

"Okay, first we need to move this coffee table." I stand and maneuver the table over to the side. "Now, we need every blanket, pillow, and cozy thing in this house."

"On it." Annabelle races back to her room and comes back out carrying as much as she can manage of coziness galore.

I laugh and help take some blankets out of her hands. "Good job. I'm going to grab the pillows and comforter off Owen's bed, and we will be set."

"Okay, try not to take so long this time." Annabelle laughs and makes kissing noises.

"You quit that." I toss the nearest pillow at her. "I'll be right back, ya goofball."

I walk in the bedroom as Owen pulls his vest over his head. "I knew you'd come back in here." Owen tries to close the distance between us.

I hold out my hands. "Wow, stop right there, buddy."

"Buddy? Really?" Owen cocks an eyebrow.

"Yeah, *really*, I told Annabelle I would be right back. I'm just here to steal your comforter and pillows."

"Sorry, darlin', they come at a price." He flashes his signature smile.

I roll my eyes. "You get five seconds," I tease.

Owen grabs my wrist and yanks my body flush against his. He doesn't say a word or waste a second, his tongue is down my throat, and his hands hold my face tightly.

"Alright, five seconds are up, buddy."

"Enough with this 'buddy' crap. I don't ever want to be your buddy." He leans down and kisses me again.

"You never were," I mumble in between kisses.

He pulls back but with his hands still cupping my face, he stares into my eyes. Our fun, teasing mood has shifted to something more. "And never will be."

"What do you want to be?" I ask barely above a whisper.

"Yours, and only yours, because goodness knows—you are *mine*."

I kiss him this time with everything I have, and then it becomes crystal clear.

I'm falling for Owen West. Hard.

"Wav! Are you coming or what?" Annabelle yells from the living room. Our lips break apart, but his forehead still rests on mine.

"I better get back out there," I whisper.

"Yeah, I need to go too." But neither of us move.

A knock comes to the door. "Uncle Owen, quit hogging Wav. It's a girls' sleepover. You're not invited."

I hold back a laugh. "Will you help me carry the comforter out there?"

"Sure." We pull apart from each other. "Alright, Annabelle, we're coming."

I grab the pillows, and Owen pulls off the comforter. When we open the door, Annabelle stands at the door with her hands on her hips.

"Quit being a sassy pants. I'll be gone all night." Owen ruffles her hair as he walks by.

I smile at her. "Come on, cutie. He's right. We've got all night."

Owen drops the comforter on the couch. "Alright, girls, I have to get to work. Please don't destroy my house."

"We are only going to destroy the living room," I say nonchalantly and shoo him out of the way, so I can spread the comforter down as our base of the sister pile.

"I can live with that. You two have fun, and you"—he points to Annabelle— "behave."

"And you"—Annabelle points back— "be careful."

"Always am, kid. Okay, I'll be back in the morning. Call me if you guys need anything."

"I will. Now go, you're going to be late." I push him out the door.

"I'll see you in the morning. Man, I like saying that," he says with a quick kiss to the forehead.

"And I like hearing it." I grin. "Bye, honey."

"Bye, Wav."

I close and lock the door behind me. "Now, let's finish the pile."

"Yes!" Annabelle claps her hands and does small jumps.

We throw every blanket, every pillow, some stuffed animals, and even pull some of the couch cushions into our pile. After about twenty minutes, it's perfect.

"Alright, let's get the pizza and our movie snacks set up, and I'll start the movie. We are doing a princess double feature."

"What's the movie?" Annabelle asks.

"*The Princess Diaries.* You're going to love it."

"I've never heard of it."

"I know, and that totally makes me feel old, but you'll love it nonetheless." I pull up the movie while Annabelle brings over the box of pizza and the bowl of snacks. "Okay, kid, you ready?"

"Ready, Freddy."

We cozy up in our sister pile and dig into our food. "No way, so she's really a princess?" Annabelle asks as she pops some Peanut M&M'S in her mouth.

"Yeah, and you have to share those bad boys." I hold my hand out for her to hand over the bag.

"I'm so jealous. I wish I was secretly a princess."

"Don't we all?"

Annabelle looks down at her lap and fidgets with her blanket. "Waverley?" Her voice is low, almost like she's afraid to speak any louder.

"Yeah?" Turn to her, the movie completely forgotten with the solemn look on her face.

"Is it wrong to sometimes wish that you were my mom," she mumbles.

"Oh, sweetie. I can't tell you how many times I wished I had a different mom at your age. It's okay, it doesn't mean that you don't love your mom." I reach out again but this time to hold her hand.

"I feel like she doesn't care. How can she be a mom and not care?" A tear falls down her face.

"She cares, Annabelle. She just has a hard time showing it."

"Is it also wrong to wish that I could stay with Uncle Owen permanently? He takes care of me and listens to me when I talk."

"Annabelle, listen to me. There is nothing wrong with these feelings. They're normal. Owen, especially, loves you so much and no matter what he will always be there for you. I think maybe you should tell him how you feel. It's good to express your feelings."

"But I don't want to hurt Mom's feelings by asking to stay here, and it's hard on Grandma too, having to come here on the nights Uncle Owen works." She wipes another stray tear. "Sorry, I ruined girls' night."

"You did not ruin girls' night. This is what girls' nights are for. Crying when we need to, sharing our secrets and feelings, talking about literally anything. I'm so glad you shared with me, Annabelle." I wrap an arm around her shoulder. "I love you, cutie. I'll always be here for you."

"Thanks, Wav." Annabelle sniffles.

"You know what we need to do?" I stand up and grab my bag from the kitchen table then plop back down next to her. I rummage through the bag. "Face masks! And of course, cute headbands to hold back our hair."

"Ah, yes!" Annabelle cheers.

"I got this one for you." I hand her the pink one that has a crown on the top. "And this one for me." I pull mine over my head then pull back my hair.

Annabelle laughs. "You got yourself a unicorn one?"

"Of course I did. It's awesome."

Annabelle pulls hers on as I rip open the two sheet masks. "Okay, here." I pull one out and place it on her face. She giggles when I struggle to get her mask to fit right.

"Okay, miss ma'am. You put mine on, see if you can do better."

"Okay, give it." She pulls out the mask, and it drips everywhere. "Oh, oh, why is this one so wet?"

I refrain from a "that's what she said" joke, the kind of jokes I hear too many of in my sixth grade classroom. Instead, I just chuckle. "It's okay. I'm ready." I lean my face forward, and Annabelle does her best to place the mask on my face.

"Okay, so it's hard." Annabelle laughs as she fumbles with the mask.

"Tell me about it." We finally get both of our masks situated as the first movie comes to an end. "Okay, cutie, I'm about to introduce you into the world of enemies to lovers. Ready to be forever changed?" I grab the remote and start *Princess Diaries 2.*

"Enemies to lovers? You mean like you and Uncle Owen?"

I snort a laugh. "Yeah, I guess so."

"I knew you two loved each other." Annabelle smirks.

"Well, I don't know about love," I say sheepishly.

Am I falling for Owen? *Yes*, but I don't know how he feels, and I feel like I should tell him before I tell Annabelle.

"Mhm, whatever you two want to tell yourselves."

"Hush, you goofball, watch the movie."

Chapter 23

Owen

I start my shift right on time. I've never been this close to being late, *ever*. I just can't help it. Being around Waverley is addicting, and knowing she's at home with Annabelle makes me happy. It's foolish to think it will always be like this. I know Annabelle will eventually move back in with her mom, but for now, it feels like we're a family.

Tonight is a little slow, so Graham, Levi, and I decide to grab a quick bite at the small twenty-four-hour diner in town. It's your standard small town diner with random knickknacks and old town pictures on the walls, and the booth cushions have rips in them from where they've been worn down.

It used to be where Natalie worked before they let her go. Not that I blame them. Natalie still hasn't gotten her butt up from the couch to get a new job. I imagine her work ethic was just as lazy.

"Well, I could if the old man would just die already," Graham says and takes a bite of his sandwich.

"I know I'm new to town, but Mr. Park doesn't seem like he will be giving up that house anytime soon." Levi shakes his head.

"What are you talking about?" I totally spaced out of their conversation.

"I want to buy the Park's house, but the old man won't let it go," Graham grumbles. "It's like a five-bedroom house, and it's just him living there. What does he need that big of a house for?"

Levi laughs. "Dude, just find another house."

"I don't want to. The old man needs to let it go. Win loves that house. She brings him leftover pastries from the store once a week, and she always talks about how much she loves that house."

"Have you asked him if he would sell? He might for a Bennett." I shrug. "Everyone in town loves Chief."

"I've asked. He wasn't interested, said he would die in that house."

"Oh, come on, dude. You want to live in a house after a man dies in it?" I wipe my mouth with a napkin.

"Yeah, he'd probably haunt the place." Levi jokes.

"I'd live in a haunted house. Hell, I'd live in a shack if it was the one Winry wanted."

"Gross, you make me nauseous." Levi pushes away his empty plate.

"I don't care. I will get her that house." Graham shoves Levi.

"Well, when Mr. Park turns up dead, we'll know who did it." I laugh.

"You idiots would help me, and you know it."

"Chief probably would too. It's a solid plan." I joke.

"True." Graham nods and takes another bite. "Anyway, how are you and Wav doing?"

"You're asking for Winry, aren't you?" I sit back in my chair.

"Maybe." He shrugs. "But she's also about to be my sister-in-law, so I've gotta ask."

"It's good—really good, actually. She's at my house now with Annabelle. They are having a girls' sleepover. I should probably check on them and make sure they haven't burnt my house down." I scoot back my chair and pull out my phone. "I'll be right back."

"Tell her I said hi," Graham says.

"Yeah, me too." Levi dances his eyebrows.

"Absolutely not." I stand and walk toward the door. Once outside, I hit Wav's name in my phone to call her.

It rings for a while. I get a little more anxious with each ring. On the last ring, Waverley answers while laughing. "Hey, sorry, I couldn't find my phone in this mess."

"Hey, Uncle Owen," Annabelle says over speaker.

"Hey, Belley. How are you guys doing?"

"We're good. We have on silly headbands and face masks," Annabelle says.

"They are not silly headbands," Waverley interjects. "I already told you, they're awesome."

"Wav, you look like a unicorn with a scary mask on your face." Annabelle giggles.

"Rude, don't hate on my unicorn. You look like a beautiful princess," Wav says.

"I'm sure you both look great." I laugh. "I just wanted to check and make sure you guys were good."

"Yes, we're good. Minor destruction has taken place in the living room but otherwise, your house is still standing."

I almost correct her and say "our house", but I stop myself. That feels *way* too soon, but I don't know, her being there feels right. I want her there, I want her to make it her home as well. "Well, good, I'll be home a little after seven. Y'all have fun."

"Okay, honey, be safe tonight."

"Yeah, honey, be safe," Annabelle mocks.

"Annabelle! Knock it off, you goof." Waverley laughs.

The smile on my face is stupid.

I want this forever.

I unlock my door bright and early at 7:15. I open it as quietly as possible and creep into the living room where there is indeed a bit of destruction. There are blankets everywhere, cushions off the couch, pillows in every corner, and some stuffed animals in the mix.

Both of my girls are dead asleep in the middle of the mess. I tiptoe to my room, take off my uniform, and hop in the shower to wash off last night's shift. When I get out, I throw on a pair of basketball shorts and go back out to check on the girls. They haven't budged so as quietly as possible, I grab two pillows and a blanket and go back to my room, then come back and ever so carefully lift Wav into my arms.

Her eyes pop open. "What are you doing?" she whispers.

"Taking you to my bed. No way are you're sleeping on the floor while I'm here."

"What about Annabelle?" Wav giggles.

"She's fine, now be quiet." I carry her back to my room and set her down on one side of the bed. She rests her head on the pillow and shuts her eyes.

I crawl in on the other side and once I'm under the blanket, Waverley rolls over, tangles her body in mine, and her head rests on my chest. I kiss the top of her head before we drift off to sleep.

Several hours later, I'm pulled from my sleep by the sound of laughter. I roll out of the bed, pull a t-shirt on, and walk out. A burnt smell hits me right away. I spot the girls in the kitchen, both bent over peering into the oven. I just lean back and watch them.

"I don't think they're supposed to be that color," Annabelle says.

"We followed Winry's recipe exactly. I'm sure they're fine." Waverley pulls out a tray and sets it on the stove top.

"Wav, they're burnt." Annabelle giggles.

"Shoot, I don't know what happened. We followed Winry's instructions."

"I told you we should have let Uncle Owen do it. He cooks everything."

I do my best not to laugh, but I definitely can't help but smile. Not to brag, but it's true. I do cook everything.

"This isn't cooking. This is *baking*. Besides, we shouldn't need Owen to bake cookies. Come on, help me get rid of these, and we'll try again. Owen doesn't need to know we burnt the first batch."

"Too late," I say behind them, and they jump.

"Goodness, Owen, you scared me." Wav hits my arm when I walk up to see the damage.

I laugh. "What happened here?"

I noticed they cleaned up the mess in the living room, but now it looks like an explosion took place in my kitchen.

"We wanted cookies, and Wav insisted we could do it without you." Annabelle walks over to grab one of the bowls off the counter. "We have more cookie dough, but I still think we did something wrong."

"Belley, we followed every step Winry sent. It's the oven's fault. It gets too hot." Wav takes off the oven mitts and grabs her phone.

"Don't blame my oven. Here, let me see what Win sent." I hold out my hand and Wav hands her phone over. I open Winry's message. "Okay, you added everything in this order right?"

"Yes, I followed her directions exactly," Wav huffs.

I glance at the burnt cookies. "What did you use to grease the pan? Did you use cooking spray?"

Wav shuffles on her feet. "No, she didn't specify, so we used butter."

"Well, there's your problem. Using butter can cause your cookies to burn. You should have used cooking spray or parchment paper."

"I told you he'd know." Annabelle hops on the counter.

Waverley rolls her eyes. "How was I supposed to know that?"

"It's alright, darlin'." I take the rest of the cookie dough from the counter and take it to the fridge. "It's also better to put it in the fridge for a bit and let it chill."

Waverley crosses her arms. "Winry, didn't say any of that. This isn't my fault."

"It's okay. I'm here now." I kiss her cheek as I reach around her to get the burnt tray of cookies. I grab an oven mitt then take the tray to the garbage and scrape off the cookies with a spatula.

"I swear, I know how to cook," Waverley huffs and Annabelle laughs. "I do!" Waverley says adamantly.

"Of course you do, Wav. You're right, it was the oven," I tease her then wink at Annabelle. "Right, Belley?"

Annabelle's head falls back in laughter. "Right, the oven."

"Uh, Annabelle, you're supposed to be on my side." Waverley smacks at her playfully.

"I said it was the oven." Annabelle smacks her back.

"The dough looked good. I'll pop a tray of them in the oven tomorrow." I put the tray in the sink, then start cleaning up the four other bowls they have on the counter. "Annabelle, Grandma is coming over tonight, but tomorrow, if you want, you can spend the night there."

"Like spend the night with Mom?" Annabelle asks, unsure.

"Only if you want. You don't have to. I don't work, so we can just go visit. If you want to try to stay, I can still come pick you up any time you want."

Annabelle glances at Waverley, and Wav gives her an encouraging smile. I feel like I'm missing something, but it seems special to them, so I don't pry.

"Yeah, okay, I'll stay the night."

"Okay, Belley, you can call me any time, and I'll pick you up. Promise you'll call if you need me?" I hold out my pinky, and she wraps hers around mine.

"Promise." Annabelle smiles and hops off the counter. "I'm going to read in my room for a bit, if that's okay?"

"Of course."

Annabelle starts to her room, then stops and wraps me up in a hug. "I love you, Uncle Owen."

While Annabelle is a big hugger herself, it almost felt like she needed this hug. "I love you too, kid. Everything okay? You know you can tell me anything."

"Yeah, just wanted to tell you I loved you." Annabelle shrugs.

"Okay, Belley. I love you too." I plant a kiss on the top of her head. She squeezes then lets me go, and heads to her room. I turn to Waverley. "Something I need to know?"

Wav smiles. "No, nothing to worry about. Just enjoy it."

"I will." I tug her by her waist closer to me. "You know what else I'm going to enjoy?"

She smirks. "What?"

"Another date with you." I tap her nose, and she scrunches her face.

"As if you would be so lucky," she mocks and wraps her arms around my neck. "You'll have to ask nicely."

I smile and roll my eyes. *This woman.* I'll do whatever she says. "Waverley, will you please go on a date with me tomorrow?"

Waverley bites her lower lip and peers off like she's contemplating her answer. "I don't know; I think I may have—"

Alright, my patience is gone. "Damn it, Firecracker. You're going on a date with me tomorrow. End of story."

Waverley's cheeks turn pink, and she smiles. "Hey, you called me Firecracker again."

"I did?" Oh no, I did. It just came out. I didn't even think, why, why did I say that? "Wav, I'm sorry it just slipped, I didn't—"

"Owen, hey, why are you apologizing? You used to call me that all the time. Don't get me wrong, I love when you call me darlin' and Wav, but I have wondered why you stopped?"

I brush her hair back behind her ears. "Two reasons. One, that name is a reminder of something I took away from you, and I will never be able to forgive myself for that—"

"Owen—" she tries to interject.

"Two, that's just not us anymore. You get a different name, because this is a different relationship. You're mine now, darlin'."

Chapter 24

Waverley

When I walk into my parent's house Wednesday morning, I look around the living room that hasn't changed since I was a kid. There's always a comfort in knowing that this house is a constant.

"Hi, the least favorite daughter is here," I holler and head toward our kitchen.

"Oh, stop it, Wav." Mom throws the dish rag she had in her hands at me as I round the corner.

"All of you girls are my favorite." Dad leans in, and I pop a kiss to his cheek.

"Thanks, Daddy."

"I hope you're hungry. Your mom made enough pancakes to feed the whole station." He grabs a plate stacked full of pancakes and carries it to the table.

"Of course she did. Mom always makes too much food." I take a seat at the table. "Where's Win and Wyla?"

"Winry is almost here, and Wyla is still asleep. Do you mind talking to her? She's been working so hard with her summer class. I'm worried she's putting too much pressure on herself." Mom carries another plate to the table.

"Sure, we'll do a girls' night soon. Win and I will check on her."

I put two pancakes on my plate and pour syrup all over them.

"Okay, and maybe try to set her up with Levi—"

"No," Dad interjects, cutting mom off.

"Griffin, there is nothing wrong with Levi," Mom says calmly.

"No, no way. Not all of my girls are going to date cops. I draw the line at Wyla." Dad takes a bite of his pancake.

"I knew Wyla was secretly your favorite." I chuckle.

"I love all of you the same, but I can't have all three of my son-in-laws working for me. Hell, that whole shift would practically be my son-in-laws. Two is the limit."

Butterflies flutter in my stomach as Dad acknowledges Owen as his future son-in-law. I know we're a good way off from that, but when I think about that future—the life we could have—it makes me happy.

"Well, I still think you should at least set her up on a date with someone. She needs to get out more." Mom shrugs.

"She's fine, Izzy. Wyla is focusing on school. She'll have plenty of time for all that shit later. Let me at least keep one a little while longer. I'm not ready to lose them all."

"Oh come on, Dad. You could never lose us. You'll always be our favorite." I smile.

"Um, hello, the woman who carried you for nine months and birthed you over here." Mom waves her hands.

Dad and I look at each other and laugh. "Sorry, Mom. What I meant was, Dad will always be our favorite guy."

"Uh huh, I know the truth," Mom sighs. "I have never been able to compete with your father. The man was destined to be a girl dad."

"I wouldn't want it any other way." Dad winks.

"Hey, I'm here," Winry hollers from the living room.

"In the kitchen. We started without you," I holler back.

Winry walks in and plops down in her chair. "Sorry I'm late, where's Wyla?"

"Behind you." Wyla yawns as she comes in and takes her normal seat. "Stayed up late studying for the final in my summer class on Friday."

"Which class is it again?"

"It's Medical Terminology," Wyla says as she loads her plate with pancakes. "It's not too hard, but there are a lot of words and acronyms."

"I'm sure you'll do great on your test, sweetie." Mom smiles at her, and I know she wants to say more, like "take a break", but she doesn't.

"Yeah, I hope so." Wyla gives her a half-smile back.

Hmm, maybe a girls' night is needed sooner than later.

"Wav, how was your sleepover with Annabelle?" Winry asks.

"So great. We had the best time. We made a sister pile and I, of course, showed her the *Princess Diaries* movies. We had a blast."

"Oh, that sounds like so much fun." Mom perks up. "How are you and Owen?"

Good. Great. Amazing. I'm totally falling head over heels for him.

I want to say all those things, but there's something holding me back, and I'm pretty sure it's the same thing that's been holding me back from taking that big step with Owen. I need to let this secret go.

"We're good," *Oh, goodness, how do I do this?* "He's great," I continue, but there's more I need to say.

"But?" Dad says.

"Um, I've been keeping something from you guys, and I think it's time I told you. And no, Dad. Owen didn't do anything, he's just part of the reason I'm telling you."

"Sweetie, what is it?" Mom sets her fork down and leans on the table.

"You guys have to promise to not say anything until I'm finished." Everyone nods except Dad. "Dad, promise?"

With one pleading look, he folds and nods.

"Okay. When I was sixteen..." And I tell them everything. Everything that happened that night and how relieved I felt when he died. I tell them how I never told anyone but Owen. I leave out the details they don't need about Owen and I, but otherwise they get the whole story.

I somehow manage to tell it without crying, I guess I'm healing more than I thought.

Mom, Win, and Wyla all are wiping tears from their faces, but Dad remains stone-cold.

"You can all say something now."

But no one says anything. Winry and Wyla simply stand and wrap me up in their arms. I cherish this moment for a minute, but I'm drawn back to Dad, who is clenching his fists and looks like he is about to go into a rage.

"Daddy, I'm sorry I—"

"I need a minute." Dad stands abruptly and walks out to the back porch.

The shock on my face isn't missed by Mom. She stands and joins our group hug.

"Oh sweetie, don't you dare apologize. Your dad just needs a minute to process."

We stay huddled in our hug for a good five minutes, none of us saying anything. I don't suppose there is much to say. We can't change what happened, and in this moment, this is what we need.

We eventually break apart and wipe the tears from our eyes.

Winry speaks first. "I'm sorry you went through this alone, Wav. We're your family, we should have known something was wrong. I always wondered why you never hung out with Jane anymore. I should have asked. I should have—"

"Don't do that, Win. I've thought 'I should have' too many times. *I should have just gone with them. I should have left when he came in*, but thinking that way won't change anything."

"I just—how could we not have known?" Winry pulls me back in for another hug.

"I hid it pretty well, and he either didn't remember or he knew what he did, so no one else knew. Jane and I were never that close to begin with, honestly. It was one of those groups that you had been friends in middle school but were slowly starting to drift apart anyway. I started slowly dating again after a while, but the relationships never went anywhere. I always tried to appear sex-positive in hopes it would make me *feel* sex-positive but, honestly, I'm terrified."

"Oh, sweetie." Mom starts to cry again, and we all go back in for another hug.

When they finally let me go. I venture out to the back porch. Dad sits in his rocking chair, staring out at nothing.

"Daddy?" He doesn't budge, so I sit in the chair next to him quietly.

We sit and stare out into the yard for a while.

When I think he will never break the silence, he finally does. "I'm not going to ask why you didn't tell me. There isn't any way that I could even begin to understand what you went through. Living with that weight every day for years, Waverley, I"—he chokes—"I'm so sorry, I don't know what to say, other than I'm sorry." He cries. "And don't you dare tell me it's okay, or that I don't need to apologize."

Tears pool in my eyes. "Okay, I won't."

Dad reaches over and takes my hand in his. "My beautiful, incredible, resilient daughter. I'm so proud of you. Knowing who you are and all you have accomplished, all while carrying this on your shoulders. You're so strong, and not a single man on my patrol could ever compare."

I chuckle as the tears fall silently. "Thank you, Daddy."

We rock in our chairs, hand in hand. "Please refrain from giving me any details, but Owen's been respectful, right?"

I smile, "Yes, Dad. You don't have to worry with him."

"Good, and that's all I need to hear. Save that other shit for your sisters."

I laugh. "Not a problem."

I don't think the weight of what happened will ever truly go away, but the power it had on me has now been lifted.

Chapter 25

Owen

In my truck, Annabelle requested the windows rolled down, and Taylor Swift is blaring on the aux. According to her, my era is *Reputation*, and hers is *1989*. I just nod along and turn it louder when she starts to dance in her seat.

"Oh, Uncle Owen, this is totally yours and Wav's song, turn it up!" she shouts over the already blaring music.

I chuckle as I see that the title of the song is "You Are In Love". I don't argue with her, I turn up the music and let her sing to her heart's content. After two more songs, we pull into mom's driveway.

I turn off the truck and turn to Annabelle. "Okay, Belley. I'll pick you up tomorrow after lunch, but you call me anytime, and I'll come get you. I promise."

"Okay, Uncle Owen. I promise I'll call you if I need you."

"No, you'll call me if you *want* to. Even if you don't *need* me, you can call me if you want to. Okay?"

"Okay, I promise." Annabelle smiles and we hop out of my truck. I grab her bag and we head inside. Mom and Natalie sit on the couch. There is some romance drama show that Mom watches on the TV, and Natalie is sitting, staring at her phone.

"Hey, guys," I say as we walk in.

"My babies, hello." Mom sits up in her recliner, and Annabelle goes up to give her a hug. I follow behind with another.

Nat finally decides to put down her phone. "Hey there, sugar. You ready to have some fun?"

Annabelle's smile grows and her eyes light up. "Yes! What are we doing?"

"Well, I thought we could watch some TV... then... maybe after dinner, we could play a board game," Natalie says, clearly making it up as she goes.

"Yeah, that sounds fun. Could we make dinner together? Uncle Owen has been letting me help with cooking. I think I'm getting pretty good at it."

"You can help Grandma cook." Natalie shrugs. "I'll watch."

In other words, she's going to sit on her phone—typical.

"Okay, kid, I'm going to head out." That familiar pit in my stomach from every time I would drop off Annabelle comes back. I remind myself that Mom will be here the entire time, but I can't help but feel anxious.

"Okay, Uncle Owen." After a quick hug she digs her Kindle out of her bag and sits down on the couch next to Natalie.

"You have any plans tonight, dear?" Mom asks.

"Yeah, I'm cooking for Waverley."

"Oh, that's nice. What are you cooking?"

"Nothing crazy, just tacos. Keeping it simple" I shrug.

"Yeah, nothing crazy. Dear, last time you made us tacos, you made two different meats, with two different seasonings, a ton of peppers and onions, and you made homemade salsa and margaritas. You don't do simple when it comes to cooking, and neither did your father."

I smile. "I did learn from the best." It's rare that we bring up Dad. Losing him like we did left a pretty big hole in our family.

"That you did." Mom squeezes my hand. I know it's hard for her to talk about him. "Now, go—go enjoy your night."

"Alright, call me if you need me."

"We will. Have a good night."

I make it back home and start on dinner. I suppose Mom wasn't wrong, I do tend to go a little overboard with cooking.

I make a pitcher of lime margaritas, then I start dicing up everything I need for the salsa.

I finish dicing the tomatoes when Waverley walks in the kitchen. "Hey, honey."

"Hey, you're early," I say as she plants a kiss to my cheek.

"Duh, you think I'm going to miss watching you cook. Take your shirt off." She hops on one of the bar stools in front of me.

"Your wish is my command." I wink and pull my t-shirt over my head.

Waverley does the cat-call whistle. "Is the oven open? Because it's hot in here." She fans herself.

"Here, this ought to cool you off." I grab a glass and pour her a margarita.

"Oh my word, you made lime margs?" she squeals.

"You always drink them with your tacos, right?"

"Well, who wouldn't drink a marg with tacos? They're a perfect pair, they just go together." She sips her drink. "You need any help?"

I finish dicing a jalapeno and set it to the side. "From the girl that burnt cookies? Nah, you sit your pretty ass there."

"Um, excuse me, sir, I happen to remember you burning bacon not too long ago."

"Yes, but you were distracting me. Both food burning instances involved you." I point my knife at her. "Stay out of my kitchen."

She slides off her stool and walks around the counter top. "I'm sorry, I didn't quite hear you. What was that again?" She has this flirty look in her eyes.

I set down my knife and take a step toward her. "I said stay out of my kitchen."

She smiles sweetly. "Fine. Okay! But first, do you want to try my marg? It's delicious."

"Yeah, I'll take a sip."

"Okay." Wav brings her drink up and for a moment I think she is going to hand it to me but then she tips it over and lets a shot of it fall on her chest. *Holy hell.*

"Oops, silly me." She smiles wickedly. "Let me try that again."

I grab a chunk of her hair and tilt her head back, then lick from her cleavage up to her neck.

I whisper in her ear, "You're right, it is delicious."

"Want another taste?" she asks breathlessly.

"Yes." I bite her earlobe and her body shivers.

She brings the drink back up and pours just a little more on her chest. I don't let a single drop go to waste as I lick it off her.

"Owen," she moans but I muffle it with my lips on her.

I take the glass out of her hands and set it on the counter, then I haul her ass over to the kitchen table.

"I want to taste my dessert now too."

I undo her jeans and pull them off. Waverley rips her tank top off revealing a matching

deep green lace bra and panties set. She smiles as I take her in.

"Fuck, darlin'. You're breathtaking."

"The green reminded me of your eyes." She blushes.

Fuck, if that doesn't do something to me. She bought this solely thinking of me. My cock twitches as I stare at the beauty in front of me.

"Owen—"

"Just let me appreciate this view for a moment longer because, in a minute, the only thing I want on you is my mouth."

I get about two seconds then Waverley hooks her legs around my waist and pulls me on top of her.

"Times up." Her lips latch onto mine.

My hands roam her perfect curves as our tongues fight each other. I grab her arms and move them up over her head.

"Keep those up there, Waverley." I start to kiss down her neck.

"Or what?" She giggles.

I reach her perfect tits. I pull back the lace and lick her nipple. "Want to play a game? Want to see how close I can get you, then stop?"

"No." Waverley shivers as I take one in my mouth.

"Then I suggest you listen to what I say and keep those arms up there." I switch to the other breast, and she writhes underneath me.

I slowly make my way down, kissing her stomach then I hook those green lace panties and yank them off of her. I tease her by kissing her thighs and getting close enough that she can feel my beard on her.

"You're driving me crazy." She shuffles under me.

"Good, the feeling's mutual." I decide to give her a little relief by licking her center then drag my tongue up lazily.

"Fuck," she pants.

I do it again, but this time I'm over being slow. I go straight up to her clit and lick and suck with no mercy. With each flick of my tongue, I can feel her body vibrate. Her legs rest over my shoulders and her hands remain above her head. This has to be one of the most glorious sights I've ever seen.

"Owen, don't stop." Her breath is jagged, and her legs shake.

"You want to come, baby?"

"Yes," she moans.

"You want to come on my tongue, or should I let you ride my fingers to find your high?" I flick her with my tongue again and her back arches as she groans.

"I want more, I want you to fuck me."

I freeze. *Did she...?* "What?"

Waverley leans up on her elbows, and we stare into each other's eyes. "I want to have sex with you, Owen."

I stand up and cup her face. "You sure this is what you want, Waverley?"

I search her sky-blue eyes for any hint of hesitation or fear.

Do I want to have sex with her? Yes. But this isn't something I'm going to take on a whim. I need to know this is what she wants.

She smiles and gives me a small kiss. "Yes, I'm ready. I want it to be you, Owen. I want this. No condom either. I'm on the pill. I want to feel all of you," she says as she slips her hand down my shorts and wraps her hand around my cock, stroking slowly.

I think my brain is short circuiting; I'm unable to form words. So instead, I scoop her up and she squeals. I carry her straight to my room and lay her down on my bed.

I brush the hair out of her face. "I want you, Waverley Bennett. I'll always want you and one day, I'm going to throw you all around this bed and fuck you every way possible, but for now, I want you to be selfish. I want you to tell me what you want. What you need and when to stop. You're in control, Wav. Nothing that you don't want to happen will happen. Understand?"

Tears well in her eyes as she nods.

"Fuck, don't cry, baby. You don't—"

"No, no, I want to. I just... thank you. Everything you just said was the reassurance I didn't know I needed. I want this, I need this." She leans up and starts to place kisses on my face and neck. "I trust you, Owen. Please."

"I got you, Wav, I promise." With a quick kiss, I stand up and take off my shorts. Waverley stares up at me. I know she's nervous, but she is doing her best to hide it. I need to boost her confidence.

"Come here, baby." I pull her up, off the bed. "Do me a favor and wrap that pretty mouth around my cock. It needs to be nice and wet to glide into that tight pussy of yours."

Her eyes light up at the anticipation, and she slides down to her knees. She wraps one hand around the base and looks up at me wickedly. There's my girl.

I'm about to sing her fucking praises. I don't want there to be a single doubt in her mind about what she does to me, or how badly I want her.

Waverley starts slow, only taking the tip in and out of her mouth. I know she's trying to get back at me from earlier, but I let her do it. I pull her hair back to keep it out of her face.

She teases for a few more seconds then surprises me and takes me to the back of her throat.

"Oh, fuck." She does it again. "That's my dirty girl. Take my cock, baby."

So she does. She picks up her pace and moans when I start to rock my hips. Her hands grip my thighs, steadying her. She takes me to the back of her throat again and this time, she pauses for a minute and starts to flick her tongue on my base.

"Damn it." I pull her back. "That mouth of yours is ridiculous."

She licks her lips and smiles confidently. *Much better.* She stands, and I capture her beautiful face in my hands. "You're in charge, Wav. What do you want?"

"It's not a want anymore, it's a need. I need you inside of me."

With a low growl of satisfaction, I lay her back down on the bed, kissing her softly. Our bodies flush against each other. I don't think I'll ever get over how good she feels against me. I lightly press against her center. "You ready?"

"Yes." She pulls me back down for another kiss as I slowly push in. Wav closes her eyes, and her lips part. She doesn't give away if it hurts, but I don't dare go any faster.

With each inch, the need to thrust in and out is overwhelming. *Fuck, she feels amazing.* When I'm all the way in she lets out a breath and adjusts under me.

"You good, baby?"

With her eyes still closed, she nods.

"Waverley, eyes open, baby. Look at me." Slowly, she opens them and looks up at me. "Are you good?"

"Yes, I'm good. I'm with you." She wraps her arms around my neck. "You can move now."

Thank fuck. I slowly pull out and then push back in, keeping a steady rhythm. Waverley wraps her legs around me, making it a little easier to glide in and out. One arm wraps around her waist holding her close, and I lean on the other as I kiss her.

"Owen," she pants. "Faster."

She doesn't have to tell me twice. I pick up my pace, and she clenches around me.

"Fuck, Waverley, This pussy is mine. It'll fit me and only me."

She moans loudly as I pick up my pace a little more.

"Yes, Wav. Let me hear you."

She moans again. "Owen, I'm so—"

"I know, baby. You can let go. Come on my cock, Wav."

Two more hard thrusts, and her walls pulse, squeezing me tight.

Waverley's back arches as she screams out. "Fuck, fuck, Owen!"

She claws at my back and I snap, thrusting into her with no restraint. I've never been with a woman without a condom, but I've also never slept with Waverley before either. I know I have a past, but this—this is exactly how I want it to be forever. With this woman and nothing between us.

When I look into her eyes, I'm done. I pump all of me into her and come so hard it takes every ounce of strength to not collapse on top of her.

I roll to the side and pull her with me, she rests her head on my chest as we both try to catch our breath.

"That was... perfect," Waverley whispers.

"Yeah, it was." I kiss the top of her head.

She lifts her head up toward me and smiles. "Can we do it again?"

Chapter 26

Waverley

Owen laughs. "You want to go again?"

"Yeah, I want to go again. That was amazing."

He laughs again. "It was."

"Then why are you laughing?" I shove his bratty ass.

"I knew once you had me you'd be obsessed with me." He smirks. "As if." I shove him again and pull away from him. "I changed my mind, I don't—"

"Get your ass back here." Owen captures me in his arms and pulls me back on top of him. "I'm kidding. If anyone is obsessed, it's me. I want to do it with you for as long as you'll let me. I just thought I could make you some tacos first."

I smile. "Can I help you cook?"

"Welllll..." Owen starts so I shove him again. He laughs. "Yes, darlin', you can help."

"Good answer." I go to give him a quick kiss, but when I try to pull away, he places a hand on the back of my neck and pulls me back in.

This kiss is lazy but sensual. His tongue tangles with mine as he holds a firm grip.

One thought is now perfectly clear at this moment. This is it. This is what I want. I want a life with Owen West.

I am, without a doubt, head over heels in love with him.

Back in the kitchen, I'm sitting on the stool, sipping my marg as Owen chops some peppers in front of me. I know I said I wanted to help, and I tried. But when Owen saw me attempting to cut the peppers, he promptly kicked me back to my stool. Owen slices them like he's some master chef. In seconds, they're cut perfectly.

"What was wrong with what I was doing?" I cross my arms and pout.

"Are you kidding? The way you were going at those peppers, you would have sliced your hand open," Owen says as he starts the last one.

"I've never cut myself cooking before, thank you very much," I say holding my head high.

"By some miracle, Wav. Come on, let us be a modern couple. I'll cook, and you reward me with a kiss when I'm done." He winks and smiles that damn sexy smile.

I roll my eyes. "Who taught you how to cook like this anyway?"

"My dad," Owen says with a bit of emotion in his tone. I know he died when Owen was in high school, but he never talks about him.

I debate pushing the subject for a moment but decide to ask him anyway. "What was he like? Your dad?"

Owen takes a breath and finishes cutting the pepper. "He was the best, everything you would want in a father." Owen shrugs.

I can't decide if he wants me to keep asking questions or move on to something else. "We don't have to talk about him if you don't want to, honey."

Owen looks up at me and his face softens. "No, it's fine. He had me in the kitchen as soon as I was old enough to hold a spoon. He said it was a skill every husband needs to know, and it wasn't fair to expect our wives to do all of the cooking."I giggle. "I like him already. I bet he would have let me help cook."

"Ha! If he saw your knife skills he would never let you enter his kitchen." Owen takes the peppers and pops them in a pan.

"Oh, come on, he would not. I bet he would try to help me rather than kick me out."

Owen cocks his head and grins. "Okay, that might be true, but I'm not as good of a teacher as he was, so you get the boot with me."

I laugh. "Tell me more about him."

"Okay, let's see. He loved sitting on the porch to watch storms. Mom would have to drag him inside when they would get really bad. He said watching a storm was therapeutic. Mom told him he was nuts," he says, still buzzing around the kitchen.

I laugh because it sounds a bit like us.

Owen pauses and looks down at the pan in front of him. "We all took it hard when he got his cancer diagnosis, and we all fell apart when he died."

I furrow my brows. "What do you mean? I thought you were still close with your mom?"

"Yeah, we are now. But it took Natalie getting pregnant to bring us back together." He takes another deep breath. "Unfortunately, Natalie didn't jump on the 'let's be better' bus with us. She took Dad's death the hardest. Not that I blame her. They were close and losing your dad at fifteen is..." he pauses, his voice thick with emotion. "I just wish I had been there for her more after it happened."

"It's unimaginable, but you lost him too. And you were what? Seventeen? You can't put that pressure on yourself, honey."

"Yeah, I know." Owen shrugs and adds the seasoned chicken to a pan.

I slide out of the stool and walk around coming up behind him. I wrap my arms around his waist and rest my head against his back. "I'm sorry about your dad. I know I didn't really know him, but I know he'd be proud of you."

Owen twists around and kisses the top of my head as he hugs me back. "Thank you." He rests his chin on top of my head and rubs my back.

I know that was probably hard for him to talk about. We've both been having hard conversations today. "Hey, I told my family today about what happened... about the rape."

"You did? How'd it go?" Owen asks, surprised. He pulls back just a little, studying my face as I peer up at him.

"Good. It felt good to tell them." I smile. "Dad took it really hard, but we talked more, just the two of us, and he was okay when I left."

Owen chuckles. "I'm surprised he let you leave. I barely want to let you out of my sight. I can't imagine how he feels."

I rest my head back down on his chest. "I think that's why what happened earlier...happened. I think telling my family was what I needed to do to let it go." Those wounds may have done some damage, but they're simply old scars now that are no longer covered up by Band-Aids.

"Hey." Owen tips my chin back up to look at him. "I'm proud of you."

I smile, and he kisses my forehead.

All I can feel right now is love. I love this man so much. His selflessness, his kindness, his patience. I want to tell him all of that, but I don't want to rush him.

I'll just say it in my head for now.

Chapter 27

Waverley

The month of August flies by. Starting back at school, I'm more confident this year in my teaching ability and in myself in general. I mean, I'm no longer carrying around my secret. I have a kick-ass boyfriend, and a job I love.

"Hey, pretty lady," Anna says as she walks in my classroom after last period on Friday.

"Hey, hey. What are you doing?" I ask as I get my bag ready to go.

"Oh, just checking in on my work bestie. I saw that sexy-as-sin boyfriend of yours picking up Annabelle, but you were nowhere to be found. You two are usually eye fucking each other in the pick-up line."

"We do not do that." I brush her off.

"Oh yes, you do, babe. What gives, why weren't you out there drooling all over that man?"

I laugh. "I've got to hurry today actually. My sisters are coming over tonight, and I still have to go to the store to stock up on wine, candy, and chocolate."

"Man, seeing you guys makes me want a sister so bad. All I have is a stupid brother." She laughs.

"Well, you can join us tonight if you want. But just a heads up, we will make you share your deepest darkest secrets." I stand up and grab my bag.

"Oh, I so would, but I'm not ready to tell you about that murder I committed that one time." She laughs.

"Darn, next time it is. Can't wait to hear all about it." I nudge her, and we both walk out to our cars.

After buying out the whole wine and junk food section, I'm finally home. I drop all of the bags on the kitchen table when my phone dings.

Honey

> **I missed you today.**

I smile ridiculously at my phone.

> **I missed you too.**

> **What are you wearing?**

I snort a laugh.

> **What am I wearing? Really?**

> **Come on, Wav. I haven't gotten to see you in two days. Just tell me you're naked.**

What would you do if I was?

Owen's name flashes on my phone immediately. "Hey, honey."

"What time are your sisters coming over?" he blurts out.

"Maybe in half an hour, possibly sooner. Why?"

I start shifting through the grocery bags, unloading everything.

"Because I'm in your driveway."

"What? No you're not—" But then I hear my door open. I walk in my living room as Owen shuts the door. "What are you doing here, you—"

"Naked, now," he demands as he walks up to me.

"Owen, my sisters could be here any minute." I laugh.

"Then we better hurry." He smirks as he backs me up against the wall and kisses me like he's desperate for it. Goodness knows I am.

I wrap my legs around his waist, pulling him in deeper. Owen's hands cup my ass and give it a well-deserved squeeze as he bites my lower lip.

He carries me over and sets me down on the couch then pulls his t-shirt off over his head.

"I said *get naked*," he growls.

I rip my shirt over my head then race to take off my jeans when my front door opens again.

"Wow," Winry says as she and Wyla walk in. "Put your clothes back on."

"Damn it," Owen grumbles. "Come back in half an hour."

"Sorry, buddy. The naked party is going to have to wait, it's sister time." Winry pings back. "Don't you have to get to work anyway?"

"Buzzkill. I'll be sure to return this favor," Owen says as he throws his t-shirt back on.

I laugh. "I'm pretty sure this is just retaliation from when Wyla and I walked in on her and Graham."

"Exactly, and one day we will do the same to Wyla." Winry shoves her, but Wyla doesn't seem to be as amused.

I pull my shirt back on and hop up from the couch. "Sorry, like she said, it's now officially sister time." I kiss his cheek.

"Yeah, yeah, I guess I better go anyway."

I walk him to the door. "Sorry, honey."

"It's okay, I'll get you all to myself soon enough. In the meantime, avert your eyes, assholes. Or watch, I don't care," Owen says to Win and Wyla then cups my face to give me another desperate kiss.

"Ow, ow," Wyla chants, and Winry whistles.

Owen lifts his hand to give them the finger. "Okay, I do have to go. I'll talk to you later."

"Okay, be safe tonight."

"Of course." With another quick kiss, he walks to his truck.

I turn back to my sisters who are both smiling at me. "What? Don't look at me like that."

"Wav, you so love him." Winry giggles.

"I—" Part of me considers lying but then I remember who I would be lying to. "Yeah, I really do."

"I knew it! I knew he was the one for you." Winry claps her hands together. "Ahh, I'm just so happy."

"Me too, he seems really good to you," Wyla adds.

"He is." I blush. "But let's get sister night started. What should we call for delivery?"

Two hours later, our Chinese food is gone, and the sister pile is in full swing. Our sweats are on and not a spot of makeup on any of us. I refill my wine glass and dip into the Peanut M&M'S I bought. Winry has a glass of wine and the bowl of her homemade cookie dough in her lap. And Wyla sits on the floor with a pillow snuggled in hers.

"Wyla, are you sure you don't want anything else? You only ate soup tonight. I thought you loved their sweet and sour chicken?" I ask her. She's been acting weird all night. She never turns down Chinese food.

"I'm fine, Wav. I'm just not very hungry tonight." Wyla shrugs.

"Okay, if you say so. So, Win, what's up next on the wedding planning?"

"Mmm, let's see. I've got all of the big stuff lined up, like the vendors and tables are all set. I've got to get invitations sent out by the end of this month. Oh, and we have to get you guys' bridesmaids' dresses."

"Oh, yay! What were you thinking you want us in?" I ask.

"I honestly don't have a clue. I'm thinking something like sage green or maybe a neutral color. But really, I want you guys to pick out your own styles. I figured we would decide when we went shopping."

"Yeah, I'm sure we will. That sounds great. Doesn't it, Wyla?" I nudge my dazed sister.

"Hmm? Oh yeah, dresses. Sounds great." She nods.

"Okay, what is going on with you? You've been acting weird all night."

"Yeah, since when do you only eat soup from Ling's Palace? You love their sweet and sour chicken."

"I'm fine, guys. I told you, I'm not really hungry." She shrugs.

"Right, because we *so* believe you. Come on, Wyla, is it school?"

"No, Wav, it's not school." She gives me the side eye. "I said I'm fine, just an off night."

"Alright, well I was thinking since things didn't work out with me and Levi, I thought we could set you two up." I pop some M&M'S into my mouth. "You said he was hot."

"Oh, that's a great idea!" Winry squeals, "Then we could all triple date."

"No, I'm good. I don't want to be set up on a date with Levi." Wyla shuffles on the floor, crisscrossing her legs.

I give her a little nudge with my foot. "What? Come on, you said he was so hot, why not?"

"Because I don't want to." she snaps, seeming to get more irritated by the second.

"Okay, geez. Well, what about someone else? Wyla, you've been so busy in school. Why don't you take a break and go on a date?"

"Yeah, I agree," Winry adds, sipping her wine.

"Guys, no dates. I don't want to go on any dates," Wyla says adamantly.

"Okay, okay, goodness. Drink some wine and stop being crabby." I grab the bottle of her wine of choice. "Seriously? Win and I are a bottle down, and you haven't even opened one?" I hand it to her.

"I just haven't wanted any." She shrugs.

"Well, you need some. Let me get you a glass," Winry says standing up from the pile.

"No, Win, I'm good, really." Wyla nearly jumps up to stop her.

I laugh. "Now you aren't drinking your wine. What, are you pregnant or something?" I say as a joke, but Wyla doesn't laugh.

In fact, she looks like she's going to throw up.

Winry turns on her heels at the silence. "Wyla Bennett, are you pregnant?"

Wyla bursts into tears. "I wanted to tell you guys, but I didn't know how." She buries her face in her hands and cries more.

Winry and I look at each other, jaws hanging to the floor. After, somewhat wrapping our heads around her answer, we move to sit on either side of her.

"It's okay, Wyla. Just start from the beginning," Winry says softly and rubs her back as she cries.

Wyla uncovers her face and wipes some tears. "Well, let's see, I'm roughly six weeks pregnant. Everything makes me sick. Oh, oh! You want to know the best part about all this, I don't even know my baby's father's full name." She buries her face again and cries harder.

"What? What do you mean you don't know his full name?" I ask.

"The guy in Nashville. My one-night stand. He's the only person I've been with in months. He's the only possible father, and I have no way of contacting him or even finding him. All I know is that his first name is Jett, that's it."

"Okay, we can work with that, that's not *nothing*." Winry takes one of Wyla's hands in hers and I take the other.

"Yeah, Wyla, we can find him." I try to sound encouraging.

"Guys, we have a first name, that's it. Do you know how many Jett's there are in this world? A lot!"

"Yeah, but we could narrow it down to Nashville, right?" I ask.

"Not really. I mean we were in Nashville for a trip, he probably doesn't even live there," Wyla says defeated.

"Wyla, it's going to be okay," Winry adds. "Do Mom and Dad know?"

"Heavens, no. I couldn't even tell you guys. How in the world am I supposed to tell Dad?" She sniffles. "'Hey, Dad, your baby here. By the way, I got pregnant by some guy in Nashville, and I have no way of contacting him.' He's going to kill me."

"He's not going to kill you. If anything, he could help you find him," I suggest.

"Yeah, maybe." She sniffles again. "How am I going to do this? I'm just twenty-two and I'm starting my last year of school."

Winry and I look at each other with pain for our sister in our eyes. I give Winry the nod for her to take the oldest sister lead this conversation. "It's going to be okay, Wyla. And you know we are about to love this baby so much, Mom and Dad included. But, you do have options. No matter what, we're your sisters and will support you always."

Wyla wipes the tears from her eyes. "I've thought of my options, but no, I'm going to have this baby. I may be scared shitless, but I have always wanted to be a mother. Maybe not under these circumstances, but I've made my decision."

Winry hugs her and I join in, wrapping our arms around her. "We are going to be the best aunts ever to this little bean."

Wyla chuckles. "I have to go to the doctor Wednesday. Will you guys go with me?"

"Of course we will." I squeeze her tight.

"We wouldn't miss it," Winry adds.

"Thanks, you guys. You're the best."

"We know," Win and I say together.

Wyla starts to cry some more. She wipes her cheeks. "Ugh, I'm so emotional."

"You're pregnant, babe, it's part of it." Winry chuckles. "Tomorrow, we'll tell mom and dad together."

Wyla nods. "Okay."

I leave Mom and Dad's after lunch. Telling them about Wyla was a bit of a rollercoaster. Poor Dad had finally wrapped his head around my secret, then he's hit with Wyla's. And considering how Wyla's happened, let's just say—we hope Dad doesn't find Jett.

Not that either of them really love how it happened or the circumstances, but eventually they came around to the fact that they are going to be grandparents, and they might as well roll with it.

I check the time on my dash, it's a little after one. I'm sure Owen's still asleep. I tell myself I'm not going to go wake him up, but then I find myself in his driveway five minutes later.

I open his door quietly and make my way back to his room. He's dead asleep on his back all sprawled out. I can't help but giggle. He's about as menacing as a puppy right now.

I ease in on the other side of the bed and try to scoot close without waking him up.

"When I open my eyes, you better not be wearing any clothes," he grumbles.

"Sorry, honey, I didn't mean to wake you."

"That's okay, you being naked can be your apology." He rolls over and captures me in his arms.

I laugh at his attack. "Where's Annabelle?"

"She stayed with her friend Madeline last night. What time is it? I should probably go pick her up."

"It was a little after one when I snuck in here."

"Damn it, yeah I need to go get her. Want to go with me, darlin'?"

"Obviously. Let's go." I try to pull out of his grasp to stand up, but he pulls me back in.

"Just one second." He takes one hand to the back of my neck and pulls me down for a kiss. The angle is a little awkward, so I whip a leg around his waist and straddle him. He hums in satisfaction.

When I feel him rock hard beneath me, I pull back. "We have to go."

"What's another half hour gonna hurt?" He tries to pull me back down, but I lean out of reach.

"Ah, ah, come on, let's go get Belley." I climb off him and his bed.

"Kids are such cockblocks," he groans. "And sisters—your sisters are fucking cockblocks, too."

"I know, honey, it's terrible. You can whine about it on the drive over."

Chapter 28

Owen

On the drive over to get Annabelle, the windows are down, and Wav has one hand out the window while the other is intertwined with mine. I bring her hand up and place a kiss on the back of it. She turns to me and smiles then pulls our hands back and does the same to mine.

We pull into the driveway, and I put my truck in park then turn to Wav. "Now, fair warning. Madeline's mom usually hits on me."

"She what?" Waverley snaps.

"Easy, killer, I already told her I was taken." I squeeze one of her cheeks.

"So, you haven't...?"

"With one of Annabelle's friend's moms? No, never. I am, on the other hand, fucking her teacher." I wink, and Waverley swats my arm and rolls her eyes.

We hop out of my truck and walk up to the door. Before I can knock, Madeline's mom opens the door. "Owen, hi. Sorry, I didn't realize you were headed over."

"Sorry, I sent a text."

"Oh, you'll have to call me next time. I never pay attention to texts." She pats my arm, and Waverley clears her throat drawing her attention.

I hold back a laugh. "Rachel, I'm sure you recognize my girlfriend. She's Madeline's and Annabelle's English teacher."

Rachel acts surprised like she just now saw her. "Oh, right. Well, um, why don't I go get Annabelle," she says sheepishly.

"Sounds great." Waverley smiles.

I hold in my laugh until Rachel walks away and pop a kiss to the top of Wav's head.

"What? I was nice."

"I never said you weren't." I smile at her.

"Then what are you smiling and laughing for?" Waverley playfully hits my stomach.

"You're just cute." I kiss the top of her head again, and I can feel her eyes roll.

Annabelle comes around the corner after a few minutes with her bag in hand. "Hey, Wav. Hey, Uncle Owen."

"Hey, kiddo. Here, let me get that." I take her bag from her. "Tell Ms. Hutchins thank you for letting you stay last night."

"Thank you for letting me stay, Ms. Hutchins. I had a fun time."

"Of course, anytime, Annabelle. Owen, just let me know when she wants to stay again," Rachel says, but this time there isn't a flirty tone behind it.

"Okay, thanks again." I wave, and we all load up in my truck.

"I take it you brought Wav to get Ms. Hutchins to finally leave you alone." Annabelle laughs in the backseat.

"What? Why would I need to do that?" I play dumb.

"Please, Uncle Owen, I'm not a baby. I could tell she likes you," Annabelle huffs out.

Waverley snickers as I shake my head. "I just came to pick you up, and it just so happened that Waverley was with me, and I *may* have made a point to introduce her as my girlfriend."

"Mhm. Well anyway, I made you something," Annabelle says, digging through her bag. "Madeline got this new bracelet machine that makes beaded friendship bracelets, so I made you one."

Man, I think my heart has exploded, and Wav's too because she puts her hand over her heart. "You made me a friendship bracelet?"

"Yeah, Madeline didn't like any of the black beads, and they reminded me of you. Here." Annabelle places the bracelet on the middle console, "I put mine and Wav's name on it too."

Waverley hands me the bracelet, it's all black beads with *Belley + Wav* in lettered beads.

"I hope it fits. I figured bigger was better." Annabelle shrugs like she didn't just give me something I'll cherish forever.

I roll the bracelet on my left wrist. "It's perfect. Thank you, Belley. I love it."

"Good, because you can never take it off."

"Absolutely not. You'll have to pry it off my cold, dead body." I reach back and squeeze her knee.

Waverley still holds her hand over her heart and looks like she's seconds away from tears, but damn it, so am I.

I roll out of bed at 3:30 Monday afternoon. This is the first time in forever that I've slept past 2:00 p.m. and that's usually my sleep-in time.

Wav and Belley should be walking in any minute now from school. Wav insisted on bringing Annabelle home from school today and told me that I better still be asleep when she gets here. I'll incur her wrath later. I just want to see her.

I throw on some jeans and a black t-shirt, then head to the kitchen to have a post-school snack ready for them.

I cut up some apples and strawberries, then I wash the blueberries and raspberries I just bought. As I do the final rinse on the berries, I hear the front door open.

"Honey, we're home," Wav hollers.

Yes, yes you are, darlin'.

I turn as Wav and Belley walk in the kitchen.

"Hey, Wav." I lean in for a quick kiss then set the berries on the counter. "I got y'all some fruit to munch on."

"You didn't have to do that. You were supposed to be sleeping." Waverley pokes my chest. "I told you to sleep in."

I chuckle. "I did, I swear. I woke up maybe fifteen minutes ago."

Waverley furrows her brow. "Okay, I'll let it slide this time but only because you made us food."

"I have to make sure my girls are fed." I kiss the top of her head, "So, how was y'alls day?"

"Good. Wav's class was the best, as usual." Belley shrugs and takes the plate of apples to the kitchen table. "Just a normal day."

"I do my best, but considering my competition, I'd say I'm pretty hard to beat." Waverley brushes her hair behind her shoulder.

"Ah, and she's humble too." I laugh and pop a blueberry in my mouth.

"Oh, hush." Waverley smacks my stomach.

"She's not wrong." Annabelle laughs. "Today, Miss Quinn made us take a pop quiz on multiplying fractions and cross cancellation." Her eyes roll to the back of her head. "I'm so glad you decided to admit you liked Wav and not Miss Quinn." She sticks out her tongue.

I grab Wav and pull her toward me. "Yeah, me too, kid."

Waverley's cheeks blush, and she smiles, crinkling her nose. "Me three."

"Hey, your mom asked if you wanted to stay the night tonight since you don't have school tomorrow. I told her it was up to you, Belley."

"Why don't we have school tomorrow again?" Annabelle mopes. Of course she's upset that there's no school tomorrow.

"I don't know, ask your teacher." I squeeze Wav in my arms.

"Ah, stop." Waverley giggles and tries to pull away. "It's a professional development day," Waverley groans. "They're as fun as they sound, trust me."

"Humph, then yeah, I'll stay with Mom. Are we still having dinner there tonight?" She takes a bite of an apple slice.

"Yeah, I'm making your favorite—lasagna. We'll head over there around five, then I'll pick you up tomorrow whenever you're ready."

"Oh, yay! Wav, can you eat with us tonight? Uncle Owen's lasagna is the best." Annabelle bounces up and down.

I glance at Wav, and she looks back at me with hesitation in her eyes. It's not that I don't want her to come because I definitely do. But Natalie will be there, and I don't want Waverley to feel uncomfortable.

"Um, we'll see. Why don't you go and pack a bag to stay the night, okay?"

"Okay." Annabelle bops to her room, and I wait for her to shut her door.

"Hey, you know I would love for you to come tonight, but if you're uncomfortable—"

"No, I want to go, if you're okay with me coming that is." Waverley shrugs. "I mean, Natalie and I will have to figure out a way to be around each other eventually. Plus, I haven't technically met your mom."

"What? You've met my mom."

"Yeah, in passing, like my dad saying 'Hey, Waverley, this is Mrs. West,' when I was like ten. I haven't been introduced as your girlfriend."

"Oh right, I should probably tell her we're dating." I scratch my jaw and shrug. "I keep forgetting to do that."

Waverley scoffs and smacks my chest. I capture her hand. "I'm kidding, darlin'. She knows all about you. I'd love for you to come tonight."

Waverley smiles, "Okay, good."

"Yeah, good." I pull her in and give her the kiss I've been wanting to give her since she walked through my door.

"Mmm. As much as I'd love to keep doing this, I want to run home and change out of my teaching clothes. Will you pick me up at my place on your way?"

"Of course. I'll pick you up a little bit before five."

"And maybe you can stay at my place after dinner?" Wav bites her lower lip.

"Oh, believe me, you were not going to be able to get rid of me tonight."

"Good."

With another kiss and a smack to the ass, she heads out my door.

I load up all of the ingredients I need for dinner, then shoot a text to Natalie.

> Two things. Annabelle is staying the night tonight, and Waverley is coming to dinner. Annabelle already said she wants to stay tonight, so no backing out. And you will be civil to Waverley.

Natalie

> Fuck you, I don't have to do any- thing.

Well, I expected that.

Natalie, stay in your room for all I care, but those two things are happening. We'll be there a little after 5.

Naturally, I get no response.

Well, this ought to go well.

Chapter 29

Waverley

When we pull up to Owen's mom's house, nervous would lightly describe how I feel right now. My stomach is in knots, and my leg was bouncing the whole drive over. I really did want to come tonight. I want to officially meet his mom, but Natalie will be here too, and we all remember how the last time went when her and I were together.

We hop out of Owen's truck, and Annabelle runs inside. I start to follow behind her, but Owen holds me back.

"Hey, it's gonna be okay. I'll be right beside you the whole time."

A little bit of tension leaves my body. He's right. "Thanks, honey."

He smiles and wraps his arm around my shoulder. "Come on."

We walk in the door, and Owen's mom stands in the living room like she's been anxiously waiting for us to walk in. She has the biggest smile on her face.

"Hi, Waverley. I'm so glad you're here," she greets.

"Hi, Mrs. West. Thank you for letting me join y'alls dinner," I smile. It's been awhile since I've seen her, but other than general aging and some gray in her hair, she looks the same. Up close though, I can really see how Natalie and Annabelle favor her. They all have blonde hair and blue eyes. It makes me wonder how much Owen would favor his dad.

"Oh please, call me Lauren. I'm so happy you're here." She clasps her hands together. "Owen and Belley talk about you all the time."

"*Mostly* good things too," Owen adds and winks at me.

I give him a little nudge, and Mrs. West swats at him. "Mhm. Don't let him lie to you, Waverley. I've never seen him so smitten."

"Okay, that's enough. We're going to start dinner." Owen tugs me toward the kitchen.

"Oh, are you actually going to let me help cook?" I ask hopefully.

Owen laughs. "You know how to boil water, right?"

"Probably not," Natalie interjects as she brushes past us, leaving the kitchen.

"Natalie," Owen warns, but I rest my hand on his arm.

"It's fine, Owen. Just let it go." He hesitates for a moment. I know he wants to stand up for me but fighting with her will get us nowhere, and it will just upset Annabelle.

Owen relents, and we head into the kitchen where Annabelle is unloading the groceries for dinner.

"Want to help us cook tonight, kid?" Owen ruffles her hair.

She brushes it back down. "Really? I can help?"

"Sure, I need someone to help Wav." Owen pretends to cover my ears. "You know how she is in the kitchen."

I scoff and elbow him in the stomach.

Annabelle giggles. "It's okay, Wav. I don't think Grandma's oven gets as hot as Uncle Owen's."

Owen snorts a laugh, and my mouth gapes. "Annabelle, whose side are you on?"

"I'm on whichever side gets me lasagna tonight." She shrugs.

"So, mine." Owen pops a quick kiss to my cheek. "Okay, let's get started."

Owen unpacks the rest of the groceries and gives us both instructions. He's a little bossy in the kitchen. I like it.

"Okay, Annabelle, want to help me do the layers?" Owen asks, pulling out a baking dish.

"Yes." She bops over to him, and I take a seat at the table, taking them in. Owen stands by Annabelle, instructing her on what to do next instead of just doing it for her. He's actually taking the time to teach her. She listens intently with the biggest smile on her face.

"Alright, kid, we're going to start with a little sauce on the bottom—"

"They're pretty cute, aren't they?" Owen's mom comes in the kitchen and takes the seat across from me.

I smile. "Yeah, they are. They're pretty inseparable too."

"Oh heavens, yes. You would think being Grandma I would hold a little pull, but nope, it's all Uncle Owen. No one else compares in her eyes."

"Kid, quit eating the sauce." Owen laughs.

"It's called taste-testing, Uncle Owen." Annabelle takes another bite of the sauce. "Don't worry, it's good."

"Obviously. I made it." Owen takes her spoon. "Alright, let me put this in the oven, it will be ready in forty-five minutes."

"Ugh, but that's so long," Annabelle whines.

"I know, but why don't we play *Bullshit* in the meantime?" Owen raises his eyebrows to Annabelle.

"Ah, yes." She jumps up and down.

"Okay, go grab the cards." He ruffles her hair and she runs out of the kitchen.

"Waverley, I swear we don't let Annabelle curse all the time, only when we play Bullshit." Mrs. West chuckles. "It's just not the same without it. Just saying 'bull' doesn't have the same effect."

"Yeah, and Belley gets so serious when she plays." Owen takes the seat next to me. "For an eleven-year-old, her bullshit detector is impeccable."

"You should play Winry and Wyla. It's almost not fun playing with them. They get so intense."

"I can only imagine." Owen pulls my chair a little closer to him.

Annabelle comes racing back to the table. "Got 'em!" She tosses the pack of cards to Owen. "Mom said to play without her." She shrugs and takes the seat by Mrs. West.

Of course she did. I hold back my eye roll and give Annabelle an encouraging smile.

"Alright, that's her choice," Owen says and starts to pass out the cards. "Okay, the person with the ace of spades goes first."

We all scan through our cards, then Annabelle sets down a card. "One ace." She smiles.

"Two twos." Owen sets down his cards, stone faced.

"One three." I set mine down.

After one full turn, I see Annabelle's eyes shift from fun to laser-focused.

"Two sixes." Owen pulls out his cards.

"Bullshit," Annabelle says before he even sets them down.

The corners of Owen's mouth turn up as he drops the cards. "Check 'em."

Annabelle furrows her eyebrows and reaches for his cards. "Ha! A six and an eight! Pick em up, Uncle Owen."

"Damn it." He scoops the rest of the cards up while Mrs. West and I laugh.

Unsurprisingly, Annabelle wins the first round, then Owen takes the second one.

"Bullshit," I say as Annabelle tries to claim two jacks.

Annabelle tenses. She only has three cards left.

"Dang it, Wav." She scoops the stack up, "Is this payback for my oven joke?"

"Yes, yes it is." I smile and glance over at Owen. He looks so content here, happy.

I win the next round and before we know it, the timer for the lasagna buzzes.

"Okay, I call mercy." Mrs. West puts down her cards and holds up her hands. "I'm starving, and I clearly suck at this game."

"Alright, good game, ladies." Owen pushes back his chair. "Annabelle, will you get the table set?"

"Yes." She gathers up the cards and puts them back in the pack.

"I'll go get Natalie." Mrs. West stands from the table next.

I slide out of my chair and walk over to Owen as he pulls out the food. "What do you need me to do, boss?"

He chuckles. "Boss? I like that."

"Mmm, only in the kitchen."

He leans in and whispers so only I can hear. "And what will you call me in the bedroom?"

I can feel my cheeks turning pink, and the thoughts racing through my mind make it feel a lot hotter in here than it is.

"Okay, table's ready." Annabelle beams. "Bring on the lasagna."

"Coming." Owen winks at me, and we head back to the table with the desired food.

As I slide in my seat, Mrs. West and Natalie come into the kitchen. The disdain on Natalie's face isn't missed, but I keep my mouth shut. She slides in the seat across from me, and Mrs. West takes the head of the table.

We can do this. We just have to be civil.

Owen cuts out portions of the lasagna and starts to put them on our plates. Belley claps and licks her lips as he hands her a plate. He makes his way around and as he goes to hand Natalie hers, she turns up her nose.

"Ugh, did you put zucchini in this?"

"Yes, Nat. That's how Annabelle likes it. Just pick it out." Owen sets her plate down in front of her when she refuses to take it.

Owen sits back down, ignoring her glare.

"So, Waverley," Mrs. West starts, trying to cover the awkward tension. "How's your family doing? I just adore your parents."

"They're doing good. Everyone is pretty much in wedding planning mode right now for Winry and Graham. They're getting married in Mom and Dad's backyard, so they both have been full-on occupied with making sure the yard is perfect."

"Oh, how lovely. I'm sure everyone is very excited. You and Owen are the maid of honor and best man, right?"

"Yes, ma'am." I smile.

"That's so great. You two will be able to get some beautiful pictures. You must get me some so I can put them up in the house." Mrs. West beams.

"Not happening," Natalie mumbles.

I can practically feel Owen grit his teeth, and I think he's about to snap at her when Mrs. West takes the lead. "Natalie, dear, I will put whatever pictures I want up in my own house."

"But I live here. Owen has his own place. Let him hang his pictures there," she grumbles.

"Well, how about this, you start paying the bills of ours that your brother pays, and I'll let you have a say in the decorations." Mrs. West shrugs.

Don't laugh, Waverley. Hold back your smile.

Natalie shuffles in her seat and wisely chooses to not say anything else during dinner. The rest of us enjoy our meal and carry on a conversation as she sulks.

"Alright, you guys cooked. Natalie and I will do the dishes," Mrs. West says, picking up some of the dishes.

"Mom, sit, we can do it." Owen stands and tries to take the dishes out of her hands.

"Absolutely not." She turns away from him. "Leave it all on the table. We'll take care of it. Annabelle, you helped with dinner too, so you're excused from dishes also."

"Yes! I'm going to read in the living room." Belley jumps up from the table and heads off to read.

"Nat, dishes." Mrs. West nods to the rest of the table.

She huffs. "Okay, I heard you." As she starts to clear the table, I don't miss the death stare aimed my way.

Owen comes up behind me and rests his hands on my shoulders. "You ready to go, Wav?"

"Sure." I nod and walk over to his mom. "Thank you so much, Mrs. West for having me over. I had a wonderful time."

"Oh, I'm so glad you came. Here, soapy hug." She turns away from the sink and holds out her sudsy hands for a hug.

I smile and hug her back.

"You're welcome here any time, Waverley." She squeezes me for a moment then lets me go.

"Thank you."

As Owen gives his mom a hug, I venture to the living room to say bye to Annabelle. I hate the idea of leaving her here tonight, especially with the mood Natalie is in.

Annabelle lays back on the couch, her eyes glued to her Kindle. I walk up to her and sit next to her legs.

"Hey, cutie. I think Uncle Owen and I are about to leave. Are you still good to stay here tonight?" I ask, even though it might not be my place to offer. I can't help it.

"Oh, yeah." Annabelle rests her Kindle on her stomach. "I'm good. I'll get some reading done. I just started this dystopian-type series. I'm really excited about it."

I smile. Of course she can see the bright side in staying here tonight. "Okay, Belley, that sounds fun."

Owen comes in and walks up beside me and reaches down and squeezes her shin. "Okay, kid, you good?"

"Yes." She rolls her eyes. "I promise I'll call you if I need to."

"Oh, the eye roll. I get enough of those from Wav. I don't need them from you too," Owen huffs.

Instinctively, I roll my eyes.

"See?" Owen points at me.

"Hush, you." I swat at him.

Owen laughs. "Come on, darlin', let's go. Bye, Belley." He blows her a kiss as we walk out the door.

We load up in his truck. As I buckle my seatbelt, Owen still hasn't started the truck. "You okay?" I ask.

"Hmm, I feel like I'm forgetting something." He furrows his eyebrows and turns toward me. "Oh, yeah." He captures my face and kisses me. I'm tempted to crawl over his dash but in his mom's driveway doesn't seem appropriate.

He pulls back and smiles. "Yup, that was it."

"I'm so glad you remembered."

When we pull into my driveway I ask, "Do you still want to come in? You don't have to stay if you don't want to, or come in if you don't want to. I just—"

"Wav, are you good if I stay?" he interrupts my derailing train.

"Yes, I would like that." I nod.

"Okay, good." He reaches to the back and grabs a backpack. "I guess I'll need these extra clothes and toothbrush after all."

"Goodness, you're such a dork." I laugh.

"Mhm, we'll see how much of a dork I am when you're screaming my name later." Owen winks and hops out of the truck, leaving me sitting there, blushing. I guess he's not wrong.

Once inside, we collapse on the couch. "Did you have a good time tonight?"

"Yeah, it was nice talking with your mom. I loved how she didn't hesitate to put Natalie in her place." I slide my legs in his lap. "Do you really help your mom with the bills?"

Owen scratches his jaw. "Yeah, I pay about a third of them. It's mainly Natalie's bills but since she lives with my mom now, I picked up a little more to help Mom out with extra living expenses."

"Owen, that's so generous of you, and on your police salary too. That's pretty amazing. I know your mom really appreciates it."

"Yeah, she does. I know a cop's salary isn't exactly a six-figure number, but I've got a good amount in savings."

"You're a good man, Owen West." I place my hand on his cheek. "I've never been so happy to be proven wrong."

Then the most adorable thing happens—Owen blushes. My smile becomes stupid big. *Ugh, this man has ruined me.*

"Come here, baby." Owen tugs me in his lap and combs my hair behind my ear then kisses me so passionately, I swear I'll combust.

I readjust on his lap, so I'm now straddling him. His hands grip my ass as I slowly move my hips. My whole body feels like it's on fire.

Owen hums in approval. "Wav? You remember how I said I couldn't wait to throw you around the bed?"

"Mhm," I practically purr.

"I think it's time to stay true to my word." He kisses down my neck.

Yes, I do want that. "But, I'm a little heavy."

Owen stops kissing my neck abruptly. "What the fuck did just you say?"

"Owen, come on, I know I'm not—"

"Waverley, stop that right now. This body is fucking perfection, and I'm telling you right now if you ever talk negatively about this body again, I'll bend your ass over and leave you with a nice red hand print."

Okay, why does that turn me on even more? It's almost tempting to call his bluff, but he's right, my body is banging.

"Okay, I won't, but Owen, you can still spank me if you want to."

Owen growls. "Fuck, yeah."

Before I know what's happening, Owen scoops me up and carries me to my room, kissing me the whole way.

He sets me down at the base of the bed and in seconds, our clothes are gone. Owen stays true to his word and tosses me like a ragdoll on the bed. He crawls on top of me then spins us around to where I'm back on top.

He pulls me down, and his tongue dives in my mouth. I'm so wet, I'm practically dripping all over his dick already. I'm so ready for him, I try to line us up, but then Owen hooks his arms under my legs and literally lifts me on top of his face.

"Hold on to the headboard, Wav and fuck my face."

"Owen."

A swift smack comes to my ass. "I said hold the headboard and fuck my face." Owen rubs the place he just smacked, intensifying the tingling sensation. "I won't tell you again, Waverley."

I do as I'm told and grab my headboard, then lower down on his face. "Fuck, Owen." I rasp at the first pass of his tongue, and my hips start to move.

"That's it baby, fucking ride."

His tongue starts to flick side to side on my clit as my hips slowly move a little faster. That knot in my core starts to grow and then another smack comes to the same spot on my ass.

"Oh, my... *fuck*." My head falls back in a mixture of pleasure and pain. "Yes, Owen."

He hooks his arms around my legs again, pulling me down a little further and locks me in place as he absolutely devours me. And fuck, if that wasn't exactly what I needed.

I let go of the head board and arch my back. "Owen, yes, right like that. Oh my fuck, fuck." My hips thrust in small quick bursts as Owen holds them tight and continues to eat me out like I'm going to be his last meal. My orgasm shatters through me as I scream out Owen's name.

When my hips stop, he releases his grip and finishes me off with a few more sweeps of his tongue. "Fucking delicious. Now"—he scoops me up again and flips me around and sets me up on all fours—"you're going to give me another one. You ready, baby?" he asks as he lines us up.

"Yes, please," I beg and push back against him.

"Good girl. Beg for it, Waverley." Owen pushes in maybe an inch. "Beg for more of my cock."

"Please, Owen, I need more, I need—" My body is practically vibrating.

"Tell me, baby, what do you need?" He presses in just another inch, and it's driving me crazy.

"I need you, Owen, I need your dick inside of me, I need your hands in my hair, and I need you to fuck me."

"Oh fuck, baby, that's so hot." Owen fists my hair, pulling my head back and pushes the rest of the way in me. We both moan at the relief.

Owen pounds into me, we haven't done this position yet, and I've got to say it's a new favorite. He tightens his grip on my hair and gives it a little tug. I fucking love it. I start to meet him thrust for thrust. His other hand grips my ass hard as his hips start to go faster.

"Oh, Owen, yes. I'm so close."

"Not yet, baby." Owen whips me around again, now to my back. He holds my legs behind my knees and pushes them down, spreading me open.

"I want to watch these perfect tits bounce as I fuck you, then I want to see that beautiful face of yours while you come all over my cock." He starts to thrust in me again and that tension shoots back up.

I moan at his words and my eyes roll to the back of my head.

"Fuck."

My word, forget seeing stars, Owen makes me see my whole future. Time bends and I

can see the life I want, the life I need with him, it's all there.

"Owen—" I feel that need grow, and I know that I'm about to fall apart all over again.

"That's it, baby, I love hearing my name on your lips while I rip you in half. Say it again," he demands. "Tell me who owns this pussy."

Oh hell, how am I still functioning? His words make every thrust of his hips more pleasurable.

"You, Owen, only you... Owen, I need—"

"I know, baby, come for me." Owen lets go of one of my legs and rubs small circles on my clit, driving me over the edge for the second time.

"Fuck, Waverley." Owen's thrusts come hard and fast and then we're both riding our high. Meeting each other's thrusts, and falling together.

As our hips slow to a stop, and Owen leans down on his forearms, careful to not put all of his weight on me. We stare into each other's eyes as we catch our breath.

"Does it always feel like this?" I whisper.

"No, Wav. It doesn't. It's never felt like this for me, and I can assure you it will feel nothing like this with any other guy. You're a part of me, Wav."

I bite my lower lip to maintain my cheesy smile.

Owen presses a kiss to my forehead. "Let me get a towel and get you cleaned up." He climbs out of the bed and heads toward my bathroom and that gives me an idea.

"Hey"—I roll over and off the bed—"better idea. You go grab a bottle of wine out of my fridge and two glasses, then meet me back in the bathroom."

"Mmm, shower?" He raises his eyebrows.

"Even better, now go." I pop a kiss to his cheek and go to my bathroom. My glorious pale pink bathroom with its big claw foot tub. The perfect size for two.

I turn the water on and add a lavender bath bomb and add some drops of orange essential oils to compliment the lavender.

Owen opens the door and sets the wine on the sink counter.

"Wav, I'm not going to fit in there."

I roll my eyes. "Yes, you will. You'll sit first, then I'll sit in your lap."

"Okay." He shrugs then starts to pour our wine.

"Okay? You're not going to argue?"

He hands me my glass. "You said you're going to sit in my lap, right?"

I nod.

"Why would I argue with that?" He takes his glass and sets it on the little stand I have next to the tub and gets in.

I smile and hold back a laugh at the sight of the 6'3 hunk covered in tattoos in a bath with purple shimmery water. *Man, I love him.*

"Okay, get your ass in here." Owen holds out his hand for me.

I whip my hair up in a messy bun and take his hand, stepping into the tub. I settle on his lap, and he wraps his arms around me.

"See, this is pretty nice, isn't it?" I rest my head back on his shoulder.

"I'll agree that it's not bad having my naked girlfriend in my lap."

"You know you like the bath too. It's relaxing." I reach up and pat his cheek. "My only regret is not getting a picture of you in here by yourself. I'll get one next time."

Owen laughs. "Only if you promise to make it your screensaver."

"Oh, without question." I lean up and reach for my glass of wine. "Do you think Belley's okay? I kind of hated leaving her tonight with how Natalie was acting."

"I know. Welcome to how I've felt for the past eleven years. I love my sister, I do, and I don't want to keep Annabelle from her. She needs her mom too, but Nat just... I don't know, I feel like I'm stuck between a rock and a hard place with her."

"Do you think she would ever give you guardianship?"

"I wish she would. I truly don't think she's a terrible mother, but I don't think she wants to be a mother either. I know I practically get Annabelle full-time anyway, even when I don't have temporary custody, but at the end of the day, I have no say in her well-being, even though I'm the one taking care of her."

I take a sip of wine. "Maybe she'll reconsider by y'alls next court date. When's that again?"

"It's coming up, just about three weeks away." Owen leans his head back.

"It will all work out, honey. At the end of the day, Annabelle loves you so much. She knows you're the one she can depend on."

"Yeah, I just wish it could be more stable for her. I know all the switching is hard, especially with me on night shifts."

"Have you asked my dad if he could switch you to days? I'm sure he could work something out given the circumstances. You do have an inside person now. I could talk to him too, if you wanted."

Owen snorts a laugh. "I knew eventually something good would come out of dating you."

I cock my head toward him, mouth gaped. "Uh, excuse me?" *Little shit.*

Owen tightens his grip around my waist. "I'm kidding, darlin'." He plants a kiss on my temple. "I'll talk to your dad about switching shifts."

"Mhm, okay, honey." I rest my head back on his shoulder again. "I can stay with Annabelle one night this week to give your mom the night off again too."

"You don't have to do that, Wav."

"I know I don't have to, but we have fun and it helps everyone out, so why not? I'm going to school anyway, so we might as well go together. Plus, I love spending time with her."

"She loves spending time with you. I think you may actually come close to rivaling me." Owen chuckles.

"Yeah, right. Please, no one could ever beat you in her eyes."

"Duh, I'm the best. That's why I said you *almost* rival me." Owen smirks, and I roll my eyes. "So, how long do we sit in here?"

"Until our wine is gone." I shrug.

"In the glasses or the bottle?"

I drain my glass of wine. "Bottle, definitely the bottle."

Chapter 30

Owen

Waverley's alarm blares at 5:30 a.m. She groans and blindly reaches over to switch it off. I roll over and spoon her, the scent of lavender lingers on her skin. Her silky smooth body feels cool next to mine.

"Morning, baby." I place a kiss on her neck.

"Mmm, good morning," she mumbles and snuggles back into me. "I need to get up."

"So, get up." I kiss her neck and ear. It may be early in the morning, but I've got a naked Waverley in my arms. You can't blame me for wanting her any time of the day. Plus, morning sex is the best way to start your day. "Come on, Wav, get up." I nibble her ear.

"How am I supposed to get up when you do that?" She giggles and leans her head back giving me better access.

"Waverley, get up," I demand but don't stop kissing her. I slide my hand down in between her legs. *Wet*. Just what I thought. "I dare you."

Waverley hooks one leg over mine, letting me glide a finger right in. I start slowly, in and out, she squirms in my arms trying to urge me to move faster.

When I don't, Waverley whips around, climbs on top, and glides me right in. "I don't have time for you to tease me this morning." She bounces her hips. "I'm in control this time."

Oh, hell yeah, I love the confidence in her eyes. "Yes, ma'am."

After leaving Waverley's place and forcing myself back to sleep for a few hours so my schedule isn't complete shit over the next few days, I head back to Mom's to pick up Annabelle.

I walk in the front door and Mom sits in her chair watching another one of her dramas on her TV. "Hey mom, where is everybody?"

"Well, Natalie is off to lunch with a new guy that she's apparently seeing now—"

"What? Annabelle didn't go with her, right?" I swear, if she took Annabelle out on some date with some random guy...

"No, she's reading in your old room. Are you kidding? Come on now, Owen, you know I wouldn't let her take Annabelle out like that."

"You're right, sorry." I walk over and sit on the couch. "So, Nat's seeing someone new?" *Great.* I wonder what winner she picked this time.

"Looks like it. I don't know much about him, considering I just heard about him today, but she says she likes him a lot." Mom shrugs.

"Yeah, I'm sure," I huff. "Did she happen to spend any time with Annabelle while she was here?"

"They ate their breakfast and watched some TV together this morning. Owen, I know your sister isn't exactly mother of the year, but she does love Annabelle."

"I never said she didn't, but would it be so bad if I kept custody of Annabelle?" I say quietly, "You know I'm the one taking care of her."

"Yes, I know, but she's your sister, Owen. I don't want to see you two no longer speaking to each other. Your sister just needs a little guidance."

"A little guidance? Mom, come on—"

"Hey, Uncle Owen," Annabelle says, interrupting me and walking into the living room. "I finished my book." She plops on the couch next to me.

"Oh yeah? How was it?" I lean back on the couch and listen as she talks about her book and recaps every bit of the story for me. She's practically beaming, like telling me this has been the best part of her day.

"But it's just book one out of three, so I still need to read the rest. I'll probably start the other one when we get home."

"Sounds like a plan, kid." I ruffle her hair. "You ready to go?"

Annabelle shuffles on the couch. She turns to my mom. "Grandma, is Mom back yet?"

"Not yet, sweetie." Mom gives her a half smile. "I can call her and see where she's at, if you want to wait on her."

"No, that's okay." Belley frowns and stands up. "I'll go get my bag."

When she walks out, I turn to Mom. "Nat doesn't need guidance, Mom. She needs to spend time with her kid. She begged me for these sleepovers with Annabelle, but now she's not even here."

"She'll do better." Mom's trying, I know she is. I get that it's hard since Dad's not here, but at the same time, something's gotta give here.

"Yeah, we'll see."

Annabelle and I get in my truck and head back to our house.

"You don't work tonight, right?" Annabelle asks.

"No, I'm off. You're stuck with me tonight, kid."

"Is Wav going to come over tonight?"

"I don't know." I hope she is. "We can ask her to."

"Yay! And maybe we could do pizza and a movie too?" Annabelle questions.

I chuckle at the high pitch of her voice. "We'll see, Belley. She might not be able to come over."

"Well, call her," she says plainly. When I don't immediately reach for my phone, Annabelle starts chanting, "Call her, call her, call her."

"Okay, okay. Geez, I was working on it." I reach over and give her a little shove then hit Wav's name to call her over CarPlay.

"Hi, honey," she answers sweetly.

"Hey—"

"Hey, Wav," Annabelle cuts me off.

Waverley laughs. "Hey, Annabelle. What are you two up to?"

"We're headed back to the house. We were—"

"Can you come over for pizza and a movie tonight?" Annabelle interrupts again, too excited to wait on me to ask.

"Yeah, that sounds fun, Belley. I'd love to. What time?"

I turn down our street. "Just head over whenever you want, darlin'. I'll order the pizza and get it delivered around six."

"Sounds good. We have one more meeting, then I'll head over soon after, but I gotta go. I'll see y'all tonight."

"Okay, see you soon."

"Bye, Wav," Annabelle adds.

"Bye, Belley. Bye, honey," she says, then she hangs up.

"Uncle Owen," Belley starts. "Do you love Wav?"

You would think this question would make me feel panicked, like I should hide how I feel about Wav from Annabelle, but what's the point in lying to her?

"Yeah, I do. Why do you ask?"

"I never hear you tell her. How come?"

"I don't know. There just hasn't been the right time I guess, and I don't want to pressure her to say it back." I shrug and pull in our driveway.

"Do you guys have sex?"

I slam on the break, blood pressure immediately rising. "What?"

"Do you guys have sex? We have a sex education class next week, but Madeline said that sex is what two people do when they're in love." She shrugs like this is a normal conversation.

Lord help me. I knew this day was going to come eventually, but I'm not ready. I'm not prepared for this. I run my hands over my face. *Pull it together, Owen. It's going to be awkward as fuck, but honesty is the best policy. Right?*

"So, do you? Or do you have to wait till someone says it?" she asks.

"Wait—always wait, even after they say it," I blurt out. *Okay, deep breath.* "Okay, kid, yes. Waverley and I do have"—I pause—"sex. *But*, we're also adults and even though I haven't said it, I do love her. It's a different kind of love when sex is involved but look, the important thing to know is that sex is an *adult* activity. Nothing you need to be thinking about for a long, *long* time. We can talk more about this later, but I want you to know you can always ask or tell me anything, Waverley too, don't ever feel like you can't talk to us because you can."

"Okay, thank you for telling me the truth. I don't have any more questions, so you can relax." Annabelle laughs. "You look pale, like you're going to be sick."

"Well, you sprung this topic on me. I wasn't prepared." We hop out of the truck and when she rounds the corner, I lock her in a hug. I need time to stop. "Just remember no one will ever love you as much as I do."

"I know, Uncle Owen. I love you too." She squeezes me tight, then we head inside.

"Okay, Wav probably won't be here for a couple hours, so help me with the chores then you can read."

"Alright, rock, paper, scissors on who cleans the bathroom?" She turns with her fist ready.

"Of course. Okay, ready?" I hold out my fist. "Rock, paper, scissors, shoot." I go for paper, but Annabelle goes scissors. "Ah, damn it. Best two out of three?"

Annabelle giggles. "Alright, I'll just beat you again."

"Yeah, yeah, okay... Rock, paper, scissors, shoot."

"Ha, paper covers rock." Annabelle takes her hand and covers my fist.

"Damn it, fine. You win, fair and square. I'll do the bathrooms and the kitchen, you got your room and the living room."

"Okie, I'll clean the living room first. Have fun cleaning the bathrooms." Annabelle scrunches her nose and sticks her tongue out.

I chuckle. "Get going, brat." I stick my tongue back out at her.

We get started on cleaning, and it honestly shouldn't take us long, I like to keep the house in pretty good shape. I finish up in the bathrooms and pass Annabelle headed to her room as she finishes the living room.

I get started in the kitchen, and I'm finishing up the dishes when my front door opens. I don't turn, I just assume it's Waverley. "Hey darlin', you're here earlier than I thought."

"Ew, you thought I was Waverley. Gross." Natalie walks in with a random guy following in behind her.

I sigh and stop doing the dishes. I really don't want to deal with this shit right now. I don't care for her little antics. Her shit is getting real old. "Natalie, what are you doing here?"

"What? I can't come see my brother and *my* daughter." She hops on the bar stool, still failing to introduce the man she's brought into my house.

When it seems she's not going to do it, he steps around the bar and holds out his hand. "Hi, I'm Derrick. Sorry, I didn't realize you didn't know we were coming."

I shake his hand because not shaking hands in the south is like a sin. "Owen. So, again, what are y'all doing here?"

"I told you, I wanted to see you guys. I wanted Derrick to meet Annabelle and since she's here, we're here." Natalie says it like it's obvious.

Yes, let's introduce Annabelle to someone who you'll date for maybe a month.

Great idea, is what I want to say but hold it in.

Annabelle comes out of her room. "All done cleaning. Oh, Mom, hey, you're here." She squeaks, happy at this surprise. She runs up to Nat and gives her a big hug.

"Yeah, I wanted to see you." Natalie actually returns her hug and smiles. Even if it's an act, I don't care. It's better than her usual pat on the head. "Belley, I want to introduce you to my boyfriend, Derrick."

Boyfriend? Oh, great.

"Hi, Annabelle." He reaches out his hand to her. "It's nice to meet you." She tentatively places her hand in his, and Derrick shakes it.

I'll give him the benefit of the doubt that he is better than the last one. He seems normal, for now. Usually, I can read people pretty well and get an idea. He isn't exactly screaming danger with his khaki slacks and cream collared shirt.

"Hi, it's nice to meet you." Annabelle glances at me a little unsure but then goes back to Natalie. "Are you guys staying for pizza?"

"Oh—" I start.

"We'd love to," Natalie says, cutting me off. "I mean, unless Uncle Owen wants us to leave."

Yeah, figures, turn this on me. I sigh. "No, you guys can stay."

While Annabelle, Natalie, and Derrick sit in the living room talking, I order the pizza, then go to call Wav.

It rings a couple times then it sends to voicemail.

"Hey, honey. I'm here," Wav says as she walks in the door. She pauses when she notices the new additions to our dinner. "Oh, hi." She smiles awkwardly.

"Hey, Wav," Annabelle says from the couch.

"Hey, Belley," Wav says, still a little surprised.

Well, so much for giving her the chance to escape this dinner.

I walk over to her and greet her with a sympathetic smile. "Hey, darlin'. Sorry, I tried to call you with a warning."

"That's okay," she says, but I know the tension between her and Natalie makes her nervous.

"You don't have to stay, Wav. It's okay," I say hushed.

"No, I'm good, really." She smiles trying to reassure me.

"Okay, Wav." We join them in the living room. "Derrick, this is my girlfriend, Waverley. Waverley, this is Derrick."

"My boyfriend," Natalie adds.

Waverley gives Natalie a small nod, acknowledging her stake of claim. "Hi, it's nice to meet you."

"You as well." Derrick shakes her hand, and we all sit back down.

"How was school today, Wav? Did you miss me?" Annabelle says, ignoring the awkwardness that fills my house.

"Of course, I missed you. We just had a bunch of boring meetings. I would've much rather had regular classes today." Waverley smiles at her.

"Oh, are you a teacher?" Derrick asks.

"Yes, I'm Annabelle's sixth grade English teacher," Waverley answers.

Derrick crosses his leg over his knee. "That's great, I'm actually a Professor at the University in Northshore."

"Oh really? I got my degree there, what do you teach?"

"The fun class, I teach Finance."

"Oof, fun indeed. I've been considering going back to get my Masters," Waverley says. "Especially since they offer online classes."

"Yeah, it can be very helpful to have as you grow in your career. A lot of work though, but I'm sure you'll be fine."

Alright, I'll give it to Derrick. He seems somewhat like a cool guy, but the night is still young.

"Wav is the best teacher," Annabelle adds. "She never gives homework and always lets us have time to read in class."

"Oh, no homework? That does sound like a good teacher," Derrick agrees and while he may miss Natalie's eye roll, I don't.

Keep your cool. Annabelle's here.

We talk for a while. Derrick asks genuine questions, and it makes me wonder how in the world he has ended up with Natalie. I want to ask, but I'm also afraid it's not a *kid-friendly* answer. Now, I'll say Natalie has been on her best behavior tonight. Only eye rolls have been given, and they only seem to be noticed by me, so I've let them go.

When the pizza finally arrives, we all gather around the small kitchen table. When Waverley sits on one side and Natalie sits on the other I can see her hesitate for a moment on where she should sit.

"Hey, Belley, why don't you sit at the head of the table?" I pull the seat out for her.

She gives me a puzzled look. "But you sit there?"

"I'm going to sit by Wav, you sit here."

She smiles and nods then sits in the chair. I push it back in and take the seat on the other side of Wav.

"So, Owen, Natalie says you're a cop here in Aster Creek." Derrick takes some pizza and puts it on his plate.

"Yes, have been since I was twenty-three, so for roughly five years now," I say and take a bite of my pizza.

"That's awesome, man. So I'll take it you enjoy it?"

I nod. "Yeah, it's definitely the job for me. I'm considering requesting a shift change to days instead of nights.

While I do love the night shift, it gets complicated with Annabelle living here."

Derrick furrows his eyebrows. "Oh, I didn't realize Annabelle was living with you." He gives Natalie a bit of a confused look, and she gives me the death stare.

How was I supposed to know he didn't know that? They're here now, in my house, while Annabelle is here.

"Um, yeah." Natalie shuffles in her chair. "But only for a few more weeks, then she'll move back in with me."

Annabelle tenses in her chair and puts her pizza down. Waverley notices her shift and reaches under the table to give Belley's knee a squeeze. *Does Annabelle not want to go back with Natalie?* Wav seems to know something I don't, so I'll have to ask her later.

"But we'll worry about that another day. For now, I'm enjoying my time with Belley. We have fun, don't we, kid?"

Annabelle nods. "Yeah, Uncle Owen's been teaching me how to cook. I'm getting better at it. Wav and I only burnt one batch of cookies, but we're pretty sure that was the oven's fault."

Waverley and I laugh. "Yeah, totally the oven." I roll my eyes and Wav swats at me.

"I'm sure it was, Annabelle." Derrick chuckles. "I believe you."

The rest of the dinner goes by as smoothly as it can. Natalie's definitely putting on her best front for this guy, but who knows? Maybe this could be the change she needs.

I take all three empty pizza boxes off the table and move them over to the counter out of the way. As I pass, I pop a kiss to the top of Waverley's head. She looks up and smiles at me sweetly. *Goodness, that smile.* It's the smile I want to wake up to and the one I want every night before bed.

I'm going to marry that smile.

"Are we still going to watch a movie tonight, Uncle Owen?" Annabelle asks and turns around in her chair.

I check the clock on the oven. It's nearly 8:30. "Sorry, kid, it's a little late to start a movie on a school night."Annabelle groans.

"We need to head out anyway," Natalie says as her and Derrick stand from the table.

"Thank you for letting us join you." Derrick gives me another handshake, then turns back to the girls. "Annabelle, it was lovely to meet you, and you as well, Waverley."

"Nice to meet you too," Waverley and Annabelle say back.

"Bye, sugar." Natalie gives Annabelle a big hug and kisses the top of her head. "I'm glad we got to stay for dinner tonight."

Now why would she say it like that? Just say you had a good time. I sigh. "Of course, Nat. Despite what you think, you are always welcome here."

She laughs. "Oh yes, I forgot about your open door policy. I didn't realize that extended to me. Just thought it was to your many lady friends."

Waverley's jaw drops. Did she seriously imply that I was still sleeping around in front of both Waverley and Annabelle? Waverley snaps her jaw shut, and I can see her gritting her teeth. Natalie hit her mark. It wasn't me she was trying to hurt.

Don't be mean, Owen. You're the bigger person here. Annabelle doesn't need to see you lose your cool. But damn it, she can't just say something like that.

Alright, two can play. "Nat, what day is your court hearing again? I want to make sure I have the right day on the calendar."

Natalie's cocky smile disappears off her face, and she shoots me her bitchiest face. "I—um, I'll have to look and tell you later."

Derrick looks at her confused, so she flashes him a quick smile trying to blow it off. "Um, we've got to go. I'll see you soon, Belley."

"Bye, Mom." Annabelle pops out of her chair and gives Nat a hug. "Love you."

"Love you too." Natalie pats her head. Oh great, back to the pats.

With a nod from Derrick and a passive aggressive goodbye from Natalie, they're out the door.

Well, that was fun.

I look over at Wav, and I can tell the jab from Natalie is replaying in her head. We've stayed clear of bringing up my past before, and I hate that it can be used as a weapon against her.

"Okay, kid, time for bed. You know the drill. Say goodnight to Wav." I ruffle Belley's hair, and she swats my hands away.

"Okay, okay." She walks over to Wav and gives her a hug. "Goodnight, Wav."

Wav smiles and hugs her back. "Goodnight, cutie, and hey, I want to prepare you. Tomorrow I'm going to have a sub. I have to take my sister to the doctor, but why don't I stay with you tomorrow night? We can make another sister pile, then get ready to go to school together in the morning."

"Oh yes, yes." Annabelle jumps up and down. "Can we please?" She turns back to me.

I chuckle at her still bouncing in front of me. "Yeah kid, that's fine, but for tonight, it's time for bed."

"Alright," she groans. "Good night, love you both."

"Love you too," we chime as she heads to her room.

I slide in the chair next to Wav and pull her chair closer to me. She gives me a shy smile as I push some hair behind her ear.

"I'm sorry about tonight, darlin'."

"No, don't apologize, honey, you didn't do anything." She shrugs.

"Wav, about Natalie's comment—"

"It's fine, really. I mean I get I'm not your first, or probably even your—"

"You're the only one that matters. The only one that is important. The only one that I want, and for damn sure the only one that I've been with since we got together."

Waverley smiles, and her tensed shoulders finally relax.

"The rest are the past, Wav. You're the future."

Chapter 31

Waverley

Winry, Wyla, and I sit in the waiting room of the OB's office. Wyla's sitting in between us, fidgeting and bouncing her leg nervously.

"Everything is going to be fine, Wyla." I place my hand on her leg and squeeze.

"What if it's not? What if there's something wrong?" Wyla bites her nails.

Winry reaches to pull Wyla's hand out of her mouth. "We're going to be with you the whole time. Everything will be how it needs to be."

Wyla shuts her eyes and takes a deep breath. "Okay, you're right. I'm just nervous."

The office door opens. "Wyla Bennett," a nurse calls.

Winry and I stand first then hold out our hands for Wyla's.

"Phew, okay. Let's do this." She takes our hands, and we pull her out of the chair. Hands intertwined, we walk toward the nurse.

"Hi, Wyla. I'm Gabby, I'll be doing your ultrasound today."

Wyla gives her a light smile. "Nice to meet you."

Gabby smiles and gestures down the hallway. "Right this way."

After having Wyla give a urine sample and getting all of her vitals, we finally sit in the ultrasound room.

"Okay, Wyla. Now it's most likely that you'll have to have a transvaginal ultrasound since you suspect you're only six weeks along, so here's a gown to change into." Gabby hands her the gown and steps out to let Wyla change.

Wyla looks at us wide-eyed. "Trans-what? Oh no, I can't do this." Wyla throws down the gown and heads to the door.

"Wyla." I step in front of her. "Everything is going to be fine. You can do this."

Winry comes up next to me with the gown in hand, and Wyla starts to shake her head. "You can, now put this on. We'll be right beside you."

Wyla takes the gown with shaky hands. "I hate you both," she mumbles.

"You love us. Now come on, hurry up."

Wyla changes and Winry and I stand on either side of her, holding her hands. Gabby comes back in and sits in the rolling chair in front of us.

She gets Wyla in position and gets the ultrasound ready. "Okay, Wyla, it may be a little uncomfortable, let me know when you're ready."

Wyla takes a deep breath then nods. As Gabby begins the ultrasound, Wyla squirms a little but then settles.

"Alright, Wyla, here is your baby." Gabby points to the little bean on the screen. Wyla squeezes our hands tight.

"Oh my gosh," Wyla cries. "It's amazing."

"And here is the heartbeat." Gabby presses a button and the fast-paced heartbeat fills the room.

And now we're all crying.

"Oh, Wyla, that's the best sound ever." I wipe some happy tears away.

"It really is. Is everything okay? It's beating so fast," Wyla asks.

"Everything seems fine. You'll meet with your doctor, she'll go over your due date, and we'll take some blood, but everything seems good." Gabby smiles, and I can feel Wyla relax.

After her ultrasound, she talked to her doctor who gave her the general "you're pregnant now" rundown, then tells her she's due April 23rd. Wyla gets some blood drawn, then we all get in Winry's car with a huge weight off our shoulders.

"Okay, where to next?" Winry asks as we pull out of the parking lot.

"It's not even lunch yet. Why don't we stop and shop for bridesmaid dresses? Northshore has some great dress stores."

I pull out my phone and search for the closest one.

"Wyla, you good with dress shopping? I don't want to take away from your day," Winry asks.

"Yes, of course I'm good with it. As long as you don't stick me in a skin-tight dress, we'll be good."

"Deal." Winry smiles.

"Okay, I found one. It looks very earthy boho, totally your style, Win."

I set the GPS to a store named Blooms, and we head that way.

Once inside, we divide and conquer, each of us pulling dresses of different styles and colors. Wyla and I split the dresses up in our sizes then we hit the dressing room.

You can imagine what happens next. It's a dressing room montage. Dresses galore.

It's a full-on fashion show.

After about ten other dresses, we try on these sage green satin midi dresses that have a flowy skirt and the sleeves are ribbons that you tie into bows.

"Okay, Win. These are so cute," I say as I tie Wyla's last bow.

"Ahh, let me see, let me see," Winry chants from the couch.

I pull back the curtain, and Wyla and I naturally strike our best pose.

"These are so cute." Winry jumps up to get a better look at the dresses. "I love the bow sleeves. It's very you, Wav."

"I know! I'm obsessed with them. Plus, this sage green color will look so good with the tan suits."

"And the flowy skirt will give me room to grow," Wyla adds.

"These are the ones for sure." Winry claps her hands. "Oh my gosh, I love them. They're perfect."

"I agree." I give her a little spin for fun.

"Me too." Wyla sways the skirt back and forth.

We all laugh, then take the dresses off and buy them. Satisfied with our productive day, we decide to reward ourselves with some lunch at a deli in the strip mall that the dress store was in.

We grab a little table out front, and talk wedding and baby until our sandwiches arrive.

"So, Wav, how's everything going with Owen?" Winry asks, taking a bite of her club.

"Good." I smile cheekily.

"Oh, come on, we need more than that." Wyla gives me a little shove.

"Okay, okay, we're really good. I mean, I never thought it could be like this, especially with Owen."

"It's great, isn't it?" Winry snickers.

"Ugh, both of y'all are in love and it makes me nauseous, and not because I'm pregnant either." Wyla scrunches her nose.

"Well, we haven't exactly told each other that we love each other yet." I shrug.

"Really? How come?" Winry asks. "You are so in love with him."

I lean back in my chair. "I don't know. I want to say it but part of me wants him to say it first. Me saying it first is too scary. What if he doesn't say it back?"

"Oh, please. He so loves you too." Wyla blows me off. "He's obsessed with you just like Graham is with Win."

Winry nods. "I agree. Graham says he talks about you all the time. And the way he looks at you, it's like you're his gift from God."

"He does not."

"Yeah, he does," Winry and Wyla say together.

"I don't know, guys. I still want him to say it first. I feel like I've been vulnerable enough during this relationship. He should say it first."

"Alright, that's fair. I get that." Winry shrugs.

"No, you don't." I laugh at her clear disapproval on this.

"I do too. I may not completely agree, but I see your side too."

"Well, I clearly don't need to be giving out any relation-ship advice on when to say the big words. I don't even know how to contact the father of my child." Wyla snorts a laugh.

"Oof, yeah. You win the biggest relationship struggle." I pat her shoulder.

"Have you talked to Dad anymore about finding him?" Winry asks, sipping her drink.

Wyla rolls her eyes. "Goodness, part of me hopes not. Dad's furious about how it all happened. He feels like Jett took advantage of me. I'm honestly a little afraid of what Dad would do if we found him."

I take a bite of my sandwich and nod. Dad may be a big softie to us but to those he feels have done us wrong. If we do ever find Jett, let's just say he'll have to work extra hard for Dad's approval. That is, if he would even want it.

After lunch, I get a bag ready to stay the night at Owen's with Annabelle then head that way. We should have about an hour until we need to pick her up from school, and I intend on soaking up every second.

I use my key to get in. I head to his room and find him still asleep. A little bummed, I decide not to wake him and go back out to the kitchen.

Well, maybe I could actually make him something to eat this time.

I look through his fridge and pantry. I spot some sugar cookie dough and some strawberries and raspberries, which gives me the idea to make the fruit cookies Ivy makes at Crossroads. Those things are so delicious and it's fitting that I redeem myself with better cookies.

I preheat the oven and get the cookie dough on a pan with the right nonstick spray this time. I pull out the cream cheese and mix it with some maple syrup, pop it back in the fridge, then pull out the berries to start cutting them up.

Not even two strawberries in and I'm bored of cutting. I dig my AirPods out of my bag, turn on some music, and start cutting again. I finish dicing the strawberries when "Slow Hands" by Niall Horan comes on my playlist.

I look around, still no Owen, so I turn it up and go back to cutting up the raspberries with a little sway in my hips and singing quietly. Well, it starts that way. As the song goes, I get a little more comfortable dancing and singing as I cut the berries.

The timer for the cookies goes off, so I dance my way over to the oven and pull them out. They look perfect. I set them on the cooling rack, then turn to go back to the fruit. When I turn, I jump and scream.

"Owen, you scared the shit out of me." I pull my Air-Pods out of my ears and put them back in the case, then it dawns on me. "How long have you been standing there?"

Owen smiles. "Oh, the perfect length of time. Whatcha listening to?"

"Nothing." I blush, a little embarrassed.

Owen races over and beats me to my phone. "Oh, I didn't realize you were team Niall." He laughs.

"Shut up, that's a good song." I try to take my phone back, but he turns away.

He smiles then restarts the song and turns up the volume. He sets it back on the counter, then holds out a hand.

"Dance with me?"

"What?"

"Come on, Wav. Dance with me. We're waiting on the cookies to cool down, right? Dance with me while we wait."

I smile. "Okay."

I take his hand, and he twirls me around then pulls me back in. His right arm wraps around my waist and the other holds my hand as we sway back and forth for a moment.

Then as the song picks up, Owen pushes me out then pulls me back twirling me under his arm. My back is against his chest and his arms are wrapped around me. He kisses my neck, then sends me back out and I giggle as he spins me some more.

When the song nears its end, Owen finishes it off with a dip, and I come back up with the biggest smile on my face.

Owen cups my face and pulls me in for a kiss that feels a whole lot like those unspoken words. It's passionate. It's demanding, yet gentle. It's a kiss that makes your stomach fill with butterflies, and your brain wonders how could you ever not be helplessly, madly in love with this person.

Owen rests his forehead on mine for a moment, and I think he might say it, but instead, he asks, "What kind of cookies did you make?"

"I'm making the fruit cookies like they have at Crossroads. I thought I'd redeem myself in the cookie department with those."

"Oh, very nice, I love those cookies. You and Annabelle better save me some." He gives me a quick kiss on my forehead. "You're still good to stay here tonight, right?"

"Yes, I brought all my stuff. I'll take her to school with me in the morning too, so you can go straight to bed." I poke him then go back to finish the raspberries.

"Aren't you the best?" He smiles.

"Yes, I am." I scrunch my nose at him.

"I have to head into work a little early today. I'm going to meet your dad to talk about switching to days."

"Oh, really? How do you feel about switching?"

Owen leans over and steals a strawberry. "Eh, it's fine. I mean, I enjoy night shift and working with Graham and Levi. I know Graham has been thinking about switching too, but ultimately, I know it will be better for you and Annabelle if I switched."

I slice the last raspberry. "Honey, you don't need to switch because of me."

"I know I don't *have* to, but I want to. I want to be on the same schedule as you. Granted, your dad might tell me no, so it might not happen." He shrugs.

"Want me to work my magic on him?" I smile.

Owen chuckles. "That's okay, darlin'. I think I got it, but I do need to go get Belley. You staying and finishing the cookies?"

"Yeah, if that's okay?"

"Of course." He gives me a quick kiss. "I'll be back."

"Okay, honey."

Owen heads out the door, and I pull the cream cheese mixture out of the fridge and start spreading it out on the cookies.

Halfway through, I hear the front door open and close.

I turn around. "Hey, you're back. Oh, Natalie, hi, um, what are you doing here?"

She jumps, startled by my voice. "What are you doing here? I didn't see Owen's truck in the driveway." She crosses her arms and takes her usual defensive stance.

"Yeah, he went to pick up Annabelle. He knows I'm here. What are you doing here? Since you clearly thought no one was home."

Natalie shuffles on her feet. "I wanted to be here when he got back with Annabelle. Can't a mother want to see her child? You know what, I don't have to explain myself to you."

"I mean, I guess you don't to me, but I imagine Owen will have some questions as to why you're here when no one was supposed to be home."

Natalie rolls her eyes. "I told you I wanted to see Annabelle. I wanted to surprise her."

Yeah, because I totally believe her. I don't know why she's really here, but I'm sure her intentions aren't to see Annabelle.

"Okay, well they'll be here soon, so you can wait here with me." I turn back to the cookies hesitantly. I have this weird feeling she shouldn't be left alone. Maybe it's just me overthinking but the look on her face when she saw me definitely gave off *I've been busted* vibes.

"Oh, joy," she says sarcastically and slides onto the stool at the bar.

I sigh and turn back to her. "What is your problem with me exactly, Natalie?"

"Excuse me?" She snarls her nose.

"Oh, come on, let's not pretend that you don't have a problem with me. You've had one with me since high school. So, what is it?" It's my turn for the bitchy defensive stance.

Natalie scoffs. "You're right, I don't like you, and I never will. You and your stupid perfect family. You know you guys aren't as great as you think y'all are."

"My family? Goodness, Natalie, what did we ever do to you?"

"It's just who y'all are, the perfect sisters, with the perfect parents. The Bennett girls always getting everything they want, loved by everyone." She rolls her eyes.

"You have no idea what my family has been through. What *I've* been through."

"Oh what, you mean it's not all sunshine and rainbows in your life? Well good, welcome to the fucking club," she scoffs. "You know one day, my brother will come to his senses and see you for the slut you are."

My eyes go wide with shock. "Slut? Natalie, I've only ever slept with your brother. What the fuck are you talking about?"

"Oh, so you're a liar too. I know you slept with Nathan while we were dating."

That name. I squeeze my eyes shut.

"Natalie, get out of my house." Owen comes into the kitchen. "Annabelle, room, now."

Annabelle scurries past her mom heading straight to her room at his tone, and Owen comes up to me wrapping me up in his arms.

Natalie doesn't move. "I'm not leaving, I'm your sister, Owen. She's the one who slept around with Na—"

"Don't you fucking say that name again in my house," Owen snaps harshly. "Not in my house, not in my presence or in Wav's, got it?"

"Owen, you're being—"

"Natalie, you have two options. Apologize to Waverley or get out. Up to you." Owen squeezes me tighter.

Natalie's jaw drops. She hops off the stool and slams the door on her way out.

Owen takes a deep breath and kisses me on the top of the head. "You okay, baby?"

"Yeah." I shake my head. "How much of that did Annabelle hear?"

"Don't worry about it. I'll talk to her."

"Okay, I, uh... I just need a minute." I push out of his arms. The look on his face is pleading for me to stay with him, but he nods. I walk past him and go into his room. I take a few minutes to collect myself and calm my racing mind. I hadn't heard anyone say that name in years, and I was hopeful I'd never have to.

I get about five minutes to myself, then Owen comes in. "Sorry, I couldn't hold back any longer."

I give him a small smile. "It's okay, I was just about to come back out there. How's Annabelle?"

"She's fine, Wav." Owen sits on the bed next to me. "The real question is—how are you?"

"I'm fine, too. I mean it caught me off guard. I'm fine, really." I take his hand and interlock our fingers. "Thank you for standing up for me."

"Wav, of course." He brushes some hair behind my ear. "I'll always stand up for you."

I stare in those green eyes. *Man, I can't hold it back anymore.* "Owen, I—"

"Uncle Owen?" Annabelle hollers from the living room.

"Coming," Owen hollers back. "Sorry, what were you saying?"

Damn it. All my confidence gone in an instance.

"I was just going to say that I think a cookie will lift my mood."

Chapter 32

Owen

After some fruit cookies and a small talk with Annabelle about what happened, I begrudgingly leave for my meeting with Chief, which is rather unfortunate because I'm stressed as hell. I have a strong feeling that kicking Natalie out of my house today is going to bring some rather unfortunate consequences that I'm not looking forward to.

I walk in the station and head straight for Chief's office and knock on the door.

"Come in," he hollers.

I walk in, and see Chief sitting behind his desk, leaning back in his chair. He motions for me to take a seat.

"So, Owen, what did you need to talk about?" Chief asks getting right to it. He has always been a straight shooter.

"I wanted to talk to you about the possibility of me switching to day shift here in the near future."

He leans back in his chair. "Oh? How come?"

"Well, with me holding guardianship of Annabelle, it's been a bit difficult with me on nights. I know I could be losing guardianship of her in the next two weeks but with how much I've watched her before, I just believe it's the better option for me to take care of Annabelle."

"And Annabelle is the only reason?" Chief raises his eyebrows.

Damn, my hands are sweating. "Waverley plays a part too. I'd like to be on the same schedule as her. I want to give both her and Annabelle the best. I think switching to days could help that."

Chief smiles. "I like hearing that, and I kind of figured it was coming, so I had already put a few feelers out to some of the guys on day shift. Stevenson said he's willing to change shifts with you. He doesn't have any kids and his wife just started nights at the hospital, so I'll let him know y'all will be switching shifts effective Monday."

"Oh, that's great. Thank you, sir. I really appreciate it." I stand to shake his hand and he returns it.

"I know you do, but I do want to talk to you about something." He gestures for me to sit back down.

Wonderful. "Okay."

"Nothing wrong, and I hope I'm not overstepping. I just wanted to let you know that if you want some help keeping guardianship of Annabelle, I'll help. I don't mean for this to come off the wrong way because I respect you and your family, but I know that girl is better off with you. Now, I'm not telling you what to do, or how to do it, but if you're thinking you may want to keep guardianship of her, know I'm here to help you. Help you do it the right way too."

I nod as I process all of that. I know deep down Annabelle is better with me, but how am I supposed to fight my own sister for custody?

"Just think about it, and if you decide to let it be and play out the way it needs to then I trust your decision. I know you'll take care of her no matter what, just like I know you'll take care of Wav."

"They're my whole world. I'll always take care of them."

"Good, I'm happy she has you, Owen. Both of them. Your dad would be proud of you."

Wow.

"Thank you, sir. That means a lot to me."

I don't know what I did to get in Chief's good graces, but I know I'm going to do everything in my power to keep it.

Chief knocks on his desk. "Alright, I'll let you start your shift. Be safe tonight."

"Yes, sir." I nod and walk out of his office. Now with a whole lot to think about.

Around midnight, I meet Graham and Levi at the diner. It's been a rather slow night, which I'm honestly thankful for. The last shift I worked was crazy. I had a DUI, a speeding ticket that turned into a drug find, and two fender benders.

I pull out one of the chairs at the table, joining them. "Hey, y'all order yet?"

"Nah, we just sat down," Graham says.

"I'm starving though. I pray this slow night continues, and we don't have to race out of here." Levi reaches for a menu.

"I know, I'm definitely down with this slow night. This past weekend was crazy."

Not to mention, I'm having an internal debate on what to do about custody over Annabelle. I really need to talk to Waverley. I need to know her thoughts and how she feels about it.

"Tell me about it. I got called on two different domestics Saturday night." Graham shakes his head. Domestics are his least favorite calls and given everything that happened with Winry and her ex-boyfriend, I get it. Graham handles them fine, but I know every time he gets one of those calls, it brings back memories that he'd rather forget.

"Yeah, sorry I couldn't assist you in those. I was tied up each time they came through." I pat his shoulder.

"Don't worry about it, I know it was a crazy night. I'll get used to them eventually." He shrugs, but I doubt he will ever not think about Winry when he gets a domestic call.

The waitress comes up to our table and we each order our usual.

"So, Owen. I hear you're leaving us." Levi leans back in his chair.

Graham looks at me and cocks an eyebrow. "Leaving?"

"I'm not leaving. I'm just switching to days. How'd you even hear about that? It just happened."

"I was talking to Sarg when Chief told him about the change. What are you switching for? I thought you liked night shift?"

"I do, but days will work better for Annabelle and Wav."

"Man, you haven't screwed that up yet?" Levi asks, wanting to push my buttons.

"No, I haven't, asshole, and I don't intend to," I reply with a condescending smile.

"Damn," Levi jokes. "I'll keep waiting."

"Yeah, do me a favor and hold your breath while you wait."

Graham and Levi laugh, and the waitress drops off our drinks. Similar to our night, the diner is slow. We're the only people here besides the cook and our waitress, so our food comes out in no time.

"Oh, hey, Win and I are buying Mr. Park's house," Graham says as he takes a bite of his food.

"Really? You finally killed him?" I joke.

"No." Graham rolls his eyes. "Turns out tenth time's the charm. He made a call the other night about some kids ding dong ditching his house. He mentioned that his son has been bugging him to move in with him because of his health. So, I just threw it out there again that I'd gladly buy the house. He said he would think about it, but he called me Monday and gave me his price."

"To which you said, 'I don't care because Win gets what she wants,'" I say and take a sip of my drink.

"Without question." Graham nods. "And don't act like you aren't the same with Waverley. You just switched shifts because you know it will benefit her."

"Annabelle too," I add, but he's right, I would do anything to make Wav happy. I meant what I told Chief. Wav and Annabelle are my whole world. Their happiness is all that matters to me.

I get home from work about a quarter after seven. The living room is all cleaned up, and I don't see the girls in the living room or the kitchen. I head back to my room when I hear laughter coming from my bathroom. I smile. What a wonderful noise.

I knock on the door. "Hey, it's me."

"Come in," Wav responds.

I open the door, and Annabelle sits on a stool as Waverley is curling the last of her hair. "Hey, honey, how was your night?" she asks me.

"Not too bad. We were slow. Happy to be home though." I lean in to give her a kiss to the cheek. "What are you two up to?"

"Wav is curling my hair." Annabelle beams.

Wav smiles and puts down the curling iron.

"And we're done," she says as she combs through the curls. "What do we think?"

Annabelle jumps out of the stool and checks her hair in the mirror.

She squeals, "Eep, I love it! Uncle Owen, what do you think?" She whips around to me.

Ugh, she looks like she's sixteen. *Don't cry Owen.*

"You look beautiful, Belley."

She smiles and jumps up and down. "I think so too."

I chuckle.

"Aren't you going to tell Wav she looks beautiful too?" Annabelle gives me a little shove.

"Of course I am." I pick Annabelle up and set her to the side clearing the path to Wav. I cup her face. "You look beautiful too." I give her a small kiss, and Annabelle giggles.

"Thank you." Waverley smiles. "Oh, hey, how'd it go with my dad?"

I let go of her face, begrudgingly. "Good, I'll start day shift Monday."

"Oh, that's great, honey!"

"You're changing shifts?" Annabelle asks.

"Yeah, I'll be working during the day instead of at night now."

Annabelle seems a little apprehensive. "Does this mean we won't do any more sleep overs?"

"Of course not." Wav wraps her arm around her. "We'll have plenty more. Uncle Owen just may be joining us in the sister pile sometimes. Ya know, he could benefit from a face mask."

Annabelle giggles.

"Oh, could I really?" I raise an eyebrow. "This face not good enough for you?"

"It's perfect." Wav smiles and plants a quick kiss on my cheek. "Okay, Annabelle, we need to get going. Why don't you grab us two fruit cookies for breakfast?" Wav winks at her.

"Okay." Annabelle rushes off to get the cookies.

As soon as she's out of the room, I haul Waverley closer and give her a real kiss. Waverley hums in approval.

"I missed you last night."

"I missed you too." She pulls me in for another lingering kiss. She pulls back a minute later. "Okay, we really need to get going. We're running late as is."

"Okay, baby, but really quick, I want to talk to you about something. Nothing bad, I just want your opinion on something. How would you feel about me asking Graham and Win to watch Annabelle tomorrow after school for a couple hours, and we can go on a date and talk about it?"

"Yeah that sounds like fun, as long as there's nothing I need to worry about. Otherwise, I'm going to need details immediately."

I chuckle. "No, no worries, I promise." I kiss her forehead.

"Okay. Then yes, a date sounds great."

"Perfect. Okay, let me help y'all out to the car." I help carry their bags and drinks while they scarf down their cookies. They load up in the car and buckle their seatbelts. "Okay, y'all have a good day."

"Okay, you too," Annabelle mumbles with a bite of cookie in her mouth.

"You get some sleep. I'll bring her home after school. I mean it, you better be asleep when we get here." Waverley gives me her *I'm serious* look.

"Alright, darlin', I will." I smile. "Y'all be careful."

"We will," they say and wave as they pull out of my driveway.

I need every morning to be like this.

Chapter 33

Waverley

After school Friday, I bring Annabelle home again. I did plan ahead and pack a couple outfit options to change into, so I can change here for our date later. I know Owen said it was nothing to worry about, but how can I not worry a little bit? Not to mention I had all day yesterday and today to jump to every possible conclusion about what we could be talking about.

Gentleman, want your girl not to go into a spiral? Don't tell her y'all need to talk about something then give her zero details.

"What are y'all doing tonight?" Annabelle asks.

"I don't know, really. I know we're going to dinner. Are you excited for Winry and Graham to come over?"

"Yes. While you're my favorite Bennett sister, Winry does have Crossroads, and that's my favorite place." Annabelle puts her feet up on my dash.

"I better be your favorite sister." I laugh.

"You are, which says a lot because Winry owns a real bookstore. A bookstore, Wav. I mean, come on."

I roll my eyes and smile at her. "Well, I'm honored. You're my favorite too.""No, Uncle Owen is your favorite." She laughs. "But I'm second."

"How about you're my favorite West girl and Owen is my favorite West guy."

"Okay, deal."

We pull into Owen's driveway. I get so giddy every time I pull in. I just love his house, and that says a lot since I'm literally obsessed with mine. I always thought I'd force the man I ended up with to move into my house, but there's something about this house that feels like home. Granted, it could just be the people in it.

Annabelle and I unload our stuff and put our bags on the hooks by the door. We find Owen in the kitchen with snacks ready for us.

"Hey, honey." I greet him with a kiss. "Whatcha make us today?"

"Nothing crazy, just chips and salsa." He shrugs like he didn't make the salsa from scratch.

I take a chip, scoop some of the salsa, and pop it in my mouth. "Well, it's delicious, as usual. Thank you."

"Yeah, thanks, Uncle Owen," Annabelle says as she starts to dig in.

Owen laughs. "You're both welcome."

"What time are Win and Graham coming over?" I ask, eating another chip.

"Around five. They said they're going to order some pizza, so don't fill up on chips, Belley."

"Then what'd you make 'em for?" Belley mumbles with a full mouth.

I hold in a laugh. I mean, she has a point.

After a couple chips and talking about our days, I talk Annabelle into putting the salsa away.

"Can I go read until Graham and Winry get here?" Annabelle asks.

"Of course," Owen says. "But I put a basket of your clothes that were in the dryer in front of your door, if you could put those away real quick first."

"Okie," Annabelle responds with no sarcasm or disdain at the request that any normal kid probably would have. She just bops off to her room, and I know she'll do exactly what Owen asks her.

"Can you teach me how to ask kids to do things and get responses like that every time?" I ask Owen. "I get about a hundred eye rolls and aggravated sighs from most of my students all day, none of which come from Annabelle, though."

"Good, but I honestly couldn't tell ya." He shrugs. "She's always been that way."

"You do realize it's because you've raised her that way, right? I'm sorry, but that's not your sister's doing."

"I'll agree that it's not Natalie's doing, but I wouldn't say it's all my doing either. Annabelle is just a good kid."

Owen grabs two bottles of water out of the fridge and hands me one.

"Thank you," I say and untwist the cap to take a sip. "And whose would you say it is? Last time I checked you're the one who takes care of her. I just want you to give yourself a little bit of credit, honey. She is a good kid, but you've played a big part in that."

Owen shakes his head and chuckles.

"What? What are you laughing at?" I swat at him. He catches my hand and pulls me into him.

One hand rests on my cheek and I lean into the touch. He smiles. "How did you go from being Waverley, the girl who tested all my patience, to *Waverley,* the girl who I'm crazy about?"

I bite back my smile. "Crazy, huh?"

He stares deeply into my eyes and his hand slides to my neck. "Madly and utterly obsessed with." He pulls me closer and kisses me just the same as his words, madly and obsessively.

"Owen," I whisper breathlessly in between kisses. It's more of a plea, actually.

He squeezes my neck slightly then pulls back from the kiss.

"Go get dressed for our date, Wav."

I open my mouth to protest, but he stops me. "Go get dressed. There's a bag for you on my bed."

"What is it?" I smile.

"Waverley." Owen's head falls back. "Get your ass in there and find out." He playfully smacks my ass and I head back to his room.

There's a pink gift bag sitting on his bed and a bouquet of flowers. I can't help the smile on my face. I sit on the bed and admire my flowers first. It's an array of bright, colorful wildflowers. My favorites. I set them back down and pick up the bag. There's a card at the top, so I open it up and there are two short paragraphs.

On the left side of the card, it reads:

Wav, you're about to be looking fine as HELL. Your boyfriend is freaking awesome for putting all of this together. Let him rip this outfit off you later!

Much love,

Your sisters.

On the right side it says:

Wav, your sisters stole half of what I was going to say, but they're right. I will be ripping this off you later. You're so incredible, darlin'.

P.S. There's no underwear for a reason.

Owen.

I can't help but feel a little sad that he didn't include love. But then again, do I want him to say it first on a card? No, I'm not going to let something that silly take away from this sweet thing he did for me.

I pull the tissue paper out of the bag and first, I pull out some black boyfriend-style jeans with slits at the knee, then

I pull out this dark green lace bodysuit top. My jaw drops, and I jump off the bed eager to get it on. It's gorgeous.

I pull it on and snap it at the bottom. I pull the jeans on, then go over to the mirror. I do indeed look fine as hell. The green matches his eyes like the lingerie I had on the first time we had sex. I tighten the straps, making sure it lifts my breasts. The cups have padding in them making it to where you don't see the goods but under the wire is full lace.

I go into his bathroom, touch up my makeup, and fluff my hair with some dry shampoo and texture spray. I finish off my look with some lip gloss and give my hair one last flip for volume. I tie up my black lace heels and take one more look in the mirror. Perfect.

I turn to head back out into the living room and find Owen watching me as he leans against the door frame. "Wow, you look..."

I smile seductively. "Fine as hell?"

He pushes off the frame and walks toward me. "That doesn't do this justice. You're breathtaking, Wav."

"Thank you," I say, blushing. "This outfit is perfect, Owen. Thank you."

"You're perfect, not the outfit. It compliments you, not the other way around." He takes a small step closer but stops with about half a foot in between us. "If I so much as graze you while you look like this I won't be able to stop myself. I need you to walk out of my room right now before I absolutely shred that lace."

A thrill shoots up my spine. I want that. I don't care that we haven't even made it to our date yet. I'll wear something else.

"Hey, we're here," Winry yells from the living room. *Damn it.*

Owen sees the disappointment all over my face.

"Later, darlin'. Promise." He winks, and we both head back out to the living room.

"Hey, guys. Damn, Wav, you look so good." Winry claps her hands and bounces.

"Thank you, and thanks for helping with it." I go up to give her a hug.

"Please, Wyla and I hardly did anything. We were more for sizes and support than we were for help. It was all Owen." Winry pats Owen on the shoulder.

"Yeah, they weren't very helpful, especially when they told the cashier that they were both my girlfriends." Owen crosses his arms, and gives Win an unamused look.

Graham's head falls back in laughter. "You did what?"

"Oh, it was great. Owen turned twenty shades of red when we said we were both his girlfriends and then argued about who loved him more while she bagged the clothes." Winry laughs, and I can't help but join in.

"It wasn't funny. The whole store heard you two. On the way out the door, this random guy tried to high five me," Owen says, and we all laugh even harder. "Alright, while you guys laugh, I'm going to change. Wav, will you let Annabelle know we're about to leave?"

"Yeah, of course." He gives me a quick kiss to the cheek then heads to his bedroom to change.

"I'm going to put these pizzas on the table," Graham says and walks toward the kitchen. I go to get Annabelle, but Win grabs my hand stopping me.

"Hold up, hot stuff."

"Oh boy, what is it?"

Winry rolls her eyes. "I just wanted to let you know that Graham and I are totally good to stay as late as y'all want. This top is meant to be ripped apart in the name of amazing sex."

"It so is, isn't it?" I put my hands on my waist and give Win a little shake.

"Oh, do that, and you'll never make it to dinner." She laughs.

"Perfect." I wink, and we both snicker.

"What are you two over there giggling about?" Graham asks.

"Nothing," Win and I say together and giggle some more.

After saying goodbye, Owen and I are finally out the door and headed to dinner. Owen has one hand on the steering wheel and the other on my thigh. I take him in. *Damn, he's so hot.* Black is just his color. He's got on black slacks and a black short sleeve collared shirt that shows off those glorious tatted, muscular arms.

"So, where are we headed?" I ask.

"Graham recommended this place, Rivulet, in Rosewood. Said he takes Win there a lot. It was their first date, too."

"Oh yes. Win talks about that place all the time. Apparently, their pasta is to die for."

"That's exactly what she told me this morning while we were shopping. Said she'd be disappointed if at least one of us didn't get it."

"I can't believe you went shopping this morning with my sisters. Have you gotten any sleep today? You worked last night." I interlock my fingers with his hand that rests on my thigh.

"I slept about two hours after dropping Annabelle off at school. Don't worry, Wav—I've gone with no sleep for over twenty-four-hours many times. Plus, I need to work on switching my sleep schedule anyway since I start days on Monday."

"Oh, yeah, are you excited?"

Owen chuckles and shakes his head. "It's the same job, Wav. It will just be daylight when I do it this time."

"I know that, but you've never done it during the day before. It could be totally different. What if you hate it? What if working in the sun is too much for you? Like a vampire, you won't survive." I tease him.

Owen laughs and it's like finding a new song you love. You just want to put it on repeat.

"I think I'll be fine, Wav."

"If you say so. Just know I'll never move on if you turn to ash in the sun." I laugh.

We arrive at the restaurant about a half hour later. Owen opens my door and helps me out of his truck. "Am I getting the princess package tonight?" I smile.

Owen glances at his watch. "For about another two hours, then I'm going to fuck that invisible princess crown off your head." Owen winks, takes my hand, and walks us toward the restaurant.

Damn. I'm one lucky girl.

We get settled at a table outside on the deck with a view overlooking the river flowing next to it. The waitress greets us right away, and Owen orders a bottle of white zinfandel.

We look over our menus, and I just can't pass up the pasta here given the way Winry talks about it. We order our food when the waitress comes back with the wine.

While he's been amazing all afternoon, I need to know what he wanted to talk about. I pick up my glass and take an encouraging sip.

"So, what is it that you want to talk to me about that you mentioned yesterday?"

Owen also takes what I imagine is an encouraging sip from his glass. "Well, when I had that meeting with your dad about changing shifts, he told me that he would be willing to help me get guardianship of Annabelle."

Alright, that wasn't at all what I was expecting.

"Okay, and how do you feel about that? Getting guardianship, or at least trying to."

"I don't know." Owen sits up in his chair. "I mean, I love Annabelle. I've been begging Natalie to let me take over guardianship of her for years, but how am I supposed to forcefully take it from her?"

"I don't think you should think of it as forcefully taking it, Owen. I mean, at the end of the day, you would be doing what you think is best for Annabelle."

"But am I? By taking her from her mom? I would obviously still let her see Natalie all the time, but I don't imagine Nat will be all that happy about it, and I know she'd just take it out on Annabelle."

Hmm, yeah, that part is probably true.

"How would you feel about it, Wav? Me getting full guardianship."

"How would I feel?" *Why is he asking me?* "Honey, it's your call."

"No, Waverley, it's our call. I know I've had Annabelle full time since we've started dating, but how would you feel about making that official? I mean, we'd have her pretty much all the time. Nights without her at the house would be few and far between."

"Owen, I love Annabelle. I didn't start dating you with the hope that she'd be moving back in with her mom in a couple months. If you want to get guardianship, then I support you one hundred percent." I reach across the table to hold his hand. "No way in the world would I ever leave because of Annabelle."

"Are you sure? I don't want to add all this stress and drama to your life."

"Bring it all, Owen. As long as you're there, I'm good."

Owen squeezes my hand and smiles. "You're incredible."

"I know." I wink at him.

Our food arrives shortly, and the pasta is most definitely to die for. My word, it's good.

Owen cuts a piece of his filet. "Do you want a bite of my steak?"

"Yes, please." I lean forward, and Owen feeds me a bite.

"Mmm, that's so good." My eyes roll back. This place is fantastic. "Do you want to try a bite of my pasta? It's delicious."

"I think Winry would kill me if I didn't." He laughs. I feed him a bite and his eyes do the same. "Fuck. We're coming back here all the time."

"Now I get why Winry loves it so much."

"Me too." Owen wipes his mouth with his napkin, and I admire his tattooed hands.

"So, how many tattoos do you have?"

"Oh man, I lost count. It's more just like one big one now."

"Well, which one is your favorite?"

Owen raises an eyebrow and thinks for a minute. "Um, I really like the card suits on my fingers. My dad loved card games and doing magic tricks with decks of cards, so it always reminds me of him."

"That's sweet. I think one of my favorites is the ravens on your shoulders, but I do also love your hands."

"You love my hands or the tattoos on my hands?" Owen smirks.

"Both." I wink.

Owen chuckles. "So, what about you? I know you have the wildflowers on the front of your left hip. Do you want anymore?"

I don't know why it makes me feel all giddy that he noticed my tattoo. I mean, it's not exactly hidden when we're participating in certain activities but still. I like that he knows exactly what's on my body without me having to point it out.

"I do. I want to get three butterflies that go from under my breast then flutter up to my ribs."

"Oh yeah? Any reason? You don't have to have one, just curious."

"Yeah, I want three obviously for me and my sisters, then butterflies because they symbolize rebirth. I don't know, I..." I trail off trying to figure out how to put into words that I have this new-found confidence and feel like a better version of myself since I've finally let go of my past.

"Wav, you don't have to justify it to me. I think it sounds great. Super sexy too."

I blush at his gaze, it's almost like he's trying to envision the tattoo on me and nothing else.

"Well, then I'll definitely have to work on getting it then," I say and take the last sip of wine in my glass.

Owen refills my wine glass with the remainder of the bottle.

"Oh no, come on. This will be my third glass. You've only had one," I protest as he slides the glass toward me.

"I'm driving, darlin'. You don't have to drink it, but only one for me."

"That's true. Okay, if you insist." I pick up the glass for another sip.

We both finish up our entrees, and I finish my wine. I slip off to the bathroom while Owen pays for dinner. I give my hair a quick fluff and put on some lip gloss before heading back out.

Owen waits for me by the hostess stand. His eyes trail up my body slowly as I walk toward him. It sends a shiver down my spine. Dinner was great, but I'm ready for the princess treatment to come to an end the way it was promised.

"You ready to go?" I ask with my best fuck-me eyes.

"Yes," he says and leans in, giving me a kiss, teasing me. "But not for that yet. We're adding a stop."

"What are we doing now?" I ask with raised eyebrows, hoping it still includes what I want.

"Patience, darlin'. You'll like this one, come on." He takes my hand and walks me out toward his truck.

We drive back to Aster Creek and the whole time, Owen refuses to tell me where we're going. Finally, we pull into Despark Tattoo Shop in town.

"We're getting tattoos?" I squeal.

"Yeah, my buddy Eddie said he had an opening tonight, and Graham said they were good to stay late, so I thought we could get our tattoos. If you want to, that is?"

"Hell yeah." I bounce in my seat, too excited. "Wait, what are you getting?"

"You'll see," he says, with excitement written in his green eyes. "Let's go."

We walk in the tattoo shop, and it's got all black walls and white swirls to make it look like smoke. The furniture is very sleek and modern. While I knew it was here, I haven't been inside before. Win and I got our tattoos at a shop in Northshore, but this place is so cool.

"Hey, man. How the hell are you?" A tall, lanky man covered in tattoos walks up greeting Owen with the usual bro-hug.

"I'm good, man, I'm good. Eddie, I don't know if you know my girlfriend, Waverley?" Owen turns toward me and pulls me in under his arm.

"One of the Bennett sisters. Of course, I do. Hi, Waverley, I'm Eddie." He holds out his hand to shake mine. "I went to school with this asshole, so I don't know what spell he's got you under, but I'm sure a few stories from high school will set you straight."

I look up at Owen, *my Owen*. "You can try, but I doubt you'll be successful."

Eddie laughs. "I like her. Come on, guys." There are three separate sections separated by black velvet curtains, and Eddie walks us over to his chair. "So, what are we wanting tonight?"

Owen gestures for me to go first.

"I want to get three butterflies starting here and floating up to here," I say and point to where I want it placed.

"Alright, how do you want the butterflies to look?" Eddie asks and picks up his laptop.

"Um, just simple. I like the outline of them and all black."

"Okay." Eddie does some typing on his laptop, then turns it around to me. "Something like this? We'll place them where we want them, do you like the design?"

I look at the butterflies, and they're perfect—simple line art butterflies.

"Yes, I love those."

"Wonderful, let me get everything set up." Eddie gestures for me to sit in his chair and then buzzes around us getting the stencil printed and getting everything in its place. He rolls over in his chair with the stencil ready then pauses.

"Okay, so how do you want to do this?" He gestures at my shirt.

"Oh, um." I panic because I can't just be topless in here. I guess I could unsnap it and try to pull it up as much as I can.

"I got it," Owen says and walks up to me.

He raises my right arm, then rips the lace from under the wire. He looks at me hungrily and winks. *Man, is it hot in here?* I think I'm melting.

"Well, that's one way to do it." Eddie laughs. We get the butterflies placed, and I lay on my side for us to get started.

"Alright, you ready?" Eddie asks.

Chapter 34

Owen

Fuck, I could sit here and watch Wav get tattooed all day. She's lying on her side, with her shirt ripped to shreds, and ink going on her body. Fuck, we might not even make it out of the parking lot. I'm barely holding it together right now.

"How you doing, darlin'?"

Wav scrunches her nose. "Good, it's really not that bad. I thought the ribs were supposed to hurt?"

"They do hurt. You're just a psychopath." I smirk at her.

She sticks her tongue out at me and I laugh.

"Are you going to tell me what you're going to get now?" she asks.

"Nope," I say, popping the P.

"You probably don't even have one picked out." She rolls her eyes.

"I do too. I'm just not telling you."

It's killing me not to touch her right now. My buddy has his hands on her now and even though it's not sexual, I want to rip his head off and take over myself.

He's on the last butterfly now, and it's the one right under her boob. She rolls over and lifts her breast slightly making it easier to do the tattoo, but it makes it a hell a lot harder for me. Mentally and physically.

"Alright, all done." Eddie slides his chair back. "Take a look."

Wav slides out of her chair and walks over to the mirror and smiles her beautiful smile.

"You like it?" Eddie asks.

"I love it. Thank you, it's perfect," Waverley replies, still admiring her side.

"Come here, let me see."

She walks over to me still grinning ear to ear and turns to show off her side. "What do you think?"

I think I'm going to fuck you in the parking lot.

"You're right, it's perfect."

"Ahh, I love it," she says giddily. "Okay, your turn."

I chuckle. "Okay, baby. Eddie, you got my text?"

"Yeah, I already got it ready, my man." Eddie cleans up his stuff and prints off the stencil of what he drew up from the text I sent him on the way over here. "You said chest, right?"

"Yeah." My arms are full from fingers up to shoulders, but my chest and torso only have some scattered about. I stand up and pull my shirt over my head.

Wav and Eddie both whistle. "Waverley, did it just get hotter in here?"

"Most definitely." She giggles.

I roll my eyes at them both, and we get the stencil set. I make sure my back is turned to Wav so she can't see.

"Why won't you show me?" she protests and tries to sneak a peek.

"Not until it's done. Get back, little Miss Impatient."

"Ugh, fine," she pouts but sits back in the extra chair.

"Okay, you like the placement?" Eddie asks, holding up a small mirror.

"Yeah, that's great."

"Alright, man. Let's do it."

Eddie finishes up about forty-five minutes later. "Okay, all done."

He holds the mirror back up.

"Oh yeah, that's awesome." I look at the fresh ink on the left side of my chest.

Wav jumps out of her seat. "Let me see now." She comes around so she can see. She brings her hand up to her mouth. "You got a wave?"

"Yeah, you like it?" I glance down at the crashing wave now permanently inked over my heart.

Waverley seems too stunned to speak, but there's a hint of a smile there.

"I'll wait at the counter up front," Eddie says, letting us have a moment alone. "Oh, please don't have sex on my chair."

I flip him the middle finger, and he laughs as he walks off.

I grab the front loop of Waverley's pants and pull her closer. "So, what do you think?"

"I love it, but Owen—"

"No buts. I told you—*you* are a part of me, Wav. Nothing will ever change that. You will always be mine." I caress her cheek with my thumb. "Now, let's get out of here. I have a promise to keep."

Chapter 35

Waverley

My whole body feels like it's on fire. I need this man in a bad way and if he doesn't hurry up and get me out of here, I will push him back into that small room and straddle him on that chair.

Thankfully, he seems just as eager as I do because he barely talks to Eddie after he pays and pulls me out the door.

As soon as we turn the corner around the building, all of our self-control is gone. Owen grips the back of my head and brings me in for a bruising kiss. The taste of him is enough to drive me to the edge. I wrap my legs around his waist, and he pushes me back against the cool brick of the building. He grinds against me, and I gush.

He pulls my head back and kisses down my neck and collarbone. "I need to be inside of you."

He thrusts against me again.

"My house is only about five minutes from here," I say as he kisses my neck.

"Get in my truck," he growls and sets me down. "Go before I take you right here against this wall."

I hurry to his truck, and he follows behind me. We climb in, and he throws it in reverse, whipping out of the parking lot.

I can't help but touch him on the drive over. I lean up over the middle dash kissing his neck, biting his ear, and running my hand over his hard length.

"Waverley," he warns.

"What? I just want to touch you," I reply, not stopping a single thing.

"You're killing me."

"Good," I whisper in his ear.

We pull in my driveway, and Owen practically jumps out of the truck and rips my door open. He pulls me to him and carries me to my front door, kissing me mercilessly.

He sets me down to unlock my door. As I'm trying to get my key in the knob, Owen kisses my neck and slides one hand down my torso and slips it under my jeans.

When his hand meets the drenched lace from the bodysuit, he growls in approval.

I somehow manage to get the door open, and I whip around and start to tear off Owen's clothes as we walk in. He undoes my jeans and rips my shirt the rest of the way off.

"You're so beautiful," he says, and I can't help feeling anything but that with the way he looks at me.

He pulls me back flush to him, kissing me hard, like he'll never get enough. This kiss makes me feel so alive and wanted. His tongue explores my mouth and tangles with mine.

I wrap my legs around him again, and he lays me down on the rug in my living room, neither of us willing to wait any longer.

Owen rests in between my thighs and pulls back from our kiss. He brushes my hair back from my face then caresses my cheek. As he stares into my eyes, our manic need shifts to something completely different. It's no longer demanding—it's intimate and soul binding.

I gently scratch his back, and he rests his forehead on mine. He takes a breath, words that have gone unsaid between us feel perfectly clear right now.

"Waverley—" He kisses me tenderly and pushes in slowly.

The urgency we felt on the way over here is long gone, now we just want to savor this moment. This feeling. I never thought I'd find something so all-consuming in the best way possible.

Owen's right—I'm a part of him and he's a part of me.

Chapter 36

Owen

By the following Friday, I've adjusted to day shift. The only real drawback to switching is that I need someone to drop off and pick up Annabelle from school, but it's still a hell of a lot better than having to find someone to stay with her all night.

Waverley insisted on being the one to take her to and from school, and wait with her until I get there on the days I work. She said it made the most sense since she works at the school anyway. I argued for a bit that it was too much of an ask, but considering it's an easy excuse to see her every day, I gave up pretty fast.

Around lunch, I hit up a drive-thru and park my patrol car to eat. As I dig into my burger, Waverley calls me.

"Hey, darlin', everything okay?"

"Hey. Yes, well—yes and no. Emergency-wise good, but I won't be able to take Annabelle home today. I now have a meeting with some parents after school. I had some girls decide they all wanted the same haircut so, now I have three girls, all now with matching botched bangs."

I laugh. "Oh, man. Please tell me one was Annabelle, so I can have plenty of embarrassing pictures to scare off potential boyfriends."

Waverley snorts. "Yeah right. She would never. But now I have three sets of angry parents to deal with after class."

"Oof, I'm sorry, Wav. I'll call my mom, she can take her to her place."

"I'm so sorry, honey. Are you sure? I can call Win or Wyla and see if they can take her home."

"Nah, don't worry about it. But hey, why don't you come over tonight? I'll pick us up some Chinese food, and we can do a movie with Annabelle. We should be back home around 7:30."

"That sounds great, thank you. But hey, I have to go. I'll talk to you later?"

"Yeah, sounds good, see you soon."

"Bye, honey."

We hang up, and I call my mom asking her to pick up Annabelle. After that's sorted, I go back to finish my lunch and watch as every car slams on their breaks when they notice me sitting here.

I walk up the front porch to my mom's house, eager to get Annabelle and get out of here without talking to Natalie. I haven't talked to her since I kicked her out of my house. While I'm dying to know why she was even in my house to begin with and how she knows about Nathan, I know she's going to make me pay for kicking her out.

Natalie meets me at the door. "Hey, bro, long time no see." She fake smiles. "I want to talk to you."

Of course. I step back letting her come out on the porch. "Yeah, I'd like to talk to you too. Like why were you at my house when I wasn't home?"

"I wanted to see Annabelle. I knew you were on your way home with her." She shrugs.

"Ah, see, I don't believe you." I cross my arms.

"I don't care if you believe me or not. Frankly, I could give zero fucks if you believe me. You threw your own sister out of your house, you picked *her* over me. That slut over your own sister."

My blood starts to boil. "Don't you fucking call her that. You have no idea what actually happened between her and that piece of shit."

She rolls her eyes. "Oh, really? I saw them, Owen. I know what happened."

My blood goes from boiling to ice cold. "You what?"

"I saw them." She looks at me like I'm stupid.

"Natalie, I'm going to need you to explain right now."

She throws her hands in the air. "Fine. I had just started seeing Nathan, I didn't tell anyone because I had Annabelle and people were already mean about the whole teen pregnancy thing, so Nathan told me to keep our relationship a secret. He called me one night on his way back from a party, told me his parents weren't home and to meet him there. So, I snuck the baby monitor into your room then went over to his place."

I run my hands over my face. "You left Annabelle alone? She was what—one?"

"You and Mom were both home, she wasn't completely alone, and she was asleep." Natalie rolls her eyes again. "Anyway, when I got there I decided to go in the back door, hoping none of the neighbors would see and then I saw them through the back window. He was—"

I hold up my hand, unable to hear another word. "Stop, just stop. You have no idea what really happened."

"I know what I saw, Owen," she snaps.

"Yeah, what you saw wasn't consensual, Natalie. Waverley told him to stop, but he didn't."

"Is that what she told you? Owen, come on, you don't seriously believe her?"

"Yes, I believe her. How can you seriously ask that question? And if you truly thought he didn't force her, then why didn't you tell anyone?"

"Nathan told me not to, said she wasn't worth mentioning," she says with a smug look on her face.

"And that didn't seem at all suspicious to you? Come on, Nat. You're smarter than that."

"You're going to take Waverly's side on this, aren't you?" Natalie huffs.

"Yes!" I throw my hands up in frustration. "Natalie, what the fuck is wrong with you? I just told you what really happened, and you're going to stand there and blame the victim."

"So that's it, it's her over me? Your sister!" she yells.

"Yeah, it's her, not another thought about it," I snap.

Natalie crosses her arms and cocks a hip.

"What about her or Annabelle?" she asks with a wicked smile on her face. Almost like she knows she's about to land a killer blow.

"What are you talking about? I'm not playing your games, Natalie." I'm so tired of her bullshit.

"Oh, but you are. Our court date is Wednesday, and you know I'm going to get custody of Annabelle back. I've followed every request the court has made. I even found a new job. I'm getting her back, and I'm taking her with me."

"Taking her with you? What does that mean?"

"Oh, you remember Derrick? Well, he has family in California, and he's moving there next month. I'm going with him," Natalie says, her smile growing bigger.

"What the fuck? You're moving across the country with some guy you've been dating for what? A month, tops? Have you lost your mind?"

"Fuck off, Owen, I'm not moving in with him. He helped me find a job over there and an apartment. I'm starting over, and I'm taking Annabelle with me."

No, just no. This can't happen.

"Unless," she starts. "You want to get guardianship of her." Natalie cocks an eyebrow.

"You know I want to keep her." I stare at her, so angry. I don't think I could get angrier than I am right now.

"Okay, then it's quite simple. Break up with Waverley."

I was wrong, I'm livid now. I scoff, "I'm not doing that."

"Oh, well then, Annabelle comes with me, and I wouldn't count on us coming back to visit. Travel is so expensive."

"Natalie..."

"Let me spell it out for you, Owen. Break up with Waverley, and I sign the rights to Annabelle over to you, and you'll never hear from me again. But if you try to get back with her, I'll file for custody again and again. Claim I made a mistake and that I want to be her mother again. You know I'm a master at playing the victim, so I don't imagine getting her back would be much of a problem."

"Why? Why are you doing this? What have I ever done to you that would make you do this? What kind of mother uses her own kid like some pawn in her little game?"

"You abandoned me, Owen! When I needed you after Dad died, you weren't there. Mom was too depressed, she practically forgot I existed. You both left me alone, and I needed you."

"Natalie, I'm so sorry I wasn't there after Dad died. I know I wasn't, but what about these last eleven years? I've done nothing but support you."

"No, you've supported Annabelle, not me." Natalie looks at me with no remorse, no emotion. She's serious about this. "Break up with Waverley, and Annabelle is yours. I may not be a good mother, but Waverley isn't going to replace me. Do it, or I take Annabelle to California with me."

"Natalie, please don't make me do this. Do you want me to beg? Because I'm begging you, don't do this."

I'm a step away from getting on my knees, how can I choose between Annabelle and Waverley?

"Oh, Owen. This isn't a good look for you. You have until Monday to do it, or I'm booking Annabelle's ticket."

Fuck. I play the only card I have.

"I could fight you for her, Natalie. Everyone knows I'm the one who takes care of her. If this is how you want to be then I can fight you for her."

"You could try but you see, I already spun my story quite nicely to Derrick, and he ever so graciously offered to pay for my lawyer. You may know her—Nancy Abrams, she's a real shark in family court. Big advocate for children staying with their mothers, especially when they really haven't done anything wrong. But go ahead and fight me. You better pray that you win, because if you lose, there is absolutely no way you will ever see her again."

Fuck. Nancy Abrams is mean as hell in court. At least that explains what she was doing in my house. I'm sure Nancy told her to collect any and everything she could use against me. "Natalie, please—"

"Uncle Owen?" Annabelle peeks her head out the front door. "I didn't know you were here."

"Hey, Belley." I take a deep breath.

What the fuck am I going to do.

"Are we going home? I'll get my bag."

Home.

Fuck. This is going to hurt.

I walk over to her and hug her. I can't help it, I need it.

"Actually, kid. I need to do something for a bit, can you stay here for a little while longer?"

"Okay, Uncle Owen." She smiles. "I love you."

"I love you too."

I once told myself I would make any sacrifice for Annabelle. But how the fuck can I do this? I think this one will kill me.

I pace in my living room. My mind is scrambling to think of any possible option that would result in me being able to keep both of them. *What the fuck can I do?* My chest hurts at the mere thought of losing either one of them. If I fight Natalie for Belley and lose... No, I can't risk losing her. I can't put Belley's well-being on a chance. I know she's better with me, I know she is, but losing Waverley? I think I'm going to be sick.

I freeze when I hear my front door open, and Waverley walks in. My beautiful girl who I'm so in love with that I seriously can't picture my life without her.

But I can't picture my life without Annabelle either.

Fuck.

Waverley smiles, and I just move to her. I grab her face and kiss her so desperately because I'm a selfish asshole and if this is the last time I get to kiss her, I'm going to do it.

Waverley can sense my pain in this kiss, and she places her hands on my arms and pushes back.

"Hey, everything okay? Where's Annabelle? I thought we were doing movie night?"

She looks around the living room, searching for her.

I take a deep breath. "Um, Belley's at my mom's. I have to talk to you about something."

Her eyes search my face for any hint of what I'm about to say.

"Owen, you're kind of freaking me out. What's wrong?"

I drop my hands from her face, I can't bring myself to look into those sky-blue eyes.

"I, uh... talked to Natalie today. Our custody date is Wednesday,"

She nods and drops her bag on the counter. "Yeah, I remember. What'd she say?"

"Well, you know she's still with Derrick? Turns out he's got family in California, and he plans on moving there next month."

I don't know if I can do this.

She furrows her eyebrows. "Okay... and?"

I take another deep breath. "Natalie wants to go with him, and take Annabelle too."

Waverley's jaw drops in disbelief. "What? That's ridiculous. She can't do that. She can't take her from you."

I run my hands over my face.

"She can, Wav. I only have temporary custody of her, and I'll most likely be losing it Wednesday since Natalie hasn't gotten into any more trouble."

Shock still mares her beautiful face. "But that's crazy, Owen. You're more of a parent to Annabelle than she is."

"I know, but I'm not actually her father, Wav. I don't have any say in if she takes Annabelle anywhere." Waverley switches from shock to panic. The determination on her face to think of an option that would work kills me even more.

"But what about fighting for guardianship? I already told you I was good with it, and everyone knows you are the one that takes care of her anyway. Owen, we have to figure something out, we can't let—"

I place my hands on her shoulders, needing to ground both of us.

"There's... one way." I don't think I can actually say the words. "Natalie said she would forfeit her rights to Annabelle to me at Wednesday's hearing, but I have to do something—"

"Well, do it, honey, I mean what could possibly be stopping you..." She trails off at the look on my face.

I'm absolutely gutted right now. I'm going to be sick.

"It's me, isn't it? You have to break up with me, and she'll give you Annabelle," she whispers.

Ow, ow, I think my chest is on fire. "Waverley..."

"Oh my word." Tears fill her eyes, and she takes a small step back, brushing my hands off her shoulders. The determination I saw on her face is long gone.

I reach for her hand, needing to hold on to any part of her.

"I don't know what to do, Wav. I could fight her, I could, but if I lost, I could lose Belley for good. If we fake break up, and Natalie finds out, she would just file for custody again. Even if she signs away her rights, she can still file to get them back. I've seen it happen before. With the right lawyer she could do it. Even then, if she doesn't manage to get full custody back, she can really make it difficult and put Annabelle through the wringer in a custody battle. I can't put Annabelle through another one of these hearings. I can't have her constantly wondering who wants her and where she's going to live. I can't lose Annabelle, Wav. You know I can't."

"But you can lose me." She wipes a tear that escapes down her cheek with her other hand.

Fuck, I think I'm dying. "I don't want to, baby."

"But you *can*." She starts to pull away from me again.

"Waverley." I follow her step and caress her cheek. I love her, she needs to know that I love her. "I lo—"

"Don't say it," she snaps, and pushes me back. "Don't you dare say that. Not now."

"But I do, Wav. I lov—"

"No, stop, just stop," she cries and holds out her hand.

This is hell. I try to wipe some tears from her face.

"I said stop!" she yells and pushes me away again.

I take a step back.

"Okay, I'm sorry." I can't bear this anymore. I have to figure something out, but I need time. "Waverley, please just give me some time to figure this out. I don't want to lose you."

She dries her tears and suddenly her voice becomes calm. "There's nothing to figure out, Owen."

No, there has to be. I can't accept that this is the end. "I don't want to let you go, Wav, please just give me some time to fig—"

"No, Owen," she says sharply, cutting me off. "This is it. You have to. We're done." The words leave her mouth, and I don't think I'm breathing anymore.

No, no, no. Fuck. No.

"Don't, don't say that. You said you wouldn't leave when it came to Annabelle."

Wav swallows down her emotions. "I said I wouldn't leave *because* of Annabelle, and I'm not. I'm leaving *for* her, Owen. I won't be the reason you lose her, or that she loses you."

I try to take a step to her, but she holds out her hands to stop me. "Waverley, please don't—"

She blinks back the tears that are fighting to fall. "I need to go."

She grabs her stuff and hurries to the door.

"Waverley, please don't leave. I'm begging you." I'm breaking, I can't do this. I try to follow her. I need her to stay. "Wav, please, I lo—"

But she slams the door on her way out.

Chapter 37

Waverley

Breathe, Waverley. Just breathe, but it's so hard. I feel like there's an anchor on my chest, and it's already shattered my heart into pieces, now it's making it difficult to breathe.

"Waverley, please just give me some time to figure this out. I don't want to lose you." Owen looks exactly how I feel. Broken and hopeless. Natalie only left us with one option.

Fuck. I don't want to lose him either, but this isn't about us. It's about Annabelle and what she needs.

"There's nothing to figure out, Owen."

"I don't want to let you go, Wav, please just give me some time to fig—"

"No, Owen," I cut him off.

Annabelle told me that if she could choose, she would stay with Owen. I can't be the reason she loses him.

"This is it. You have to... We're done." As the words leave my mouth I want to take them back, but I push through.

Owen shakes his head almost like he can't accept this as the answer. "Don't, don't say that. You said you wouldn't leave when it came to Annabelle."

I try to keep my voice even and free of emotion, but I'm dying. "I said I wouldn't leave *because* of Annabelle, and I'm not. I'm leaving *for* her, Owen. I won't be the reason you lose her, or that she loses you."

He tries to take a step closer, but I hold my hands up stopping him. I can't have him get closer.

"Waverley, please don't—"

My heart is gone; it's torn to shreds. Tears are threatening to spill over. I need to get out of here. "I need to go."

I grab my things and head straight for the door.

He follows a few steps behind me, so I move faster. "Waverley, please don't leave. I'm begging you. Wav, please, I lo—"

But I slam the door, drowning out the words I can't bear to hear.

My tears start to flow immediately. The life I wanted—gone. Everything I wanted with him, gone in an instant.

I back out of his driveway. I don't even know where to go now. Home doesn't feel right because my home is with Owen.

So I head for Winry's.

I turn down the main road in town, and my tears just keep falling. So hard I can barely see. So hard that I don't see the car driving on the wrong side of the road, coming right towards me, until it's too late. Glass shatters and I'm jerked forward, colliding with the airbag.

When the initial impact stills, it's like I can feel the urgency. But calmness takes over my body. There's no pain. My eyes flutter for a moment, they're so heavy right now. Objects move around me, but I can't bring myself to care.

I just need to close my eyes for just a minute.

And then, it's all black.

Chapter 38

Owen

It's been an hour since Waverley walked out my door and *fuck*. I think I'm having a heart attack.

The pain in my chest is pure agony. Watching Waverley walk out my door absolutely gutted me. How am I supposed to move on from her? How could I possibly see her in town and not want to grab her and kiss her? Fuck, how in the world could I ever see her with someone else? I can't. I don't want to be without her, but what am I supposed to do? I can't lose Annabelle, but I think losing Wav is going to kill me.

I love her. Damn it, I love her so much. I have to find another way to keep them both. I just can't be without either of them.

They're my girls. My family. My home.

My entire world revolves around them.

I'm going to fix this. I grab my keys and head toward my truck. I have to get Waverley back. As I pull out of my driveway my phone starts to ring. Chief's name flashes on my screen.

Fuck.

I grit my teeth and prepare myself for the ass-chewing I deserve.

"Hey, Chief, listen I'm—"

"Owen." His voice sounds pained and stressed. "I need you to come down to the hospital."

My stomach drops. "What happened?"

"I'll be waiting for you in the lobby when you get here," he says before hanging up the phone.

I slam on the gas. I don't think I have ever driven so recklessly in my life. My heart is pounding— I can feel it throughout my whole body.

I whip into the first parking spot I see, not caring that it's shitty parking and race inside. I scan the lobby and see the family I prayed I wouldn't. All of the Bennetts huddled together. When they spot me, I can read the hurt, the concern, all over their faces. Graham has his arms around Winry as she wipes some tears from her face. Chief stands pacing, while Wyla and Mrs. Bennett sit holding each other's hands.

"What happened? Is she okay? Where is she?" I ask, panicked.

"Owen, I think we need to talk over here first," Chief says, pulling me to the side. Graham follows behind us.

"Someone tell me what is going on right now. Is Waverley okay?"

Chief looks like he's going to be sick. He runs his hands over his face.

"Somebody say something!" I shout, not caring if it causes a scene.

Why the fuck is no one saying anything?

Graham grabs my shoulder. "She's alive, but she's in a coma right now."

My whole body goes numb, I can't stand. I fall into the chair behind me.

Graham sits next to me. "She has two broken ribs, a broken leg, fractured wrist, and a traumatic brain injury from hitting her head. The paramedics said she was barely responsive at the beginning but has now slipped into a coma. They are doing a CT scan and MRI now to assess how bad."

I stare at the ground—this is all my fault. I should have never let her leave. I should have fought for her.

"How? How did this happen?" I choke out.

Graham and Chief look at each other but say nothing again.

"How the fuck did this happen?" I demand.

"It was a head-on collision." Chief grips my shoulder. "Your sister. She was driving the other car. She..." he pauses. "She didn't make it, Owen. She died on impact. We're so sorry."

The words shoot through me like a bullet.

This can't be happening.

"I've called your mom, and she's on her way. Owen, they believe that Natalie was under the influence of alcohol at the time—"

I shut my eyes and drown it all out, willing this to be some awful nightmare. How am I supposed to tell Annabelle?

"I've called the judge and CPS, they are extending your temporary custody, but you'll have another hearing in a month to gain full guardianship. I've also called a family lawyer on your behalf, and he's going to take care of everything."

I can't form words with this lump lodged in my throat. I bury my face in my hands. What the fuck am I supposed to tell Annabelle? How will I ever survive Wav not waking up? She has to wake up. Please God, let her wake up.

Chief looks over my shoulder at the entrance doors of the hospital. "Son, your mom and Annabelle are here. I know this is going to be gut wrenching, but they need you. Annabelle needs you."

Chief squeezes my shoulder, and the following hour is one of the worst hours of my life.

Annabelle cries in my lap until she passes out. I hold her tight, because she's the only thing holding me together right now.

"Chief Bennett." A doctor comes up to our group. Chief stands and follows him back down the hallway.

"Here, let me take her. You go with Chief," Graham says, reaching for Annabelle.

"Okay." I nod and hand her over. I hate leaving her, but I have to know if Waverley is okay.

I follow the direction Chief went and find them down a hallway, standing outside a room. Wav's room. I walk up as the doctor walks away.

"What'd he say?" I ask not wasting a second.

Chief turns to me with tears in his eyes. Fuck, I can't do this.

I hold my breath until he finally says, "They believe she's going to be okay. They said the tests didn't show any bleeding or severe swelling. She's still in a coma, but they're hopeful she'll wake up in the next twenty-four hours."

It's a miracle I'm still standing. Relief floods me.

"They said they are about to finish casting her leg and her wrist, but we can go in and see her for a minute, if we'd like. He only pulled me aside because he doesn't want to overwhelm her if she were to wake up, but I think just us two will be okay."

I nod and follow him in her room.

I've seen terrible things as a police officer, truly awful things—Chief even more so, I'm sure—but we both freeze when we see Waverley lying unconscious in the hospital bed. She's hooked up to countless machines, oxygen under her nose, and her leg and wrist are splinted together. She has a scratch on her face and some on her arms, likely from where the glass shattered.

Still frozen in my spot, I can't bring myself to move. Chief takes a deep breath then walks up to her bedside.

"Hey, Wav," he chokes out. "I know my strong girl is in there. When you're ready to wake up, we'll all be here, ready to see your smile again." Chief takes her non-splinted hand in his and holds it for a moment.

With one more look at her, Chief lets her hand go and walks back toward me.

"I'm going to go update everyone. We've got Annabelle, so take all the time you need."

"Chief," I say. "How am I supposed to do this? My niece just lost her mother. I lost my sister. I can't lose Wav, too. How am I supposed to take care of Annabelle like this? How am I supposed to be here for Wav? How am I—"

"Son, she's going to be okay. None of us are going to lose her. She's strong, you know that." Chief grips my shoulder. "You'll take care of Annabelle like you always have. I'm sorry you lost your sister today, and I know this situation is tearing you apart inside, but you need to focus on the things you can control right now. You're going to take five minutes for yourself to talk to the woman you love, then you're going to take Annabelle home."

"I'm not—"

"Yes. You're going to leave and let Annabelle sleep in her bed. I will call you if anything changes. Then tomorrow, you'll let Graham and Winry watch Annabelle for a few hours while you visit with Wav again. The lawyer is taking care of everything regarding Annabelle's custody, but he is not to call you until Monday, and Isabel is helping your mom with all of Natalie's arrangements."

Without thinking, I hug Chief. "Thank you, I don't know what else to say other than thank you for everything."

"There's no need to thank me. Take good care of my daughter, that's all I ask."

He claps my back.

"I will, I promise."

"Good. Now take your five minutes." Chief walks out, leaving me alone with Waverley.

I stare at my beautiful girl and find the will to walk up to her. I take her hand in mine.

"Hey, darlin'. I know you're mad at me right now. I'm mad at myself. I never should have let you walk out of my house today, and I'll forever blame myself for this, but you have to wake up, baby. I need you to wake up. I know you think I can lose you, but I can't..."

Every emotion that I've held back for the past three hours is finally coming to a head.

"I know you told me not to say it earlier, and when you wake up you can yell at me all you want, but I love you so much, Waverley," I cry. "I love you so much that I can't think of life without you. I need you to wake up."

I squeeze her hand, but she doesn't squeeze back. She doesn't move or even flinch.

"Waverley, please wake up, baby."

But nothing changes. I hold her hand tightly and pray a million prayers that she'll wake up. Eventually the doctor comes back in and says they need to get her casts placed.

Not one part of me wants to let go of her hand, but Chief's right. I need to take Annabelle home for the night.

With one last kiss to her hand, I let her go and head back to the lobby.

The next morning, Annabelle and I sit at the kitchen table, exhausted. Neither of us really got any sleep last night. Halfway into the night, Annabelle woke up screaming from a nightmare and asked me to stay with her, so I spent the rest of the night tossing and turning on her floor. Chief and Graham text updates every hour but nothing has changed.

I take a sip of my coffee. "Do you want me to make some breakfast?" I ask her.

"I'm not very hungry," Annabelle whispers.

"Yeah, me neither."

"Is Wav going to be okay?" Annabelle looks down at her lap.

The pain in my chest is immeasurable, but I do my best to keep my emotions off my face. Annabelle doesn't need to know that I'm barely holding it together.

"The doctors are hopeful that she'll wake up. Do you want to talk about your nightmare? You know you can tell me anything, Belley."

Annabelle shakes her head and some tears find their way down her cheeks. "This is all my fault, Uncle Owen." She brings her hands up to her face and sobs uncontrollably.

I go to her immediately, kneeling by her and wrapping her in a tight hug.

"Kid, there is one thing I know for sure, there is no possible way that this is your fault."

"No, it is," she cries, "I heard you and mom arguing about me moving away from you, and I didn't want that to happen, so I told Mom I wanted to stay with you, and then she got upset and left with a—"

"Annabelle, hey, it's okay." She continues to sob on my shoulder. "This is not your fault."

"Yes, it is," she chokes out.

I pull her back and cup her face, wiping the tears. "No, it's not, and I want you to stop thinking that right now. I'm serious, I don't want to hear you say that ever again."

"But if I hadn't made her upset—"

"Annabelle, listen to me. This is not your fault. You should have never been put in the position where you felt like you had to choose to begin with." I take a deep breath. "We can't change what happened, but I know, without a shred of doubt in my mind, that this was not your fault. And know that I will always be here. I'm never going to leave you, ever. I love you so much, Belley."

"I love you too." She squeezes me as hard as she can. "Can I go with you to see Wav today?"

"Of course you can. Come on, let's get ready, and we'll go."

She lets me go from her hold and wipes her eyes. "Okay."

Back at the hospital, I find Chief and Mrs. Bennett still sitting in the lobby.

"Hey, how's she doing?" I ask as we sit next to them.

Chief takes a deep breath. "Not much has changed. She's pushing the fifteen-hour mark now. They said two more hours, and they'll repeat an MRI and CT to make sure nothing has changed. For now, her vitals are good, and they said they're still hopeful."

"Wyla, Winry, and Graham are in the room with her now," Mrs. Bennett says, holding back a lot of emotion. "I'll text them to come switch with you."

I nod. I know I should probably say no, let them have their time, but I need to see her. I need to hold her hand and see that she is still breathing.

After a couple minutes, they all come back into the lobby. I stand, too anxious to get back to her.

Winry and Wyla both give me and Annabelle hugs. While I appreciate them, I really only need one Bennett sister in my arms right now.

"Hey," Winry says to Annabelle. "Graham and I were going to run to Crossroads to get everyone some breakfast. We sure could use some help, if you want to come with us? And maybe grab you a book to read while we wait."

Annabelle looks to me for approval, and I nod. "Sure, kid. I'll be here when you get back."

"Okay, yeah. I'll go with you." Annabelle gives me a quick hug and heads off with Winry and Graham.

Chief comes up behind me and pats my back. "Please go wake her up."

I nod. *Fuck, I'm going to try.*

I make it to her room, and I hesitate at the door knob. *Please, dear God, let her wake up. I need her.*

I twist the knob and walk in her room. Nothing has changed, other than her casts being put on. Otherwise, she's still hooked up to about five different machines, and the oxygen is still around her pale face.

"Hey, Wav." I pull a chair up next to her and intertwine her hand in mine. "Ya know, I was thinking about how much I love you. I thought I had fallen in love when I walked in my house after working all night and there you and Annabelle were, dead asleep in this mess in my living room. But the more I think about it, the more I realized that I started falling in love with you long before that. I think I fell a little bit when you insisted on changing your flat tire by yourself. I think I fell a little bit more every morning you would teach Annabelle how to braid her hair. With every snarky comment and every evil eye, I fell for you. Please wake up for me, baby, so I can fall countless more times. I need you, Waverley."

But she doesn't.

Chapter 39

Annabelle

We walk back into the hospital carrying food and coffee for everyone. I'm holding a bag that has mine and Uncle Owen's cinnamon rolls and a book Winry let me borrow, while Graham and Winry carry the rest of the stuff.

Truthfully, I didn't want the cinnamon roll or the book. Right now, I just want the last twenty-four-hours to be a nightmare that I'm going to wake up from.

Winry passes out everyone's stuff, and I sit back down in my chair. I pull my knees up to my chest and try to hold back my tears.

"Hey, Annabelle. Would you like to take Owen his food and go see Wav?" Winry asks with her hand reached out.

I do want to see Wav, but I'm scared. I don't want to lose her either. A little unsure, I take Winry's hand as we walk back down a long hallway.

We reach a room, and Winry goes in first. I take a deep breath then go in behind her. Uncle Owen sits next to Waverley. A very broken Waverley. She's got wires coming all out of her, something around her face, and casts on her leg and hand.

"Hey, Belley. She's okay. This stuff just makes sure all of her vitals are good, like her heart and her breathing. It's not hurting her," Uncle Owen says, as if he can read my mind.

I nod and walk up to him slowly. I hand him the bag with our cinnamon rolls in them, but I haven't been able to stop looking at Wav.

"I got you a cinnamon roll," I mumble.

"Thanks, kid." He takes the bag and stands up out of his chair. "Do you want to talk to her?"

"Can she hear me?"

"I think so." He sighs, "It doesn't hurt to try."

"Okay." I take his seat, and he walks over to talk to Winry. I take Wav's non-injured hand in mine, like Uncle Owen did. "Hey, Wav. I don't know if you can hear me, but I really wish you would wake up." I take another deep breath. "My mom isn't going to wake up, but Uncle Owen says you can. I don't really understand any of this, but if you can wake up, why don't you? I don't want to lose you too. Uncle Owen and I need you."

I feel the tears slide down my face, I don't think I can do this.

I loosen my grip on her hand, but then Wav squeezes my hand before I can let go.

"Belley?" Wav whispers as she blinks her eyes.

"Oh my gosh, oh my gosh! Uncle Owen, she's awake!"

Chapter 40

Waverley

My word, my head is pounding. What is going on? Why can't I open my eyes? They feel like they are glued shut.

"Hey, Wav. I don't know if you can hear me, but I really wish you would wake up," I hear somebody, but it's muffled and I can't make out who.

Okay, focus, Waverley.

Some more muffles come through, and it's starting to get a little clearer.

"I don't really understand any of this, but if you can wake up, why don't you?"

I don't know why. I can't seem to open my eyes.

"I don't want to lose you too. Uncle Owen and I need you."

Owen and I... Annabelle.

Damn it, Waverley, open your eyes.

With every ounce of strength. I open my eyes. My eyelids fight me on it, so I'm blinking quite a bit, but a blurry Annabelle comes into view.

"Belley?" I whisper, and I feel her starting to pull away so I squeeze her hand.

"Oh my gosh, oh my gosh! Uncle Owen, she's awake!" she yells.

I wince. *That's loud, kid.*

"Oh, thank God." *Owen. I hear Owen.* "Winry, go get a doctor."

Doctor? Where am I? I continue to blink my eyes trying to get them to focus, but it's so hard; my head is pounding.

Everything is still a little blurry, but it's getting better. Annabelle steps to the side and someone else takes her place. I blink my eyes a few more times, and Owen starts to come into view.

"Hey, baby," he cries. "I love you, Wav. I'm so sorry."

Why is he sorry? Why is he crying? Where am I?

"I love you so much, Waverley." He cups my cheeks and gives me a tender kiss.

I want to tell him that I love him too, but my head hurts so bad, I can't manage to form the words. More people enter the room, people I don't recognize.

"Sir, we're going to need you to step out so we can assess her," a lady says to Owen.

"I'm not leaving her," he snaps.

"Sir, we need to check her out, then you can come right back in once we are done," she argues.

I squeeze Owen's hand the best I can. It's the only thing I can manage. I feel my eyes getting heavier. I shoot my eyes back open when I realize I shut them again.

"Okay, I'll wait outside her door." Owen relents and squeezes my hand back before walking away.

Everything next is a mixture of people buzzing around me, taking my blood, and checking my vitals and reflexes. I've gathered that I'm in a hospital, but how I got here is still a mystery. The last thing I remember is going to Owen's house for movie night, but I don't even remember getting there.

"Hi, Waverley." A man I'm assuming is the doctor says as he walks up to my side. "How are we feeling?"

Words are still hard to form, but I manage the word, "Confused."

The doctor chuckles. "I'm sure. Do you remember how you got here, Waverley?"

I shake my head gently.

"That's okay. It's pretty normal to have a little amnesia. It should resolve itself, but it may take a little time."

Amnesia? What? The doctor must be able to read my further confusion.

"Waverley, you were involved in a pretty serious car accident that resulted in two broken ribs, a broken leg, a fractured wrist, and a mild traumatic head injury. You've been in a coma for sixteen hours."

A coma? Oh my gosh. I try to sit up, but the pain in my ribs says absolutely not. Again the doctor can read my face.

"We'll get you some more pain medication. Your family is here, but I'm going to limit your visitors to two at a time for now. I don't want you getting overstimulated. Are you okay if he comes back in here?"

Owen. Yes, I need Owen. I nod.

"Okay, Waverley. You'll be here for at least the next couple days, so you'll have plenty of time for visiting. Don't force yourself to stay awake and get some rest."

I nod again. My eyes still feel heavy—I don't know how much longer I'll be able to keep them open.

My eyes blink open again, and this time it's not blurry. My body feels numb, but my brain finally feels awake. I lift my arm and inspect the cast. I guess it wasn't a dream.

I look around my room. Owen sits in a chair next to me, his head hangs—in what I can't imagine is a comfortable position—dead asleep.

Suddenly, it all comes flashing back to me—the break up, my heart being torn to shreds, then headlights.

My head starts to throb at the return of the memories.

"Ahh." I wince.

Owen jolts awake. "Wav? Hey, baby, are you okay?" He leans up, and his hands hover like they want to touch me but are afraid to.

I nod and pinch the bridge of my nose with my non-broken hand. "I was just remembering everything. What are you doing here, Owen?"

He looks exhausted and defeated. "Baby, I'm so sorry. I never should have let you walk out of my house the other night. Waverley, I love you so much, I'll never let you go again."

But he has to. Damn it. I'm not strong enough to do this again. "But what about Annabelle? Owen, you can't lose her."

"I can't lose you either, Waverley." He takes my hand in his and brings it closer to him. "Um, do you remember how you ended up here?"

There's so much pain in his green eyes.

I want to pull my hand away but I can't, so I nod. "A car wreck, right?"

"Yeah, head-on collision." Owen hangs his head and takes a deep breath. "Natalie was the other driver. She died on impact."

"What!" My body instinctively wants to lean up at the shock. *Ow, too much.*

Owen eases me back down. "Easy, darlin'. It's okay. I mean it's not okay. Just please, take it easy."

"What... what happened? Was it...my—" I choke on the words.

Did I cause this? I try to pull my hand back, How could he or Annabelle ever forgive me?

Owen tightens his grip on my hand, pulling it back to him. "No, baby, no. Natalie was drinking. Annabelle had heard mine and Nat's argument and tried to tell her she wanted to stay with me."

Owen shuts his eyes for a moment and takes a deep breath. "Nat didn't..." he pauses. "She didn't take that well. She took one of Dad's unopened whiskey bottles that Mom had never been able to throw away. I knew she had a problem, but I didn't think she'd—"

I squeeze his hand. "Owen, honey, this isn't your fault either."

"I'd rather carry that burden. Annabelle thinks it's hers, and it breaks me."

No, she can't do that, neither of them need that burden. I look around the room.

"Where is she? Can I see her?"

A shadow of a smile crosses his face briefly. "She's at my mom's house. It's almost midnight, you've been asleep for about twelve hours." Owen holds my hand to his heart, and I can feel it pounding on the back of my hand. "Baby, I'm so sorry."

I'm dying to forgive him and tell him that I love him, but...

"What happens now? With Annabelle? With us?"

"Well, your dad is working on getting me official guardianship. I have temporary for now, and the lawyer your dad hired is supposed to call me Monday. I shouldn't have much trouble getting guardianship. As for us, Waverley, I love you. If these past thirty hours have been any indication, I can't live without you. Just the thought of losing you sent me into a complete breakdown. I need you, Wav, forever. I know I messed up. I should've fought harder. I know I should be the man that says I'll let you go if you wanted, but Waverley, I don't want to let you go. I love you and—"

Tears well in my eyes, and my heart reaches for him. "I love you too, Owen, so much."

Owen lets out a breath and smiles, "I love you, baby." He leans up and cups my face. "I'm going to kiss you now."

"Okay."

Chapter 41

Waverley

One month later - Oct. 20th

"This dress is prettier than I remember." Winry fans her face to keep her from crying.

Today's the day she and Graham are officially getting married.

"You look beautiful, Win." I reach for her hand, sacrificing a hug because I don't want to risk messing up any part of how she looks right now. I'm not exactly sturdy on my feet just yet, my left leg is still casted. Walking down the aisle with crutches isn't exactly how I envisioned today, but at least I was able to get the cast off my hand in time.

"Thank you, Wav. You look beautiful too." She smiles.

"Win, are you sure you still want me to go down the aisle on crutches? I don't want to take away from your moment."

"You're walking down the aisle. No ifs, ands, or buts about it. Mom is going to take your crutches when you get up there so you can stand normal. That's the plan," Winry snaps. "You're my maid of honor—you have to walk down the aisle."

"Okay, okay. I was just making sure." I swat at her.

"You really hit the bridesmaid jackpot, Win. I mean you got one sister hobbling down the aisle then the other can barely get her dress zipped," Wyla says, as mom is trying to zip up her dress.

"Suck it in, Wyla." Mom struggles.

"Suck it in? Mom, I can't suck it in. I'm pregnant, not bloated."

Wyla's about to enter her second trimester and is already starting to show a little, but since her nausea has passed, she eats everything in sight. At her last appointment she did a blood test to find out the gender and none of us were shocked to find out it's going to be a girl.

"Here, let me help." I limp over and hold the top of her dress together while Mom forces the zipper up.

"Ah, got it," Mom exclaims.

"Thank goodness." Wyla turns around and runs her hands over her little lump of love. "Do you think people will know I'm pregnant? Or do I just look like I ate too much for lunch?"

"Which one do you want them to think?"

"Good point." Wyla shrugs. "Do we have any more donuts?"

"Wyla! That will be your fourth donut," Mom chastises.

"What?" Wyla shrugs. "It's the baby. She's hungry."

Winry and I laugh.

"Let my perfect niece have a donut," Winry says.

I rub Wyla's belly. "She can have all the donuts she wants."

"Fine, fine, but don't get anything on your dress." Mom turns to me next. "How are you feeling, sweetie? Do you need to rest before we start? Maybe you should sit down."

"I'm fine, Mom, really. The doctor even cleared me for a 'light increase in activity,' I just have to be easy on my leg."

"Light increase in activity." Winry laughs. "That means Owen's getting lucky tonight."

"Okay, I don't need details." Mom plugs her ears.

I laugh because, yeah, Owen is totally getting lucky tonight. I wanted to do it a week ago, but Owen's been so overprotective, he's shot down all of my attempts. But not tonight.

"Okay, girls, time for final touches. We're about to line up," Emily, the day-of-coordinator says as she peeks her head in our childhood bedroom.

"Ahh, this is so exciting," Wyla mumbles with a bite of donut in her mouth. "Mm, I need to fix my lipstick."

Five minutes later, we are lined up behind some drapes on the back porch.

"Okay, Mr. Bennett, you're going to help Waverley down the stairs, then come back up to walk Winry down." Emily pulls Dad to the front. "We start in one minute."

Dad walks up beside me. "You look beautiful, honey. Crutches and all."

I snort. "Please don't let me fall down the stairs."

"I promise I'll pick you right back up."

"Daddy!" I swat his shoulder and nearly lose my balance.

Dad catches and steadies me. "I promise I won't let you fall."

"Okay, we're ready, Wyla, go now. Waverley and Mr. Bennett, you can go when she gets halfway." Emily pulls back the drape, and Wyla starts down the aisle.

Dad takes my crutches in one hand then wraps the other around me to steady me down the stairs.

By some miracle, we don't tumble down them. "I love you, my strong girl." Dad kisses my cheek and hands over my crutches.

"I love you too, Daddy." I place my crutches under my arms.

"Now, don't fall." Dad smiles and I roll my eyes.

I start down the aisle, and thankfully, they decided on a small wedding, so the eyes on me are minimal. But there is one pair of eyes I can feel locked on me.

Meeting Owen's gaze, everything else fades away. He's in a tan suit with a sage green tie that matches my dress, and he looks too damn good. Here I am, hobbling down the aisle, but Owen's eyes are filled with nothing but adoration as he watches me.

I make it to the front and smile at him. He smiles back and mouths, "I love you."

"I love you too," I mouth back as I take my place.

Mom steps up to move my crutches out of the way.

Okay, Wav, just got to stand on your own two feet for twenty minutes, no biggie. You can do this.

The song changes to "Stand By Me," the Skyler Grey version, and everyone stands and turns back to watch Winry walk down the aisle.

She looks so beautiful walking down, with a smile a mile wide on her face. I want to watch her, but I can't help but watch Graham as he struggles to keep it together. His smile is also just as wide, but tears stream down his cheeks.

When Graham steps to the front to take Winry's hand, my gaze locks on to Owen's. He smiles at me, and I can't help but think about what our day would be like. Where would we have it? What would he wear? Black, definitely all black. Would he cry as I walked down the aisle? Yeah, he probably would. My smile grows at the thought. I love this man, and I can't wait to marry him.

Graham and Winry walk back up, and she reaches back to hand me her bouquet, then takes Graham's hands.

The ceremony starts, and there isn't a dry eye in the crowd as Graham and Winry say their vows.

"Winry, my everything, my buttercup. I love you so much, and I'll continue to love you for the rest of our lives. I vow to not only be your husband, but your partner. I'll be your confidant, your friend, and your shoulder to lean on. I promise to always have awful, corny jokes ready when you need them, or whenever I just want to hear your laugh. Winry, everyday I'm in awe of you. Of your strength, your beauty, your kindness, and your ability to light up every room you enter. I thank God every day that he brought you to me, and I can't wait for our future. No matter what life throws at us, Win, I'll be by your side, following you blindly every step of the way."

"Graham, you're my best friend, my soulmate, my saving grace. There was a time that I didn't think I deserved a love like yours, but no one makes me feel more beautiful, more confident, more loved and adored than you do. I vow to love you with everything in me and to always beat you in every game possible. You are the best thing that has ever happened to me, and I'm honored to become your wife. I plan to love you a little bit more with every day that passes, and I can't wait to grow old with you."

They exchange rings and say their "I do's," then it's time for the best part.

"Graham, you may now kiss your bride," the officiant says and we all erupt—hootin', hollerin', and whistlin'—as Graham kisses Winry for the first official time as a married couple. "It's with great pleasure that I introduce to you Mr. and Mrs. Graham Taylor."

Everyone stands and cheers, then throws flower petals up in the air as they make their way back up the aisle.

Once it's time for me to make my way back up the aisle, Mom stands to bring me my crutches but the next thing I know, Owen's there scooping me up in his arms.

"Owen, what are you doing?" I squeal.

"Carrying my girl. Hold on tight, darlin'." He smirks and proceeds to carry me back up the aisle and over to where we are to take pictures before the reception. He goes to set me down gently but still holds me flush to him. "You look so beautiful, Wav."

"Even with the pink cast?" I snort a laugh.

"Nothing could ever take away from your beauty." He brushes my hair behind my ears and kisses my forehead.

"I love you," I say and melt in his arms.

He holds me tight. "I love you too."

Chapter 42

Owen

November

I carry out another box to the moving truck as Graham tapes up the last of them. This should be the last of their stuff out of their apartment. We've been helping them move into their new house all weekend.

I come back in to grab another box. "So, do you think we should start like a moving company or something? This is the third time I've moved your shit, and fourth we've moved all together."

"It has not been that many," Graham says as he picks up a box labeled kitchen.

"Yeah, it has. Once moving you next door, second moving you in with Win, and now this. I'm tired of moving your shit."

"Yeah, yeah quit your bitchin', I'll be helping you move Waverley in, if you would ever ask her."

We set the boxes in the moving truck. "I'm going to ask her tonight at dinner, asshole."

Graham rolls his eyes. "Yeah, you also said you were going to ask her last week after Annabelle's birthday party."

"She got sick, I couldn't exactly ask her to move in while her head was in the toilet."

Graham pulls down the door, closing up the back of the moving truck. "I don't see why not? You've also had all week to ask her, and you still haven't. She's not going to say no, so just ask her already."

"She might say no—she loves her house."

"Owen, when was the last time she stayed the night at that house and not yours?"

Well, that's a good point. She's maybe spent three nights at her house total since she came home from the hospital. All of her clothes are practically at my house already.

"Alright, alright. I told you I'm asking her tonight."

"Yeah, we'll see," Graham says and pulls out his phone. "Damn, the girls have already unboxed the load we just dropped off."

"No one can quite get the job done like the Bennett sisters."

"Ain't that the truth. Okay, come on, let's get this load to the house."

We head over to their new house, it's a nice white old farm style house with five bedrooms.

"So, what exactly are y'all doing with five bedrooms?" I ask as we pull up their driveway.

"No real plan, fill two or three of them with kids one day. The rest are extra. I tried to talk her into having one be the designated sister pile room so they wouldn't tear up my living room every time, but Win said sister piles only happen in the living room."

"Nice try." I laugh. "Have they forced you to join one of those too?"

Graham gives me a look that answers my question.

"Face mask and all?"

"Obviously. Neither of us are exactly good at telling them no."

"No, we're not." I chuckle.

As soon as we open the truck doors, we hear music blaring from inside. We look at each other and shake our heads.

We start to carry in boxes, and we walk into the girls all dancing around the living room.

Graham and I say nothing, just watching them for a minute. Annabelle notices first.

"Hey, they're back," she cheers.

Winry pauses the music. "Hey, babe. Sorry we got bored."

Graham walks over to her and gives her a kiss. "Don't apologize, Win. Y'all keep having fun while we unload the truck."

"Oh no. No more dancing for me," Wyla says, falling back on the couch. "I'm exhausted."

"Take a break, momma." Waverley says and rubs her belly as she passes by. "Hi, honey."

"Hi, Wav." I give her a kiss. "You need to take a break too. How's your leg feel?" She only got that cast off last week.

She rolls her eyes. "It feels fine, Owen. Dr. Holcomb said it's all healed and that I'm completely free of all restrictions, remember? You asked him three times."

Now, I roll my eyes. "Well, excuse me," I say sarcastically and pull her into me, tickling her.

She squeals and laughs while she tries to get away.

"Stop it, you two. You're making me nauseous. Both of y'all, all happy and in love... bleh," Wyla says and sticks out her tongue.

Annabelle giggles and sits next to her. "They're like that all the time."

Wyla wraps an arm around her. "Poor you. I'll have to start stealing you away so you can get a break from that nonsense."

"Yes, please." Annabelle smiles, and I don't even care that it's a bit of a jab because she's smiling again.

After Natalie's funeral, Annabelle went into a bit of a depression. Waverley, Win, and Wyla have really helped a lot by taking her in and making her feel like she's one of them, but she was still carrying around the idea that it was her fault. Winry had her therapist recommend some different therapists that specialize in child trauma.

I was able to get official guardianship of her last month. Thanks to the help from the lawyer Chief hired, it was a breeze. They tried to reach out to her biological father, but I didn't even sweat that. That asshole didn't even respond.

"Okay, we're going to start bringing in the rest of the boxes," Graham says and claps me on the back.

I kiss Wav on the temple, and we all get back to work.

After nearly three hours, we officially get Graham and Win unpacked. I finish helping Graham move the furniture into its place then head to find my girls to take them home.

I smile when I find them rocking in the rocking chairs on the front porch. "Hey, slackers. what are y'all doing?"

"Taking a break from a manic Winry." Wav laughs. "It looks like it's going to storm tonight. We should probably get going before it starts."

"Well, you're in luck because I believe we're done. Y'all ready to go?"

"Yes, please," they beg together.

We say goodbye and hit up a drive-thru on the way back to the house. We scarf down our food in the truck and make it in the house right as thunder rolls in.

"I'm exhausted," Annabelle whines. "I'm gonna read for a bit then go to bed."

"Okay, kid. Thank you for helping today," I say as she heads to her room.

"You're welcome. Goodnight, Uncle Owen. Goodnight, Wav. Love you."

"Love you too," we say before she closes her door.

I turn toward Wav, and she comes to give me a hug.

"Hey, want to go sit on the front porch and watch the storm for a bit?" she asks.

"Yeah, that sounds nice, come on."

We go out to the porch, and I pull her in my lap, not giving her a chance to sit on the other chair.

Rain starts to steadily fall.

"I love your porch. It's so much better than mine."

She rests her head on my shoulder and shuts her eyes.

Our porch, baby. It's our porch. "Hey, Wav?"

"Mhm?" she replies and snuggles closer, eyes still closed.

"Move in with me," I say, more of a demand than a request. She sits up in my lap. "I know you stay here pretty much every night anyway, and I know you love your house, but I want you here all the time. I want your stuff here. I want you to have no other option but to crawl in bed with me every night, even when I piss you off. I want you here in *our* home."

She smiles. "You're sure? You really want me to move in?"

"Waverley, what did I just say? I made a big speech—"

She cuts me off with a kiss.

"Is that a yes?"

"Of course, it's a yes. I do love my house, but this house is my home. You're my home."

I brush some hair behind her ear and stare into those sky-blue eyes. "I love you so much, Waverley."

"I love you too, honey." She smiles and rests her head back on my shoulder.

We stay out there watching the rain fall and listening to the thunder until Wav falls asleep. I carry her back inside our house and lie her down in our bed.

As I lie next to her I can't help but feel like her moving in isn't enough. I guess I'll be making a visit to talk to her dad sooner than either of us expected.

Chapter 43

Waverley

Christmas Eve

"Owen, will you let it go? I burned cookies *one time* and I'll never live it down around here." I shove him away from the mixer and add some more chocolate chips to the cookie dough.

"Not a chance, darlin'. Why in the world would I stop bringing it up? Annoying you is my love language."

Owen wraps his arms around my waist from behind and kisses my cheek.

"Well, you're fluent in it. Start learning a new language."

Annabelle giggles as she finishes a spoonful of cookie dough that she stole mid-mix.

"I think our new tradition should just be eating the cookie dough, no need to bake the cookies. That way there's no chance of burning them."

"Ah, Belley, I'm not going to burn them." I shut off the mixer and remove the bowl wrapping the top in saran wrap. I pop it in the fridge to chill while we eat the pizza

Owen made from scratch in our sister pile—or now, our family pile. Owen says it can't be a sister pile if he's there.

Owen and I, mostly I, thought it'd be fun to start a new Christmas tradition and what better way than making a mess of the living room, eating pizza, and baking cookies on Christmas Eve. With matching pajamas. Owen's thrilled about those, but hey, he put them on.

"Belley, why don't you start getting all the blankets and pillows out of your room, and I'll get ours," I say.

I officially moved in a couple weeks ago, and my parents worked out a deal with Wyla that she has to stay home for the first year after the baby is born, then the house will be all for her and her little love muffin.

"Okie." She hops off the counter and bops to her room.

"And you." I turn to Owen. "You move the coffee table and clear the spot for all things cozy."

"It's gonna cost ya, baby." Owen has a cocky smile on his face.

I roll my eyes. "I'd like to think the price I paid to get you in these pajamas should cover this cost."

Owen chuckles. "This price still requires your mouth, but just a kiss will cover it this time."

"Mhm, I think I can manage that." I go up on my tiptoes and place my lips to his with a small kiss then pull back, teasing him.

"Absolutely not, get back here." Owen lifts me up, bringing me up to meet his lips. My leg naturally does that little pop thing like it did when he kissed me in his kitchen when we first started dating.

He sets me back down after a moment and rests his forehead on mine. "I love you, Wav."

"I love you too, honey."

"Hey, Wav," Annabelle says, coming back in the kitchen. "Can you braid my hair before we start the sister—sorry—family pile? Yours always hold better than mine when I try to sleep in them."

"Sure, the stuff is in our bathroom." I let go of Owen. "We'll be right back. Coffee table moved, please," I say as sweetly as I can manage.

"I got it, I got it. Now, go." Owen gives me a quick kiss to the cheek, and Belley and I head back to the bathroom.

"Okay, Belley, what kind of braids do you want?" I ask, brushing through her blonde hair.

"Two Dutch braids please."

"Let's do it." I section out her hair and start the braids.

"Wav, are you happy?" she asks. "Like living here with us?"

Well I wasn't expecting that question. "I'm very happy, Belley. There's nowhere I'd rather be than with you two. Are you happy?" I ask a little hesitantly.

I know it's been a rough couple of months for her, and my heart aches every time I think about how abruptly her life was altered.

"Is it wrong if I say yes?"

Ow, heart hurting. "No, of course not. Annabelle. You deserve all the love and happiness, never feel bad about that."

Annabelle gives me a half smile.

I stop mid-braid and wrap her up in a hug. "Owen and I love you so much, Belley."

"I know. Y'all tell me that all the time." She snorts a laugh.

I smile. "Well, we do, and we don't want you to forget it." I squeeze her tight.

"I love you too, Wav."

I blink back some tears. "Look, you've got me all emotional. I have to start over." I redo her braids like three times, and each time I have to redo it because Annabelle has said something so sweet that I have to stop to hug her some more. About ten minutes later, we head back out.

When we walk out the living room, my jaw drops. A moment ago the only thing lighting the living room was our Christmas tree. Now, there are about a hundred lit candles scattered about.

Owen stands in the middle of the living room smiling at me.

"W-wh-what's going on?" I stammer, too mesmerized by the sight.

Annabelle giggles next to me then gives me a quick hug before racing to her room.

"Come here, Wav." Owen holds out his hand for me.

I don't know how my legs start to move, but I make my way slowly to him, still in a bit of shock. "Owen..."

"Waverley." Owen takes my hand. "My beautiful, strong Wav. You took me by surprise, one day you were—while still beautiful—this girl that drove me absolutely crazy."

I try to hold back a laugh, but it slips out, and Owen smiles.

"But then, you became this woman that drove me absolutely *insane*. I'm madly, utterly, and insanely in love with you. You're a part of me, Wav, and I couldn't possibly see any other life than one with you by my side, with family piles in the living room, and the smell of burnt cookies in the kitchen."

I roll my eyes. I'll make him pay for that one later, but not right now.

Owen gets down on one knee.

"I don't want to go another minute—no, another second—without officially making you mine forever. Waverley, will you marry me?" Owen opens the ring box and my jaw drops again. How it's still attached is beyond me, but the ring...it's my Mamaw's wedding ring. Her beautiful three stone ring but now the diamonds on the sides are now green emeralds.

"Oh my... Owen, how did you..." Happy tears begin to fall down my cheeks.

"When I asked your dad for his blessing, he gave it to me. The diamonds on the side were loose, so I had them replaced with emeralds. If you don't like them, I'll—"

I can see the panic on his face. "No, Owen, it's perfect. I love it." I wipe my tears.

"So, is that a yes?"

"Yes, of course it's a yes." I hold out my left hand, and he slides the ring on my finger. I squeal happily at the sight, and Owen stands scooping me up in his arms and kisses me.

"Can I come out now? I'm dying in here!" Annabelle hollers from her room.

Owen chuckles. "Yes, get your butt out here, kid."

Annabelle races out her door and runs into our waiting arms. "I'm so excited! Can I be a bridesmaid?"

"Without question." I squeeze her tighter.

We celebrate with our pizza and cookies—that I didn't burn, thank you very much—then we pile together in our family pile. Owen and I may have snuck off for a bit after Annabelle crashes, but then we're back in the living room all huddled together. With Belley on my right, and Owen on my left, I have absolutely everything I need.

Annabelle

Epilogue - One year later (November)

"Hey, Belley." Wav knocks on my door. "You ready? Everyone should be here soon."

"Yeah, I'll be out in just a minute," I say and tuck my big envelope in one of my canvas book bags. I carry it out to the living room and slide it in between the couch and the side table. Owen and Wav are busy setting up the table for dinner, so thankfully they don't notice.

I walk in the kitchen and help them carry all of my favorite foods to the table. I requested an Italian themed dinner for my 13th birthday, and Uncle Owen being Uncle Owen, he of course made a five-course meal.

"Belley, are you sure you don't want a party or something for your birthday this year?" he asks as we finish setting the table.

"Nah, this is all I want." When they asked me what I wanted to do this year, the only thing I could think of was to have dinner with them, Grandma, and everyone who I like to call my new family.

After my mom died, Wav's family really took me in. Even before they got married this past June, Wav's sisters always included me on sister nights. They take me shopping, and they do all the fun things aunts do. Wav's parents treat me the same as their real granddaughter, and they call and check on me throughout the week and buy me gifts all the time, just because. They even insist I call them Papaw and Mamaw. So, now I have aunts and grandparents, but some roles are still missing.

When everyone gets here, they all wish me a happy birthday and give me big hugs. We gather around the table as close as we can get. It's chaos, but I love it.

I stay quiet through most of the dinner, and I know Uncle Owen can sense that something is off. I do my best to avoid his questioning looks, and Papaw does his best to distract Uncle Owen talking about work. Papaw is the only one who knows what I really have planned. I needed his help getting everything I'd need. It's killing me to not blurt it out right now.

Finally, we all finish our food, and we head into the living room for presents. I open bag after bag of clothes and books; every gift is perfectly suited to me, and it only reassures me that this is the family I am meant to have.

After I open the last present, Wav stands up off the couch. "Okay, let me get the cake."

"Wait, Wav," I say, catching her before she heads to the kitchen. "Can you sit back down? I have something I wanted to talk to you guys about."

"Oh, is everything okay?" she asks and sits back down next to Uncle Owen slowly.

"Yeah, everything's good. Really good actually." I stand up and take a deep breath. "When my mom died, I felt guilty for so long—well, I felt guilty long before that. But anyway, I love my mom, I always will, but she wasn't the one who raised me or took care of me. She wasn't there in the moments I needed her."

I reach for my bag and pull out the envelope and hand it to Uncle Owen. He gives me a puzzled look wondering where I'm going with this. He opens the envelope and his eyes quickly scan the paper. "Belley, this is..."

"Uncle Owen, I don't think I want to call you uncle anymore. I think Dad is more fitting. Would you and Wav officially adopt me and become my mom and dad?"

"Oh my goodness, Annabelle." Wav wipes tears from her face, and Uncle Owen does the same.

"Is that a yes?" I ask sheepishly.

Uncle Owen stands up from the couch and wraps me in a hug. "Without question."

Wav comes to the other side and joins the hug. "We love you so much. We would love to officially be your parents."

Now everyone is crying, including me. I give my dad a tight squeeze. "Thank you for always taking care of me."

"Always, Belley. I'll always take care of you. I love you so much." He squeezes me back, then lets me go so he can wipe more tears from his face. The man may look like he'll kill you, which he might, but for me and my new mom, he's the biggest softie in the world.

"I love you too, Dad."

Acknowledgements

Wow. I don't really know what to say other than thank you. I'm so incredibly thankful for this journey and all of the amazing opportunities I've had in 2023. I do have some specific people to thank but before I do, I want to tell anyone reading this that I am beyond thankful for you and the time you took to read this story. You are truly amazing, thank you!

Krischan, Maverick, and Lena. Thank you for being my rocks, my constants, my family. You three are everything I could have ever asked for in this world. Thank you for loving me through all of the mess and chaos that I bring. P.S. kids I'm sorry for when your friends make fun of you for writing smut. Love you all.

Mom and Gracie, if it wasn't for you two so many parts of these books would cease to exist. I'm so thankful for you two and for mom forcing us to all be close. I can't wait to fill more books with stories that have happened to us and then have people write reviews to say "that would never happen in real life." Yup, we truly are unbelievable.

To my beta readers. I put you through it and I'm not sorry. I have loved every comment, every suggestion, and every friendship that has come out of this process. You are all so incredible and I appreciate you. Alpha/beta/proof-readers: Kristen, Bria, Annie, Nicole, Isabella, Ashley, Lilly, Hazel, Kayla, Romi, Dany, Sarah, Maria, Bobbi, Maria, and Katy.

Thank you to my group, my girls, my author family. I've truly grown as a writer and so much of that is because of you all. You are all badasses and I hope you never forget that. Thank you Dany C., Maria R., Sarah G., Kat S., Adeline M, Bobbi M,. and Karley B.

Dany, my Sippin' Stories sister, my true other half. How have we only known each other for 6 months? I'm so thankful for you! May all of our author dreams come true so we can buy our land and stick the husbands and kids in one house and us in the other.

Kristen, thank you for your friendship and your willingness to always help me no matter the circumstances. I can't wait to continue not only working together, but our friendship as well.

Special thanks to:

Caroline Palmier - copy editor

Taylor Wilson - PA

Again thank you to all of my readers! I can't express my gratitude enough. Thank you for reading Wav and Owen's story, I hope you enjoyed it!

The Dick-tionary

For those that want to avoid or find (when in need) the smutty scenes in Bring It All. The chapters listed below are the chapters that go into explicit detail. The subject of sex or sexual situations may be mentioned in other chapters but contain minimum details or is closed door.

- **Chapter One** (end of chapter)

- **Chapter Sixteen**

- **Chapter Seventeen**

- **Chapter Twenty-five** (end of chapter)

- **Chapter Twenty-nine** (middle of chapter)

- **Chapter Thirty-five**

Also By Mollie Goins

Despite It All (Book 3 in the Aster Creek Series)
Coming 2024
Feel It All (Book 1 in the Aster Creek Series)
Available now on Amazon and Kindle Unlimited
Feel It All – Amazon
Blurb for Feel It All

Winry lives a cozy, quiet life in the small town of Aster Creek where she runs Crossroads Books and Café with her longtime friend and business partner, Ivy. She has a loving, close-knit family including her sisters Waverly and Wyla. Unknown to her family, Winry has fought a secret battle with mental health issues. She keeps her walls firmly in place and pushes the worst of her struggles down for the sake of her family.

Graham enters her world, and Winry feels intense attraction. He has special "golden retriever boyfriend" vibes and seems equally interested in getting to know her. Winry feels the need to be cautious, but a run-in with her ex leads her straight into Graham's arms.

As the two grow closer, Winry can feel Graham trying to tear down her walls. She's kept her battle a secret for so long, but Graham may be the one who can break her walls down. When trouble brews in their relationship and obstacles come at them from both sides, will they be drawn together, or will they drift apart?

Readers who enjoy a cozy small-town romance with some spice will delight in Feel It All. A charming and courageous kind of romance novel, Feel It All dives into the challenges that lovers who deal with mental health struggles will face. Feel It All is a swoon worthy journey that will leave readers feeling hopeful and uplifted.

About the Author

Mollie Goins is a contemporary romance author, whose debut novel, *Feel It All*, not only hit Best Seller in an e-book category, the book also hit number one in New Releases for paperbacks in the Feel-Good Fiction category. *Bring It All* is the second book in the series and will be followed up with one more novel and one novella.

Mollie currently resides in a small town in Tennessee with her husband, two children, and three dogs. Family is very important to Mollie and the inspiration for the sister's in the Aster Creek series comes from the relationship she has with her mother and sister. When not writing, Mollie enjoys taking the kids and dogs for walks, reading, and watching tv series with her husband.

Keep up with Mollie and her books:

Instagram - @authormolliegoins

Tiktok - @author.mollie.goins

Website - authormolliegoins.com

Made in the USA
Las Vegas, NV
21 August 2024

94206190R00226